PREFACE

As per revised syllabus of **'Bachelor of Pharmacy'** from academic year 2013-2014, with incorporation of **'Pharmacognosy and Phytochemistry-I'** for third semester the course contents of the subject also have been updated by taking into consideration the developments in pharmacy profession.

Pharmacognosy and Phytochemistry-I is meant to illuminate relevance and significance of phytochemistry to pharmaceutical and industrial utility.

Authors have made an attempt and also have tried to make justice with the intention of framing the course contents.

Authors are thankful to Publisher Shri. Dineshbhai Furia, Jigneshbhai Furia and Staff members of Nirali Prakashan for their full co-operation in bringing out this book.

June 2016   **Authors**

1. **Plant metabolites:** (3 Periods)

   Primary and secondary metabolites: Meaning, types, and their functions in plant; Comparative account of primary and secondary metabolism; Role of secondary metabolites in plants; Rationale behind use of secondary metabolites as medicinal compounds; Overview of historical contribution in development of phytochemistry.

2. **Pharmacognostic scheme for study of crude drugs:** (4 Periods)

   Meaning, component, and significance of individual Pharmacognostic parameter

3. **Primary metabolites of Pharmaceutical and industrial utility:** (17 Periods)

   General consideration: Definition, classification, occurrences, properties, nomenclature, chemistry (including general biogenesis, qualitative/quantitative analysis) and pharmaceutical and industrial applications of carbohydrates, lipids and proteins and their derived products.

   A. **Carbohydrates:**

      a) Systematic Pharmacognostic study of : Agar, Guar gum, Acacia, Isabgol, Sterculia, Tragacanth and Okra mucilage.

      b) Source, extraction, properties and uses of : Starch, Pectin, Inulin, Chitosan and Cyclodextrins.

   B. **Lipids:**

      a) Systematic Pharmacognostic study of : Castor oil, Linseed oil, Neem oil, Hydnocarpus oil, Codliver oil, Shark liver oil, Rice Bran oil, Cocoa butter, Kokum butter, Wool fat, and Bees wax;

      b) Source, extraction, properties and uses of: Lecithin, Polyunsaturated fatty acids, and Carotenoids.

   C. **Proteins and Enzymes:** Source, method of preparation, properties and uses of :

      Thaumatin, Papain, Bromelin, Streptokinase and Gelatin.

   D. **Natural fibers:** Source, method of preparation, properties and applications of Cotton, Wool, Silk and Jute.

4. **Secondary metabolites for medicinal utility:**

   A. **Glycosides:** (15 Periods)

      General consideration: Definition, classification, occurrences, properties, nomenclature, and chemistry (including general biogenesis, qualitative/ quantitative analysis) of glycoside containing drugs.

      Systematic Pharmacognostic study of

      a) *Saponin glycosides:* Liquorice, Ginseng, and Dioscorea

      b) *Cardioactive glycosides:* Digitalis, Squill, and Strophanthus

      c) *Anthraquinone glycosides:* Aloe, Senna, Rhubarb and Cascara

      d) Others: Kalmegh, Gentian, Citrus peels, Artemisia, Visnaga

   B. **Tannins:** (6 Periods)

      General consideration: Definition, classification, occurrences, properties, nomenclature, and chemistry (including general extraction, qualitative quantitative analysis) of tannin containing drugs.

      Systematic Pharmacognostic study: Gambier, Black catechu, Amla, Beleric and Chebulic Myrobalan. ❖❖❖

PHARMACOGNOSY AND PHYTOCHEMISTRY-I

For

Second Year Degree Course in Pharmacy

Semester - III

S.B. Gokhale

M. Pharm. AIC.

Former Co-ordinator
R. C. Patel College of Pharma Sciences and Research
Shirpur 425405.

Mrs. Aditi Kulkarni - Joshi

M. Pharm.

Assistant Professor, HOD, Pharmacognosy,
JSPM's Jayawantrao Sawant College of Pharmacy and Research,
Hadapsar, Pune 411 028.

NIRALI PRAKASHAN
ADVANCEMENT OF KNOWLEDGE

N1319

PHARMACOGNOSY AND PHYTOCHEMISTRY-I — ISBN 978-93-5164-971-7

First Edition : **June 2016**

© : **Authors**

Published By :   Polyplate

NIRALI PRAKASHAN

Abhyudaya Pragati, 1312, Shivaji Nagar,
Off J.M. Road, Pune – 411005
Tel - (020) 25512336/37/39, Fax - (020) 25511379
Email : niralipune@pragationline.com

☞ **DISTRIBUTION CENTRES**

PUNE

Nirali Prakashan : 119, Budhwar Peth, Jogeshwari Mandir Lane, Pune 411002, Maharashtra
Tel : (020) 2445 2044, 66022708, Fax : (020) 2445 1538
Email : bookorder@pragationline.com, niralilocal@pragationline.com

Nirali Prakashan : S. No. 28/27, Dhyari, Near Pari Company, Pune 411041
Tel : (020) 24690204 Fax : (020) 24690316
Email : dhyari@pragationline.com, bookorder@pragationline.com

MUMBAI

Nirali Prakashan : 385, S.V.P. Road, Rasdhara Co-op. Hsg. Society Ltd.,
Girgaum, Mumbai 400004, Maharashtra
Tel : (022) 2385 6339 / 2386 9976, Fax : (022) 2386 9976
Email : niralimumbai@pragationline.com

☞ **DISTRIBUTION BRANCHES**

JALGAON

Nirali Prakashan : 34, V. V. Golani Market, Navi Peth, Jalgaon 425001,
Maharashtra, Tel : (0257) 222 0395, Mob : 94234 91860

KOLHAPUR

Nirali Prakashan : New Mahadvar Road, Kedar Plaza, 1st Floor Opp. IDBI Bank
Kolhapur 416 012, Maharashtra. Mob : 9850046155

NAGPUR

Pratibha Book Distributors : Above Maratha Mandir, Shop No. 3, First Floor,
Rani Jhanshi Square, Sitabuldi, Nagpur 440012, Maharashtra
Tel : (0712) 254 7129

DELHI

Nirali Prakashan : 4593/21, Basement, Aggarwal Lane 15, Ansari Road, Daryaganj
Near Times of India Building, New Delhi 110002
Mob : 08505972553

BENGALURU

Pragati Book House : House No. 1, Sanjeevappa Lane, Avenue Road Cross,
Opp. Rice Church, Bengaluru – 560002.
Tel : (080) 64513344, 64513355,Mob : 9880582331, 9845021552
Email:bharatsavla@yahoo.com

CHENNAI

Pragati Books : 9/1, Montieth Road, Behind Taas Mahal, Egmore,
Chennai 600008 Tamil Nadu, Tel : (044) 6518 3535,
Mob : 94440 01782 / 98450 21552 / 98805 82331,
Email : bharatsavla@yahoo.com

niralipune@pragationline.com | www.pragationline.com

Also find us on **f** www.facebook.com/niralibooks

CONTENTS

Chapter 1

PLANT METABOLITES

Plants are biochemical and biosynthetic laboratories which produce diversity of organic compounds from air, water, minerals and sunlight. These vast number of organic compounds enable them to live, grow, and reproduce. A series of enzyme mediated and regulated chemical reactions are used for this purpose. These reactions are collectively called as metabolism. Cell metabolism involves extremely complex sequences of controlled chemical reactions called metabolic pathways. Various metabolic pathways within a cell form the cell's metabolic network.

Major metabolic pathways are lsited below:

Cellular respiration

Glycolysis, Anaerobic respiration, Kreb's cycle / Citric acid cycle, Oxidative phosphorylation

Formation of organic compounds from non-living matter

Photosynthesis (plants, algae, cyanobacteria), Chemosynthesis (some bacteria)

Other pathways include

Fatty acid oxidation (β-oxidation), Gluconeogenesis, HMG-CoA reductase pathway (isoprene prenylation), Urea cycle etc.

Biosynthetic reactions involve different organic reactions like catalytic reactions, phosphorylation, hydride transfer, oxidation, elimination, acylation, alkylation, reduction, condensation, rearrangement etc.

Primary metabolism

The pathways that involve modifying and synthesising carbohydrates, proteins, fats, and nucleic acids are found to be essentially the same in all organisms, apart from minor variations. These processes are collectively described as **primary metabolism**, with the compounds involved in the pathways being termed as **primary metabolites**.

Primary metabolism comprises the chemical processes that every plant must carry out every day in order to survive and reproduce its line like

Photosynthesis	Synthesis of structural material	Transamination
Glycolysis	Duplication of genetic material	Synthesis of proteins and enzymes
Citric Acid Cycle (Krebs cycle)	Reproduction of cells (growth)	Synthesis of coenzymes
Synthesis of amino acids	Absorption of nutrients	

Secondary metabolism: Secondary metabolism comprises metabolic pathways that are not essential for growth, development or reproduction. **Secondary metabolites** are those chemical compounds in organisms that are not directly involved in the normal growth, development or reproduction of an organism. In the sense they are "secondary". These compounds are an extremely diverse group of natural products synthesised by plants, fungi, bacteria, algae, and animals. Most of the secondary metabolites, such as terpenes, phenolic compounds and alkaloids are classified based on their biosynthetic origin. Secondary metabolites, are found in only specific organisms, or groups of organisms, and are an expression of the individuality of species. Thus every type of secondary metabolite is characteristic for each oganism or group of organismis. Secondary metabolites are frequently produced at highest levels during a transition from active growth to stationary phase. The producer organism can grow in the absence of their synthesis, suggesting that secondary metabolism is not essential, at least for short term survival.

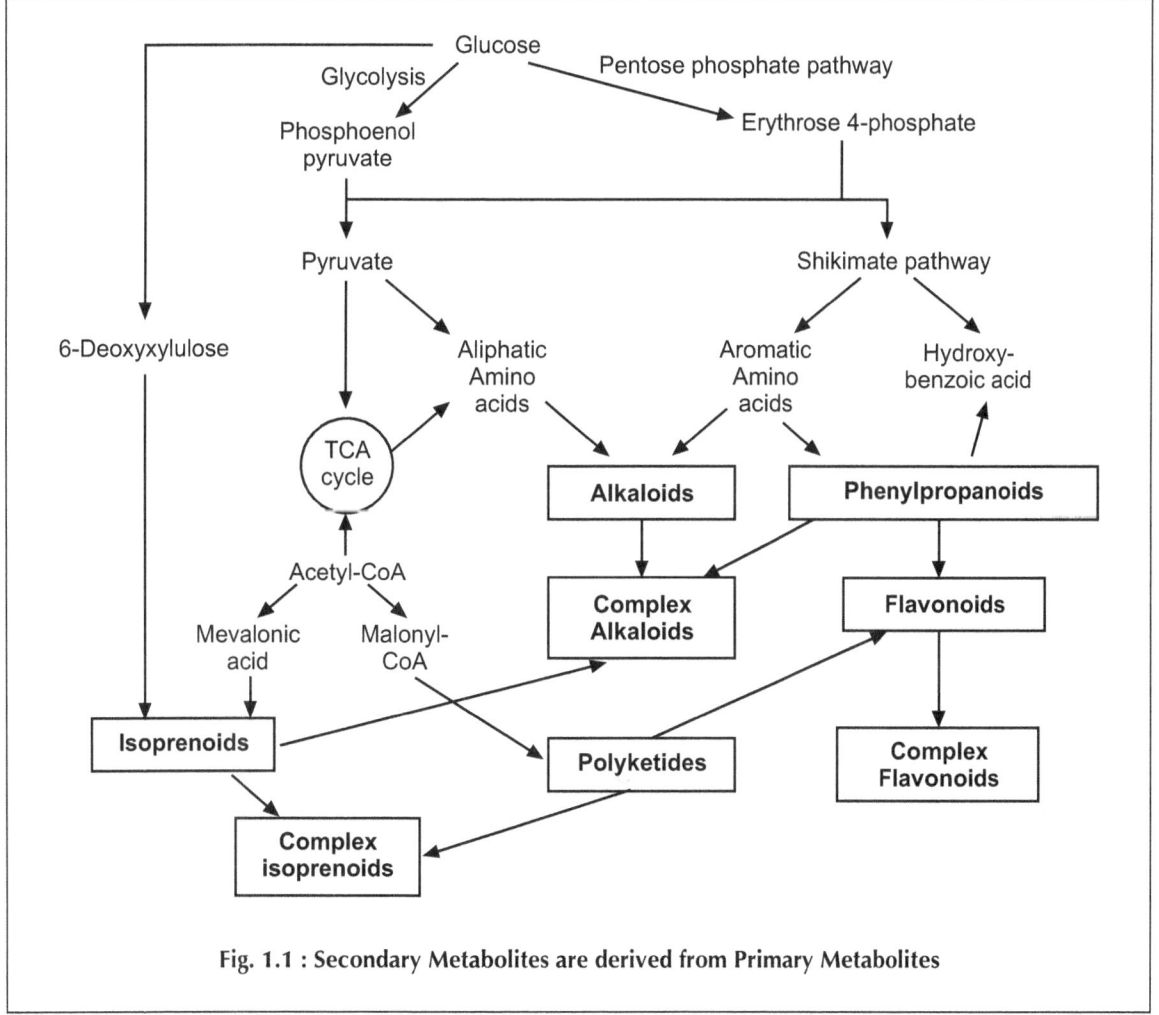

Fig. 1.1 : Secondary Metabolites are derived from Primary Metabolites

Role of secondary metabolites in plants

1. **Role of secondary metabolites in defense mechanisms of plants:** The function or importance of these compounds to the organism is usually of an ecological nature. They are used as defenses against predators, parasites and diseases on the basis of their toxic nature and repellence to herbivores and microbes. Some of the secondary metabolites are also involved in defense against abiotic stress (e.g. UV-B exposure).

2. **Secondary metabolites as attractants and repellants:** Secondary metabolites may be involved in attraction of animals for pollination (fragrance and colour of plants) or seed dispersal. The secondary metabolites may combine role of both as attractants and repellants e.g. anthocyanins or volatile terpenes can be attractants in flowers but are also insecticidal and antimicrobial.

The types and number of secondary metabolites reported from higher plants are presented in the Table 1.1.

Table 1.1 : Secondary Metabolites

Nitrogen-containing Secondary Metabolites	Approximate Numbers
Alkaloids	21000
Amines	100
Glucosinolates	100
Non-protein amino acids (NPAAS)	700
Cyanogenic glycosides	60
Alkamides	150
Lectins,peptides,polypeptides	2000
Secondary Metabolites without Nitrogen	
Monoterpenes including iridoids	2500
Sesquiterpenes	5000
Diterpenes	2500
Triterpenes, steroids, saponins	5000
Tetraterpenes	500
Flavonoids, tannins	5000
Phenylpropanoids, lignin, coumarins, lignans	2000
Polyacetylenes, fatty acid, waxes	1500
Anthraquinones and othes polyketides	750
Carbohydrates, organic acids	200

Based on their biosynthetic origins, plant secondary metabolites can be divided into three major groups

1. Terpenoids

2. Flavonoids and allied phenolic and polyphenolic compounds.

3. Nitrogen-containing alkaloids and sulphur-containing compounds.

1. Terpenoids

Terpenoids are the largest and the most diverse family of natural products, ranging in structure from linear to polycyclic molecules and in size from the five-carbon hemiterpenes to natural rubber, comprising thousands of isoprene units. All terpenoids are biosynthesised through the condensation of isoprene units (C5) from acetyl-coA or glycolytic intermediates. They are classified by the number of five-carbon units present in the core structure. A vast majority of the different terpene structures produced by plants as secondary metabolites that are involved in defense as toxins against a large number of plant feeding insects and mammals. Many flavour and aromatic molecules, such as menthol, linalool, geraniol and caryophyllene are formed by monoterpenes (C10), with two isoprene units, and sesquiterpenes (C15), with three isoprene units. Other bioactive compounds, such as diterpenes (C20), triterpenes (C30) and tetraterpenes (C40) show very special properties and will be also discussed in this chapter later.

i) (a) *Monoterpenes (C10):* Many derivatives are important agents of insect toxicity. For example, the pyrethroids (monoterpenes esters) occur in the leaves and flowers of *Chrysanthemum* species show strong insecticidal responses.

In Gymnosperms like Pine and Fir, monoterpenes mainly as α-pinene, β-pinene, limonene and myrecene, all are toxic to numerous insects including bark beetles.

ii) *Sesquiterpenes (C15):* A number of sesquiterpenes have been till now reported for their role in plant defense as antiherbivore agents of family Composite.

ABA is a sesquiterpene that plays primarily regulatory roles in the initiation and maintenance of seed and bud dormancy and plants response to water stress by modifying the membrane properties.

iii) *Diterpenes (C20):* Phorbol (diterpene ester), found in plants of Euphorbiaceae act as skin irritants and internal toxins to mammals. Gibberellins, a group of plant hormones are also diterpenes, that play various detrimental roles in numerous plant developmental processes such as seed germination, leaf expansion, flower and fruit set.

iv) *Triterpenes (C30):* Several steroid alcohols (sterols) are important components of plant cell membranes, especially in the plasma membrane as regulatory channels and maintain permeability to small molecules by decreasing the motion of the fatty acid chains.

Another triterpene, limnoid, a group of bitter substances in citrus fruits act as antiherbivore compounds in members of family Rutaceae and some other families also.

v) *Polyterpenes (C5)n:* Several high molecular weight polyterpenes occur in plants. Larger terpenes include the tetraterpenes and the polyterpenes. The principal tetraterpenes are carotenoids family of pigments.

2. Flavonoids and allied phenolic and polyphenolic compounds

Phenolics range from simple, low molecular-weight, single aromatic-ringed compounds to large and complex tannins and derived polyphenols. They can be classified based on the number and arrangement of their carbon atoms and are commonly found conjugated to sugars and organic acids. Phenolics can be classified into two groups: the flavonoids and the non-flavonoids. They could be an important part of the plants defense system against pests and diseases including root parasitic nematodes.

e.g. Coumarin, Furano-coumarins, Ligin, Flavonoid, Isoflavonoids, Tannins.

i) **Coumarin:** They are simple phenolic compounds, widespread in vascular plants and appear to function in different capacities in various plant defense mechanisms against insect herbivores and fungi. They are derived from the shikimic acid pathway. These cyclic compounds behave as natural pesticidal defense compounds for plants with higher anti-fungal activity against a range of soil borne plant pathogenic fungi.

ii) **Furano-coumarins:** These are also a type of coumarin with phyto-toxicity abundantly found in members of the family Umbelliferae. E.g. Psoralin.

iii) **Lignin:** It is a highly branched polymer of phenyl-propanoid groups, formed from three different alcohols coniferyl, coumaryl and sinapyl which are oxidized by plant enzyme-peroxidase, to form lignin. Lignifications block the growth of pathogens and are a common response to infection or wounding.

iv) **Flavonoids:** Flavonoids are polyphenolic compounds comprising fifteen carbons, with two aromatic rings connected by a three-carbon bridge. The main subclasses of flavonoids are the flavones, flavonols, flavan-3-ols, isoflavones, flavanones and anthocyanidins.It is one of the largest classes of plant phenolic, perform very different functions in plant system including pigmentation and defense. They protect cells from UV-B radiation because they accumulate in epidermal layers of leaves and stems and strongly absorb light in the UV-B region.

v) **Isoflavonoids:** Isoflavonoids are derived from a flavonone intermediate, naringenin. They are secreted by the legumes and play an important role in promoting the formation of nitrogen-fixing nodules by symbiotic rhizobia.

Table 1.2 : Classification of Flavonoides

Type	Representative compounds	Example
1. Flavonols	Myricitin	Apple, olive
	Quercetin	Orange
	Kaempferol	Black tea
2. Flavanols	Catechin	Pear
	Epicatechin	Green tea
3. Flavones	Apiginin	Celery
	Luteolin	Olives
	Fisetin	
4. Isoflavones	Genistein	Soya-bean
	Daidzein	
5. Flavanones	Hesperidin	Orange
	Naringin	Grape fruit
	Hesperitin	

Some important flavonoids are

Quercetin

Hesperidin

Naringin

vi) **Tanins:** They are a group of survival plant phenolic polymers with defensive properties. Most tannins have molecular masses between 600 and 3000. Tannins are general toxins that significantly reduce the growth and survival of many herbivores and also act as feeding repellents. They cause a sharp, astringent sensation in the mouth as a result of their binding of salivary proteins. Mammals such as cattle, deer and apes, characteristically avoid plant with high tannin contents

3. Nitrogen-containing alkaloids and sulphur-containing compounds

The alkaloids are a large and structurally diverse group of compounds and are derived from amino acids. The names of these molecules tend to end in the suffixes –ine. With a few exceptions, alkaloids are most soluble in hydroethanolic media and they generally occur as salts (e.g., chlorides or sulfates) or as N-oxides in plants. Most of them have a heterocyclic nitrogenous ring or ring system and a basic (alkaline) character. The alkaloids are potent medicinal molecules as well as toxic or even potentially fatal ones. There are many different ways of classifying alkaloids like

Table 1.3: A. Heterocyclic Alkaloids (True Alkaloids)

	Type	Basic ring structure	Examples
1.	Pyrrole and Pyrrolidine		Hygrine, coca species
2.	Pyridine and Piperidine		Arecoline, anabasine, coniine, lobeline, pelletierine, trigonelline

Condt...

	Type	Basic ring structure	Examples
3.	Pyrrolizidine		Echimidine, senecionine, seneciphylline, symphitine
4.	Tropane (piperidine. N-methyl pyrrolidine)		Atropine, hyoscine, hyoscyamine, cocaine, pseudo- pelletierine, meteloidine
5.	Quinoline		Quinine, quinidine, cinchonine, cinchonidine cupreine, camptothecin.
6.	Isoquinoline		d-tubocurarine, berberine, emetine, cephaeline, papaverine, narcotine, narceine
7.	Phenanthrene		Morphine, codeine, hydrastine
8.	Aporphine (reduced isoquinoline-naphthalene)		Boldine
	Type	**Basic ring structure**	**Examples**
9.	Indole (Benz pyrrole)		Ergometrine, ergotamine, reserpine, vincristine, vinblastine, strychnine, brucine, physostigmine
10.	Imidazole		Pilocarpine, Isopilocarpine, Pilosine
11.	Norlupinane		Cytisine, laburnine, lupanine, sparteine

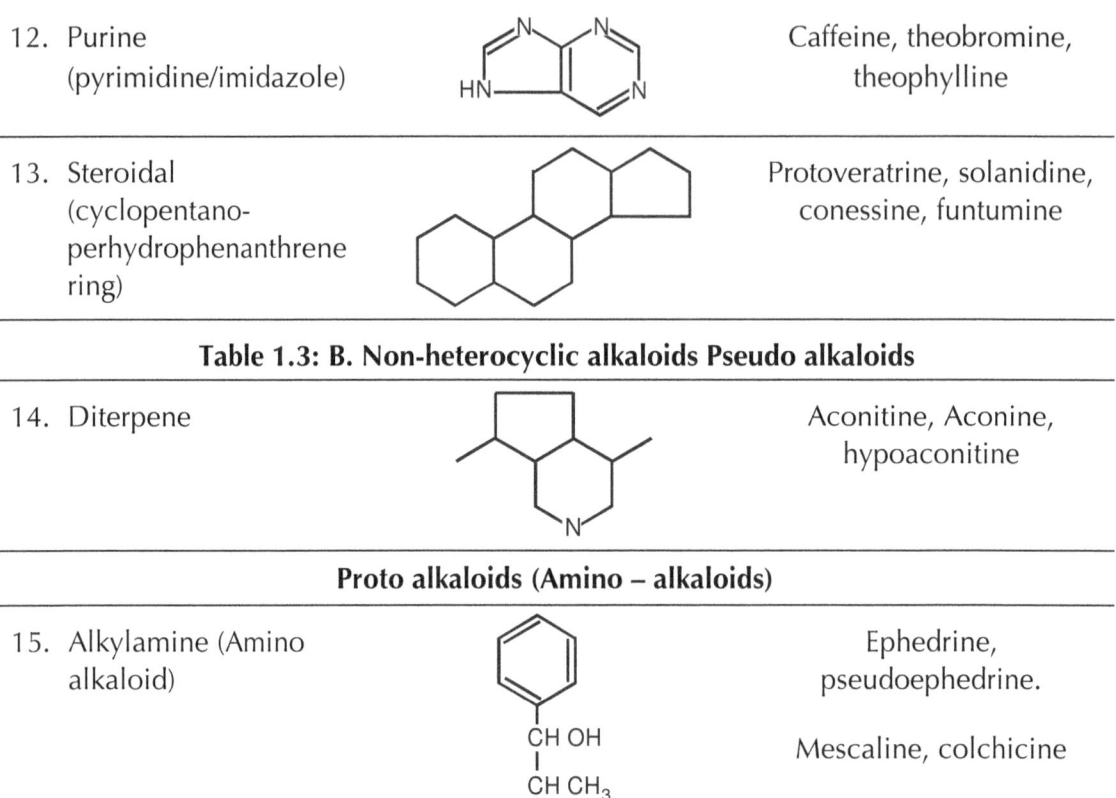

12.	Purine (pyrimidine/imidazole)		Caffeine, theobromine, theophylline
13.	Steroidal (cyclopentano- perhydrophenanthrene ring)		Protoveratrine, solanidine, conessine, funtumine

Table 1.3: B. Non-heterocyclic alkaloids Pseudo alkaloids

14.	Diterpene		Aconitine, Aconine, hypoaconitine

Proto alkaloids (Amino – alkaloids)

15.	Alkylamine (Amino alkaloid)		Ephedrine, pseudoephedrine. Mescaline, colchicine

Use of secondary metabolites as medicinal compunds.

The crude drugs are subjected to suitable methods of extraction and purification for the isolation of phytopharmaceuticals, which could be incorporated as active ingredients in the modern system of medicine.

The anthracene glycosides such as sennoside are extracted in the form of their stable calcium salts from the leaves and pods of Senna. The indole alkaloids such as ergometrine and ergotamine are commercially extracted as their salts from the fungus of ergot, known as *Claviceps purpurea*. Ergometrine maleate is an oxytocic, whereas ergotamine tartarate is used in combination with caffeine for the treatment of migraine. Caffeine is extracted from tea or tea waste, whereas Nux vomica seeds serve as the raw material for the extraction of strychnine. The antihypertensive and tranquillising agent reserpine is commercially obtained from the roots and rhizomes of *Rauwolfia serpentina*. The miracle discovery of the recent years is the extraction of vinca alkaloids, especially vinblastine and vincristine sulphate from *Catharanthus roseus*.

Vinblastine sulphate is used for treatment of neoplasms and is recommended for generalised Hodgkin's disease and choriocarcinoma resistant to other therapy, whereas vincristine sulphate is recommended for the treatment of leukemia in children.

The commercial supply of tropane alkaloids, particularly scopolamine, is from different species of *Duboisia* such as *D. myoporoides*, and *D. leichhardtii*, whereas other tropane alkaloids l-hyoscyamine and atropine are obtained from *Atropa belladonna* and *Datura metel*. The drug, 8-methoxy psoralen, used in the treatment of leucoderma is extracted commercially from the inflorescence of *Ammi majus*. Pectin of pharmaceutical grade is only obtained from the vegetative source, especially the inner part of the rind of citrus fruits, apple pomace and sun flowers. Isoquinoline alkaloids such as morphine, papaverine, codeine and thebaine are extracted from opium latex obtained from poppy capsules. The cardio-active glycoside, digoxin is commercially extracted from leaves of *Digitalis lanata*, whereas digitoxin, gitoxin and their aglycones are obtained from both *D. lanata* and *D. purpurea*. The ester pesticides obtained from pyrethrum, *Chrysanthemum cinerarifolium* are pyrethrin I and II. Several semi-synthetic analogs of these esters are being used as contact poisons for insects. In addition to pyrethrins, nicotine, sabadilla alkaloids and rotenoids are also used as contact insecticides and are derived from vegetative sources.

The alkaloids quinine and quinidine are commercially obtained from the bark of different *Cinchona* species. Quinine sulphate is an antimalarial drug. In recent years, it has regained considerable importance in the treatment of chloroquine-resistant *Falciparum malaria*. Quinidine sulphate occurs as fine needle like white crystals and is a cardiac depressant. It is used particularly to inhibit auricular fibrillation.

A steroidal sapogenin, hecogenin, is commercially extracted from *Agave veracuz* and *Agave cantata* (Amaryllidaceae). Hecogenin is used as the starting material for the manufacture of cortisones and sex hormones. Podophyllotoxin from *Podophyllum hexandrum* and anacardic acid from *Semecarpus anacardium* are two promising phytochemicals as anti-mitotic drugs. Asiaticoside is the glucoside useful in treatment of leprosy and extracted commercially in very small concentrations from aerial parts of *Centella asiatica*.

The wonder drugs of plant origin reported in recent years are ginsenosides from *Panax ginseng* and have acquired commercial significance in view of their stimulative, alterative and general tonic properties. 18-β glycyrrhetinic acid from liquorice is the drug of choice in the treatment of peptic ulcers and hyperacidity.

Pilocarpine nitrate, a drug useful in the treatment of glaucoma, is extracted from leaves of *Pilocarpus jaborandi*.

Tannic acid of pharmaceutical grade is obtained from galls and myrobalans. The genus *Solanum* (Solanaceae) comprises of widely distributed species, some of which contain steroidal glycoalkaloid solasodine. The berries of *Solanum khasianum* are rich in solasodine content, which is used as starting material for the production of sex hormones. Steroidal sapogenin, diosgenin, obtained from several *Dioscorea* species and *Costus speciosus* also serve as the starting material for the manufacture of corticosteroids.

A number of essential oils and their chemicals used as medicinal and flavouring agents are obtained from plant sources. Some of the examples of this category are the volatile oils of peppermint, spearmint, clove, eucalyptus, ginger, citronella, thyme and vetiver. The volatile products produce the characteristic odour of flowers, spices and perfumes. The most, exotic and expensive of the volatile oils are those used in perfumery. Geraniol, linalool and citronellal isolated from a number of volatile oils are widely used as components of perfume formulations. Citral from lemon grass oil is itself used in perfumery and soaps. It can also be converted to the ionones, one of which serves as an intermediate in commercial synthesis of vitamin A, while the other provides a substitute for the extremely expensive oil of violets.

The majority of spices, condiments, teas and other beverages such as coffee, kola and cocoa owe their unique and characteristic properties (aromas and flavours) to physiologically active secondary metabolites that they contain. Although today several of their purified principles (e.g. vanillin and caffeine) are produced by semi or total synthesis, high prices are still paid for compounds or mixtures extracted from their natural sources, especially if they are intended for use as flavouring agents or food additives. Spices are usually more diversified than the perfume principles containing not only terpenes, especially from dill, caraway, fennel, celery etc. but also aromatic aldehydes (cinnamic aldehyde from cinnamon), phenols (anethal from anise, eugenol from clove and safrole from *Sassafras*) and sulphur compounds (*Allium*).

Plants continue to be important sources of new drugs, as evidenced by the recent approvals of several new plant derived drugs and synthetic drugs based on secondary plant metabolites. Etoposide is a new semi-synthetic antineoplastic agent derived from subterranean parts of *Podophyllum peltatum* reported to be useful in chemotherapeutic treatment of refractory testicular carcinomas, small cell lung carcinomas, non-Hodgkin's lymphomas and non-lymphocytic leukemias. The technical-know how for indigenous production of etoposide is claimed to have been developed by Indian Institute of Chemical Technology, Hyderabad. Cannabinoids are being developed for use in neurological disorders (e.g. epilepsy and dystonia) and as antihypertensives, antiasthmatics and potent analgetics. Atracurium besylate is a new synthetic skeletal muscle relaxant, which is structurally and pharmacologically related to curare alkaloids. Plant-derived drugs of clinical significance discovered in recent years include artemisinin, a rapidly acting antimalarial agent from chinese drug, *Artemisia annua*; forskohlin, a naturally occurring labdenone di-terpene with antihypertensive, positive inotropic and adenylcyclose - activating properties from *Coleus forskohlii* and sanguinarine an antiplaque alkaloid with both preventive and therapeutic effects on dental plaque. The other bioactive compounds of therapeutic significance include organosulphur compounds of garlic and onions as cardiovascular agents, guggulipids with antiarthrytic property from *Commiphora mukul*; ellagic acid as a prototype anti-mutagen and cancer preventing agent; vasicin as oxytocic agent from *Adhatoda vasica*. Intensely sweet plant metabolites such as stevioside, glycyrrhizin, hernandulcin are already used in Japan and Europe.

The technology involved in the extraction of phytochemicals of pharmaceutical significance in majority of the cases is the guarded secret of a pharmaceutical or chemical firm. An overall approach to the method of extraction of these phytopharmaceuticals represents the co-ordination of research work carried out by scientists of different disciplines. With the advancement in analytical techniques and instrumentation technology in last three decades, it has been possible to devise commercially feasible techniques for the extraction of several phytochemicals.

Table 1.4 : Promising phytopharmaceuticals with their activity

No.	Phytopharmaceuticals	Natural Source	Activity
	ANTI-ULCER		
1.	Catechin	Leaves of *Artocarpus integra*	anti-ulcer
2.	Cyanidanol	Stereoisomer of catechin from seed coat of *Anacardium occidentale*	anti-ulcer (inhibiting action on histidine decarboxylase)
3.	Isoliquiritin	Rhizomes of *Glycyrrhiza glabra*	anti-ulcer
4.	Sophoradin	*Sophora subprotostata*	anti-ulcer
	ANTI-PROTOZOAL		
5.	Quinine microcapsules in oral formulation	Bark of *Cinchona* species	anti-malarial
6.	Pycnamine	*Triclisi* species	anti-malarial
7.	Immuno toxins like pokeweed antiviral proteins	Seeds of *Phytolacca maricana*	anti-trypanosomal, anti-leishmanial
	CARDIOVASCULAR TREATMENTS		
8.	Colenol (forskolin)	*Coleus forskohlii*	Hypotensive
9.	Digoxin	Enzymatic conversion and further selective 12 β-hydroxylation of thevenerrin and nerrifolin from yellow oleander *Thevetia nerrifolia*	Cardiotonic

10.	Aescin	Seeds of *Aesculus hippocastanum*	anti-inflammatory
11.	Nimbidin	Seeds oil of *Azadirachta indica*	anti-inflammatory
12.	Curcumin	Rhizomes of *Curcuma longa*	anti-inflammatory
ANTI-VIRAL AGENTS			
13.	Castarospermine	*Castarospermum australe*	anti-HIV
14.	Lyophilised infusion of hypericum	*Hypericum perforatum*	Influenza A and B
15.	Calanolide A	*Calophyllum lanigeum*	anti-HIV (reverse transcriptase inhibitor)
IMMUNOMODULATORS AND ADAPTOGENS			
16.	Sitoindoside VII and VIII	Roots of *Withania somnifera*	antistress
17.	Polysaccharide fraction	*Echinacea angustifolia* and *E. purpurea*	immunomodulator
18.	Syringin and cordiol	*Tinospora cordifolia*	immunomodulator
ANTI-CANCER			
19.	Bryostatin	Macrolide from bryozoans	anti-cancer (Partial agonist of protein kinase C)
20.	Rhizoxin	fungal metabolite	anti-cancer (antimetabolite)
ANTI-DIABETIC			
21.	Polypeptide P (P-Insulin) and charantin	*Momordica charantia*	anti-diabetic
22.	Gymnemic acids 1 - 4 and gurmarin	*Gymnema sylvestre*	anti-diabetic (both in insulin dependent and non-insulin dependent diabetis mellitus)

Historical contribution:

The term "Pharmacognosy" was introduced by C.A. Sydler, in 1815 in Germany. This name is formed from two Greek words "*Pharmakon*" which means drugs and "*gnosis*" means knowledge. This term was most comprehensively described by "Fluckiger" as "Pharmacognosy is the simultaneous applications of various scientific discipline with the object of acquiring knowledge of drugs from every point of view".

Then pharmacognosy may be defined as "an applied science that deals with the biologic, biochemical, and economic features of natural drugs and their constituents".

The survey of past records are extremely helpful to recognize those who have contributed to the subject matter that constituted the field of pharmacognosy.

"Papyrus Ebers" is the well known document written in 1500 BC and was found in tomb of mummy. It is now preserved at the university of Leipzig.

Dioscorides, a Greek physician, wrote "De Materia Medica" in 78 A.D. in which he described about 600 plants that were known to have medicinal significance. For example, Aloe, bellodonna, ergot, colchicum, hyoscyamus, opium etc. are few that are still used for their medicinal properties.

Galen (131-200 A.D.), a Greek pharmacist physician. He described the method of preparing formulae containing plant and animal drugs. As a tribute to his knowledge and contribution the term "galenical" pharmacy was originated.

In historical development of pharmacognosy as a subject the role of certain individuals is of considerable importance.

Jonathan Pereira (1804 – 1853) First British pharmacognosist who gave pharmaceutical basis to the subject and is considered as founder of British pharmacognosy.

Daneil Hanbury (1825 – 1875) and E.M. Holmes (1843 – 1930) both were renowned applied pharmacognosists.

H.G. Greenish (1855 – 1933) and T.E. Wallis (1876 – 1973) transformed old academic pharmacognosy and made extensive use of microscope for elimination of adulteration from powered drug.

Microscopical examinations are thus, important for pharmacipoeial identification and quality control.

The isolation techniques offer phytoconsitituents in pure form.

The era of pure compound began with the isolation of morphine between 1803 to 1806 by Friedrich Serturner.

Examples of isolated constituents are as follows :

-   Morphine (1806)   –   Friedrich Serturner
-   Strychine (1817)   –   Joseph Caventou
-   Quinine (1820)   –   Pierre Joseph
                               Pelletier and Joseph caventou
-   Caffeine (1820)   –   Pierre Jean Robiquet, and Runge
-   Nicotine (1828)   –   Wilhelm Heinrich and Karl Reinmann
-   Atropine (1833)   –   Runge
-   Curcumin (1842)   –   Vogel
-   Cocaine (1855)   –   Friedrich Gaedacke
-   Puysostigmine (1864) - Jobst and Hesse

In 19th century, the chemical structures of many of isolated compounds were determined, which are of medicinal significance.   ❖❖❖

Chapter 2

PHARMACOGNOSTIC SCHEME FOR STUDY OF NATURAL DRUGS

INTRODUCTION

The pharmacognostic study of crude drugs involves the use of several technical terms. It is necessary to make students familiar with these terms by quoting suitable examples. The sequence for illustration shall be as follows (Fig. 2.1).

1. Official titles

2. Synonyms

3. Biological source

4. Geographical distribution

5. Cultivation and collection

6. Plant protection

7. Organoleptic characters

8. Microscopic characters

9. Chemical constituents

10. Chemical tests

11. Therapeutic and pharmaceutical uses

12. Commercial varieties, substitutes and adulterants

13. Storage and Preservation of natural drugs.

1.   Official titles : Unless otherwise mentioned, it means the title by which it appears in the Indian Pharmacopoeia, any other pharmacopoeia or standard books. The drugs of outstanding therapeutic value are standardised in the national pharmacopoeias, of which about forty are published at intervals by different countries in the world.

In the first edition of Indian Pharmacopoeia (1955), all official titles were in Latin, while in the second and subsequent editions official titles are given in English.

2.   Synonyms : These are the frequently used alternative terms identical in sense to the official titles of the drugs. While prescribing the drugs, many a times, they are abbreviated and such abbreviated terms of commonly known drugs in various languages are known as synonyms. Indian Pharmacopoeia recognises English and Hindi synonyms only. e.g. LIQUORICE root in English or GLYCYRRHIZA RADIX in Latin and Mulethi in Hindi.

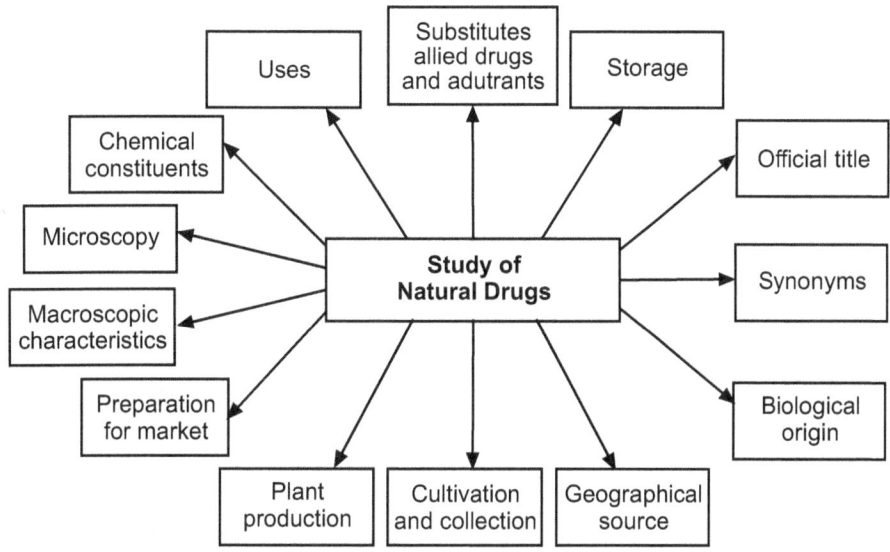

Fig. 2.1 : Study of Natural Drugs

3. **Biological origin :** In biological source, the details of the following aspects are covered.

(a) **Nature of the drug :** Whether it consists of dry or the fresh form of the drug.

(b) **Part of the plant used :** Particular part of the plant i.e. flower, bark, seed, fruit, root, wood, leaves or entire organism be mentioned carefully.

(c) **Systematic name :** Its scientific and systematic name may be botanical or zoological, depending upon the source of the drug, with family, varieties and species, if any.

(d) **Limit for active constituents :** Many a times, pharmacopoeias make a reference to the minimum contents of active constituents of drugs.

(e) **Miscellaneous details :** As and when it is necessary, the official books also mention, alongwith the source, whether the drug is collected from cultivated trees or otherwise. Sometimes, the method of preparing the drug to meet the official standards is also mentioned. At times, the season of collecting the drugs is also mentioned in the text.

Examples

(i) **Colchicum seeds** consist of the dried ripe seeds of *Colchicum luteum*, family : Liliaceae. It should contain not less than 0.3 % of colchicine.

(ii) **Fennel** consists of dried ripe fruits of *Foeniculum vulgare* Mill, family : Umbelliferae.

(iii) **Strophanthus** consists of dried seeds of the plant *Strophanthus kombe*, deprived of its awns, family : Apocynaceae.

(iv) **Cinnamon** consists of dried inner bark of the shoots of a cultivated, coppiced trees of *Cinnamomum zeylanicum*, family : Lauraceae.

(v) **Castor oil** consists of fixed oil obtained from the dried seeds of *Ricinus communis*, family Euphorbiaceae, drawn by cold expression method.

4. **Geographical distribution and history :** Habitat or geographical source indicates wherefrom the drug is obtained commercially. It may also provide history of transplantation and the original source of drugs. History of a crude drug reveals about its introduction to mankind.

5. **Cultivation and collection :** Most of the crude drugs are obtained from cultivated plants. It is experienced that the plants obtained from cultivated source yield more in all respects and hence, the system of cultivation of medicinal plants should be thoroughly studied. The normal requirements for the systematic cultivation are to be studied with reference to the soil, rain, altitude and other climatic conditions. The suitability of any of the above or all is identified and during cultivation all these requirements are provided. The fertilisers are required to be fed after taking into consideration the part of the plant to be used in medicine. For example, rhizomes are very exhaustive to the soil and hence, need heavy dose of fertilisers. Many a times, specific micronutrients or plant hormones are required to be provided to the plants.

The **collection** of the crude drugs also calls for the knowledge of their chemical constituents responsible for therapeutic uses. Thus, the choice of collection of drug depends upon constituents of the plants and not on the suitability or availability of the labour. Generally, the plants are collected when they are rich in their chemical constituents. In certain cases, they are also collected in the specific season or at the specific time and mostly, in dry weather. The reasons for this are self-explanatory. Either the plants are sensitive to the high temperature or to damp climatic conditions due to high relative humidity. The drugs containing thermolabile substances and volatile oils can be conveniently collected at low temperature.

6. **Plant protection :** Unless the cultivated plants are protected properly, the purpose of cultivation is not served fully. The destructive pests to the plants may be pathogenic fungi, insects, rodents or other animals. The agents used to protect the plants include insecticides, herbicides, rodenticides, miticides etc. The methods for controlling them are classified as mechanical, biological, chemical and agricultural methods.

(a) **Mechanical method :** It includes the operations like pruning or burning of pest infested part of the plant or trapping of pests.

(b) **Biological method :** It depends upon the type of pest. For example, many a times, flies, rabbits and even rats are troublesome to the plants. Cats, owls and hawks are natural enemies of rats and mice; frogs and birds constantly feed on insects.

These are some of the examples of natural biological control. The recent approach in pest control is development of juvenile hormone (JH) mimicking agents.

(c) **Chemical method :** Several organic or inorganic compounds are used to destroy or inhibit the action of pests. Pesticides are usually toxic to human beings. The insecticides may be of two types, i.e. contact insecticides and stomach poisons. The contact insecticides are D.D.T., B.H.C., endrine, parathion, malathion etc. These act by their contact with insects. The stomach poisons are thimet, arsenic trioxide, Paris green and fluorides like sodium fluoride and sodium fluorosilicate.

(d) **Agricultural method :** This method includes efforts of plant breeders to develop selected crop that could resist attack of pests. The efforts in hybridizing varieties that resist bacterial and fungal attacks have been proved successful in recent years.

7. Macroscopic characters or morphology (organoleptic studies) : Identification of the crude drug by organoleptic characters is one of the important aspects of pharmacognostical study. Morphological study follows a special terminology which must be known to a pharmacognosist. The morphological terminology is derived from botany and zoology, depending upon the source of the drug. In general, colour, odour, taste, size, shape and the special features of the crude drugs are to be studied under morphology.

8. Microscopic characters (Histology) : In the organised crude drugs of plant origin, the study of histological features is the main criterion for their evaluation. The arrangement of the tissues in the transverse and longitudinal sections and types of cells and cell-contents are revealed by suitable microscopic study of a crude drug.

A special reference is made to the presence or absence of stomata, trichomes, calcium oxalate crystals, starch grains and other specific characteristics. A reference should be made to the presence or absence of fibres, stone cells and to the cellular arrangements in detail alongwith the sizes of cells.

9. Chemical constituents : The utility of the drugs is due to the chemicals which they contain. Sometimes, these drugs contain several constituents which are inert therapeutically. Therefore, a pharmacist should know about the active and inactive constituents of the crude drug. For example, caraway contains volatile oil, fixed oil and proteins, volatile oil being the active constituent. Cinnamon contains volatile oil, tannin and mucilage. Mucilage and tannin are inactive constituents of cinnamon.

10. Chemical tests : The organised drugs can be identified by their histological characters. But, the unorganised drugs which do not have microscopic characters are confirmed by chemical tests. The solubility, physical characteristics and chemical tests are important parameters for the study of unorganised drugs. The aloes, being an unorganised drug, can be confirmed by the chemical test for anthraquinone derivatives and castor oil, by its solubility in three and half times volume of ethyl alcohol. The chemical tests are also useful in the identification of powdered organised drugs.

11. Therapeutic and pharmaceutical uses : Basically, drugs are used for two different purposes, that is

(i) Preventive (prophylactic) and

(ii) Curative (therapeutic).

Therapeutic activity means the action of drug on the human or animal body with specific intention to cure the disorder. For example, fennel is a carminative, senna is a purgative, while catechu is an astringent and opium is used as a hypnotic.

The **pharmaceutical use** of drug may be in isolation of desired constituent from crude drug or even, it may be to impart colour, odour, taste, or thickness to the pharmaceutical preparations. For example, lemon peels are used for isolation of pectin. Cinnamon is used as a flavouring agent. Turmeric is a colouring agent. Honey is a sweetening ingredient and acacia is used as an emulsifier (Table 2.1).

Table 2.1 : Natural Drugs as Pharmaceutical Aids

Sr. No.	Name of Natural Drugs	Use
1.	Guar gum	Thickening agent
2.	Agar	Binder
3.	Tragaanth	Suspending and
4.	Acacia	Emulsifying agent
5.	Sterculia gum	Emulsifying agent
6.	Cardamom	Flavouring agents
7.	Lemon	
8.	Orange	
9.	Caraway	
10.	Cochineal	Colouring agent
11.	Carmine	Colouring agent
12.	Turmeric	
13.	Honey	Sweetening agents
14.	Stevia	
15.	Glycyrrhiza	
16.	Cotton	
17.	Talc	Filter aids
18.	Kieselguhr	

Contd...

19.	Honey	
20.	Castor oil	Vehicles
21.	Sesame oil	
22.	Lavender oil	
23.	Rose oil	Perfume and in cosmetics
24.	Citronella oil	

12. Commercial species, varieties, substitutes and adulterants : Commercial varieties are of paramount importance in the study of pharmacognosy of a crude drug. When several varieties of the same plant are available commercially, their systematic identification is of great significance. Digitalis has several species of commercial significance like *Digitalis purpurea, Digitalis lanata, Digitalis thapsi* etc. *Digitalis purpurea* is an official drug in several pharmacopoeias, while *Digitalis lanata* is recognised by B.P.C. and U.S.P. *Digitalis thapsi* is a substitute for both. In case of liquorice, the official drug is *Glycyrrhiza glabra*. Several varieties are available, other than official drug, commercially. *Glycyrrhiza glandulifera* and *Glycyrrhiza violacea* are the drugs of second choice.

Substitutes : The word substitute itself is self-explanatory. If the official drug is not available, a substitute may serve the purpose. Substitutes are used in place of genuine or official drug, even though they may be therapeutically less effective. Substitutes resemble to a great extent to the authentic drug in morphology and chemical constituents. *Cinnamomum burmanii* and *C. loureirii* are substitutes for *Cinnamomum zeylanicum*.

Adulterants : The adulterants are somewhat similar to genuine drug with respect to morphological appearance. They may show similarity of colour, size, shape, smell etc., but it does not mean that the adulterants have either the identical or similar physiological actions, if they are taken internally. The seeds of *Strychons nux vomica* are adulterated with that of *Strychnos nux blanda* or *Strychnos potatorum*, which do not contain strychnine.

13. Storage and preservation of crude drugs : Storage of the crude drugs is as important as the cultivation, collection and preparation of the drug for the market. Proper storage is necessary for maintaining the potency of the drugs. The knowledge of nature of the drug and its chemical constituents is necessary for proper storage of crude drugs. For example, colophony is required to be stored in big masses as it gets oxidised and looses its solubility in ether, if powdered. Digitalis, being very sensitive to moisture should be stored in a container containing dehydrating agents. In several other cases, storage conditions of the drug are specific. The storage of squill, ergot, cardamom etc., is specifically mentioned and so merits special attention.

Chapter 3

PRIMARY METABOLITES OF PHARMACEUTICAL AND INDUSTRIAL UTILITY

A primary metabolite is a kind of metabolite that is directly involved in normal growth, development and reproduction.

A. CARBOHYDRATES

Formerly, carbohydrates were defined as a group of compounds composed of carbon, hydrogen and oxygen in which the later two elements are in the same proportion as in water and were expressed by a formula $(CH_2O)n$, i.e. hydrates of carbon. The word carbohydrate can be traced back to Germans, who called them 'kohlenhydrates'. It was then termed carbohydrates in English. The definition did not remain valid as it was misleading with a few compounds like (1) acetic acid expressed as CH_3COOH (i.e. $C_2H_4O_2$) and lactic acid as $CH_3CHOHCOOH$ (i.e. $C_3H_6O_3$), which are not carbohydrates and (2) sugars like rhamnose and fucose represented by the formula $C_6H_{12}O_5$.

The carbohydrates are defined as *polyhydroxy aldehydes* or *polyhydroxy ketones* or *compounds that on hydrolysis produce either of the above*.

They are substances of universal occurrence and are much abundant in plants, rather than in animals.

Carbohydrates are grouped into two major classes: simple sugars (saccharides) and polysaccharides. Low molecular weight carbohydrates are crystalline, soluble in water and sweet in taste; e.g. glucose, fructose, and sucrose. The high molecular weight carbohydrates (polymers) are amorphous, tasteless and relatively less soluble in water e.g. starch, cellulose, gums, pectins, inulin, etc. Depending upon the chemical structure, saccharides are subdivided as monosaccharides, disaccharides and trisaccharides.

[A] MONOSACCHARIDES

Monosaccharides are sugars, which cannot be further hydrolysed to simple sugars. However, they are classified according to the number of carbon atoms in sugar molecules.

Glyceraldehyde   **D-erythrose**   **D-threose**

1. **Bioses:** They contain two carbon atoms. They do not occur in a free state in nature.

2. **Trioses ($C_3H_6O_3$):** They contain three carbon atoms, but in the form of phospheric esters, e.g. glyceraldehyde.

3. **Tetroses ($C_4H_8O_4$):** They contain four carbon atoms, e.g. erythrose and threose.

4. **Pentoses ($C_5H_{10}O_5$):** They are very common in plants and are the products of hydrolysis of polysaccharides like hemicelluloses, mucilage and gums, e.g. arabinose, ribose and xylose.

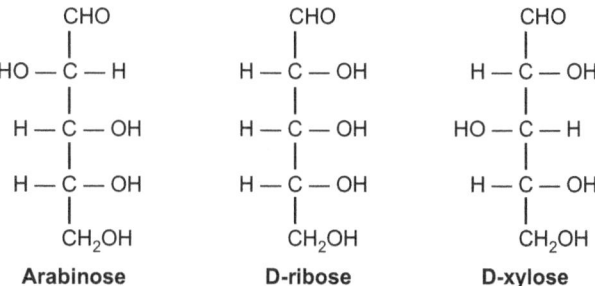

5. **Hexoses:** They are the monosaccharides containing six carbon atoms and are abundantly available carbohydrates of plant kingdom. They are further divided into two types - aldoses and ketoses, obtained by the hydrolysis of polysaccharides like starch, inulin, etc.

Aldoses: Glucose, mannose, galactose

```
      CHO                    CHO                    CHO
       |                      |                      |
HO — C — H            H — C — OH            H — C — OH
       |                      |                      |
HO — C — H            HO — C — H            HO — C — H
       |                      |                      |
 H — C — OH            HO — C — H            H — C — OH
       |                      |                      |
 H — C — OH            H — C — OH            H — C — OH
       |                      |                      |
    CH₂OH                  CH₂OH                  CH₂OH
  D-Mannose             D-galactose            D-glucose
```

Ketoses: Fructose, sorbose and rhamnose

```
     CH₂OH                  CH₂OH                    CHO
       |                      |                      |
      C = O                  C = O            H — C — OH
       |                      |                      |
 HO — C — H            HO — C — H            HO — C — H
       |                      |                      |
  H — C — OH            H — C — OH            HO — C — H
       |                      |                      |
  H — C — OH            HO — C — H            H — C — OH
       |                      |                      |
    CH₂OH                  CH₂OH                   CH₃
  D-Fructose             D-Sarbose            D-Rhamnose
```

6. Heptoses: They contain seven carbon atoms, vitally important in the photosynthesis of plants and glucose metabolism of animals and are rarely found accumulated in plants, e.g. glucoheptose and mannoheptose.

[B] DISACCHARIDES

Carbohydrates, which yield two molecules of monosaccharides upon hydrolysis, are called as disaccharides.

Sucrose $\xrightarrow{\text{Hydrolysis}}$ glucose + fructose
(Cane-sugar)

Sucrose $(C_{12}H_{22}O_{11})$

Maltose $\xrightarrow{\text{Hydrolysis}}$ glucose + glucose
(Malt-sugar)

Maltose

Lactose $\xrightarrow{\text{Hydrolysis}}$ glucose + galactose
(Milk-sugar)

Lactose

[C] TRISACCHARIDES

As the name indicates, these liberate three molecules of monosaccharides on hydrolysis.

Raffinose $\xrightarrow{\text{Hydrolysis}}$ glucose + fructose + galactose (in beet and manna)

Raffinose
$(C_{18}H_{32}O_{16})$

Gentianose $\xrightarrow{\text{Hydrolysis}}$ glucose + glucose + fructose (gentian roots)

Scillatriose (squill), mannotriose (manna) and phanteose (psyllium) are the other examples of trisaccharides.

Table 3.1 : The examples of trisaccharides along with their products of hydrolysis

Sr. No.	Name	Source	Products of Hydrolysis
1.	Gentianose	*Gentiana* sp.	Glucose + glucose + fructose
2.	Planteose	Isapgol, Psyllum seeds	Glucose + fructose + gelactose
3.	Rhamniose	Rhubarb (*Rhamnus infectoria*)	Rham + rhamnose + gelactose
4.	Scillatriose	Squill (*Urgenia maritima*)	Glucose + glucose + rhamnose
5.	Manneotriose	Manna (*Fraxinus* – sp.)	Glucose + galactose + galactose

[D] TETRASACCHARIDES

Stachyose or manneotetrose is an example of tetrasaccharide. Its products of hydrolysis are-

Stachyose (manneotetrose) $\xrightarrow{\text{Hydrolysis}}$ glucose + fructose + galactose + galactose

The examples of plants containing tetrasaccharide are *Stachys japonica* and manna *Fraxinus urnus*.

[E] POLYSACCHARIDES

On hydrolysis, they give an indefinite number of monosaccharides. By condensation, with the elimination of water, polysaccharides are produced from monosaccharides. Depending upon the type of product of hydrolysis these are further classified as pentosans and hexosan. Xylan is a pentosan, whereas starch, inulin and cellulose are the examples of hexosans. Cellulose is composed of glucose units joined by β -1, 4 linkages, hydrolysable by an enzyme cellulose present in animals, whereas starch contains glucose units connected with α-1, 4; α-1, 6 units.

Polyuronides i.e. alginic acid, pectin), gums and mucilages are the other pharmaceutically important polysaccharide derivatives. Gums are the pathological products consisting of calcium, potassium and magnesium salts of complex substances known as **'polyuronides'**. On prolonged boiling with dilute acids, they yield a mixture of sugars and uronic acids. Mucilages are physiological products related to gums and they are generally sulphuric acid esters, the ester group being a complex polysaccharide. Both gums and mucilages are considered as decomposition products of cellulose. Pectin is a neutral methoxy ester of an aldobionic acid-pectic acid, obtained as a water soluble compound from the inner portion of the rind of citrus fruits. Gums and mucilages are closely related to hemicelluloses in composition, except that the sugars produced by hemicelluloses are glucose, mannose and xylose, instead of galactose and arabinose.

Gums are either hydrophobic or hydrophilic high molecular weight molecules, usually, with colloidal properties, in a appropriate solvent or swelling agent. They produce gels, highly viscous suspensions or solutions.

Depending upon types of occurrence, gums can be classified as follows.

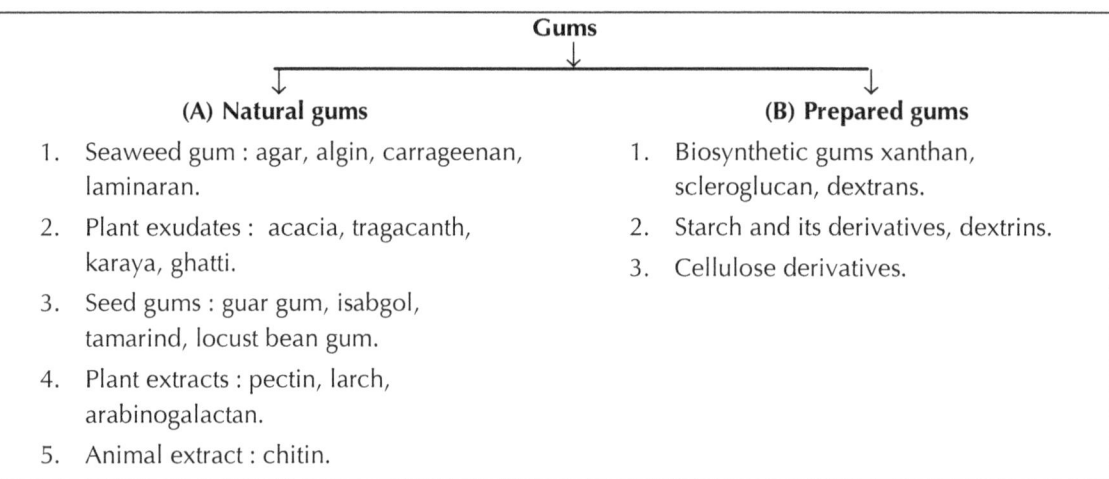

Gums

(A) Natural gums
1. Seaweed gum : agar, algin, carrageenan, laminaran.
2. Plant exudates : acacia, tragacanth, karaya, ghatti.
3. Seed gums : guar gum, isabgol, tamarind, locust bean gum.
4. Plant extracts : pectin, larch, arabinogalactan.
5. Animal extract : chitin.

(B) Prepared gums
1. Biosynthetic gums xanthan, scleroglucan, dextrans.
2. Starch and its derivatives, dextrins.
3. Cellulose derivatives.

Biosynthesis of Carbohydrates

Production of monosaccharides

Photosynthesis

- Photosynthesis is defined as the process of absorption of carbon dioxide (CO_2) and formation of carbohydrates by plants.

- It is the indirect source of all organic matter on earth. It is the source of oxygen needed for respiration. The biological world runs at the expense of energy and materials accumulated by photosynthesis. Photosynthesis in the green plants consists of two classes of reactions.

  - One class consists of the so-called *light reactions* that usually convert electromagnetic energy into chemical potential.

  - Other class consists of the enzymatic reactions that utilise the energy from the light reaction to fix carbon dioxide into sugar. These are referred to as the *dark reactions* and can be summarised as follows

$$2H_2O + CO_2 + Light \longrightarrow C(H_2O) + H_2O + O_2 \uparrow$$

Through the above mentioned photosynthetic process, various monosaccharides are produced, via phosphorylated sugars e.g. Glucose-6-phosphate and fructose-6- phosphate.

The latter monosaccharide phosphates are then utilised by the plant cell either as energy or as a building units.

Production of sucrose

- Sucrose has considerable metabolic importance in higher plants. It is not only the first sugar formed in photosynthesis but also the main transport material.

- Newly formed sucrose is therefore probably the usual precursor for polysaccharide synthesis.

- Sucrose is formed by the reaction of uridine diphosphate glucose (UDP-G) with fructose-6-phosphate.

- Once formed, the free sucrose may either remain in situ or be translocated via the sieve tubes to various parts of the plants.

- A number of reactions e.g. hydrolysis by invertase or reversal of the synthetic sequence, convert sucrose to monosaccharides from which other oligosaccharides or polysaccharides may be derived.

UDP-G

Fructose phosphate
synthase

UDP

Sucrose-6-phosphate

Sucrose phosphatase

Pi

Sucrose

Isomerisms : Stereochemical consideration

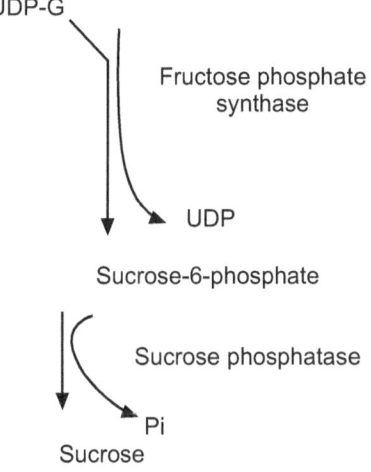

Aldohexose
(D-glucose)

(β-D-glucopyranose)

CH$_2$OH
|
C=O
|
HO—C
|
C—OH
|
C—OH
|
CH$_2$OH

Ketohexose
(D-fructose)

H$_2$O$_3$POCH$_2$ O   OH

HO

CH$_2$OH

OH

D-fructose-6-phosphate
(furanose ring)

CH$_2$OH

O   H

OH

HO   OH

OH

α-D-glucopyranose

O   H

OH

OH

β-D-glucopyranose

HO   CH$_2$OH

HO

O

OH

OH

β-D-glucopyranose
(another representation)^4 C

α-D-(+)-

O

OH

OH

Stereo isomerism in sugars

1. D & L Configuration

- The open chain structures of sugars was proposed by Fisher in 1880's, while in 1926 Howarth proposed the cyclic structure (pyranose and furanose rings).
- The configuration of sugars is designated by the symbols D & L.
- Monosaccharides are designated as D & L on the basis of the configuration of the highest numbered asymmetric carbon, D if the -OH is on the right and L if the -OH is on the left.
- (+) -Mannose, (-) -arabinose are assigned to the D- family because of their relation to D- (+)-glucose and D-(+) glyceraldehydes.
- Sugars configurationally related to D glyceraldehyde are said to be members of the D-family, and those related to L-glyceraldehyde belong to the L-series. The symbols d and l or (+) and (-) are used to designate sign of rotation of plane-polarized light.
- Monosaccharides existing in the form of heterocycles are classified with respect to the size of the ring system i.e. 6 -membered ring structures considered to be related to pyran are called **pyranoses**, and the 5 -membered ring structures related to furan are called **furanoses**. This type of nomenclature can be applied to oligosaccharides and glycoside derivatives, e.g. maltose can be named 4-D-glucopyranose-α-D-glucopyranoside, sucrose is 1-α D-glucopyranosyl-β-D-fructofuranoside, and lactose is 4-D- glucopyranosyl-β-D-galactopyranoside.

2. α and β anomers

The cyclic structure of glucose is retained in solution, but isomarism takes place about C-1, by which the position of –H and –OH groups are changed around C-1. This is accomplished with change in optical activity.

3. Optical isomerism

When beam of polarized light is passed through a solution exhibiting optical activity, it will be rotated to right or left according to the type of sample. If a compound which rotates plan of polarized light to right is said to be dextro rotatoxy (d) and designated with (+) sign. If rotation of beam is to the left hand side, is known as levo-rotatory (/) and designated by (–) sign. When equal account of dextrorotatory and levorotatory isomers are present the resulting mixture has no optical activity, such mixture is said to be racemic or (dl) mixture.

4. Epimers

Isomers formed as a result of interchange of the –OH and –H on carbon atoms 2, 3 and 4 of glucose are known as epimers. Mannose is C-2 epimer of glucose and galactose is C-4 epimer of glucose.

α-D-galactose   α-D-Glucose   α-D-Mannose

CHEMICAL TESTS FOR CARBOHYDRATES:

1. Molisch's Test

All carbohydrates give positive Molisch's test. They impart a purple colour when treated with α-naphtha and conc. sulphuric acid. With a soluble carbohydrate this appear as a ring if the sulphuric acid is gently poured in to from a layer below the aqueous solution. With the insoluble carbohydrate such as cotton (cellulose) the colour will not appear until the acid layer is shaken to bring it in contact with the material .

2. Reduction of Fehling's solution

To a heated solution of the carbohydrate, a mixture of equal parts of Fehling's solution A & B added. In certain cases reduction takes place near the boiling point and is shown by a brick-red ppt. of cuprous oxide. Reducing sugars such as all monosaccharides, many disaccharides e.g. lactose, maltose, cellobiose & gentiobiose react readily while the non-reducing sugars include some disaccharides e.g. sucrose and polysaccharides can reduce Fehling's only after hydrolysis with acids and neutralization.

3. Osazone Formation

Osazones are sugar derivatives formed by heating a sugar solution with phenylhydrazine hydrochloride & sodium acetate.

They are yellow crystals insoluble in water having a definite shape, when examined under the microscope , help in the identification of certain sugars such as maltose, lactose, glucose, fructose and mannose (the last three sugars have the same osazone).

4. Resorcinol Test for Ketoses

A crystal of resorcinol is added to a solution of the sugar and is warmed on a water bath with an equal volume of conc hydrochloric acid. A rose red color is produced if a ketose sugar is present (fructose, honey or hydrolysed inulin).

5. Test for Pentoses

Heating a solution of the sugar in a test tube with an equal volume of hydrochloric acid containing a little phloroglucinol, results in formation of a red colour indicating pressence of pentose.

6. Test for Deoxy-sugars : (Keller-Kiliani test)

The sugar is dissolved in acetic acid containing a trace of ferric chloride and transferred to the surface of concentrated sulphuric acid. At the junction of the two liquid a reddish-brown colour is produced and acetic solution gradually becomes blue

7. Chromatography

Chromatographic methods can be used for the examination and identification of sugars in extracts. They are used to identify carbohydrates present in plants as well as their hydrolytic products.

Thus, thin layer as well as paper chromatography are usually used. Aniline hydrogen phthalate is used for detection. Volatile derivatives of sugars can be prepared and detected by gas chromatography.

8. Polarography

The specific optical rotation of some sugars and polysaccharides are sometimes used for their identification e.g. glucose, fructose and gum acacia.

E.g. The British Pharmacopoeia requires that a 10% solution of gum acacia is levorotatory.

SCHEME FOR STUDY OF CARBOHYDRATES
AGAR

Synonyms

Agar has several synonyms: Agar-agar, Japanese-Isinglass, Vegetable gelatin.

Biological Source

It is the dried gelatinous substance obtained from *Gelidium amansii* (Gelidaceae) and several other species of red algae like, *Gracilaria* (Gracilariaceae) and *Pterocladia* (Gelidaceae).

Geographical Source

Agar is produced commercially in Japan, Australia, New Zealand, the USA, and India. In India, it is produced in the coastal regions of Bay of Bengal.

Preparation

In Japan, the red-algae are grown on the bamboos spread in the ocean. The collection of the material is done between May and October. The seaweeds are scrapped from the bamboos, dried and shaken. This is necessary to bleach the product to some extent and remove and foreign material like shells, sand, etc. The entire material is then taken to the high altitudes where it is washed and bleached by exposing to sun. It is boiled for 5 - 6 hours with large quantity of dilute acidified water (about 1 part of algae with 60 parts of water). The extract is then strained while hot through the cloth and transferred to wooden troughs. On cooling, jelly is produced. These rectangular solid pieces of jelly are then passed through the netting under pressure. Narrow strips, thus formed, are allowed to melt during the daytime in the sun, which removes the excess of water. This operation is continued for several days to remove the excess of water. The manufacture of agar takes place in the winter, and moisture is removed by successively freezing, thawing and drying at about 35°C. Japan is taking the advantage of natural climatic conditions since centuries for the preparation of agar. In America, the modern method of deep-freezing is being utilised for the same purpose.

Description

Colour	-	Depending upon the shape and the form, it is yellowish-grey or white to nearly colourless.
Odour	-	Odourless
Taste	-	Mucilaginous
Shape	-	It is found in various forms like strips, sheets, flakes or coarse powder.
Size	-	Sheets are 45 - 60 cm long and 10 - 15 cm wide. Bands are about 4 cm. wide, while strips are 4 mm in width. Strips are translucent, lustrous and slender while the flakes are greyish-white in colour.

In India, the raw material being used is known as *Galidiella accrosa* and indigenous production of agar is estimated to be about 200 tones. In India, the process has been developed for the extraction of agar from the species of *Hypnea*.

It is insoluble in cold water, but forms a gelatinous mass after cooling the hot solution. It is soluble in boiling water and insoluble in organic solvents.

Standards

Acid-insoluble ash	-	Not more than 1.0 per cent
Sulphated ash	-	Not more than 5.0 per cent
Foreign organic matter	-	Not more than 1.0 per cent
Loss on drying	-	Not more than 18.0 per cent
Starch	-	Negative with iodine solution

Chemical Constituents

Agar consists of two different polysaccharides named as agarose and agaropectin. Agarose is responsible for gel strength of agar and is composed of D-galactose and 3.6

unianhydro L-galactose units. It contains about 3.5% cellulose and 6% of nitrogen containing substance. Agaropectin is responsible for the viscosity of agar solutions. It is believed to be a sulphonated polysaccharide in which galactose and uronic acid units are partly esterfied with sulphuric acid.

Agarose

Identification

1. Boil about 1.5 g agar with 100 ml. water. Cool the solution to room temperature. It forms a stiff jelly.
2. When mounted in the solution of ruthenium red and examined under microscope, the mounted particles acquire pink colour.
3. To 0.2 per cent solution of agar in water, add solution of tannic acid; no precipitate is produced.
4. Add dilute hydrochloric acid to incinerated ash and see under microscope, skeleton and sponge spicules of diatoms are observed.

Uses

Agar is used as an emulsifying agent and bulk laxative. It is used in the preparation of jellies, confectionery items and in microbiology, it is employed in preparation of bacteriological culture medium.

Substitutes and Adultrants:

1. **Danish agar :** It is indigenous to the coastal region of Denmark. and has gel strength which is half its gel strength of Japanese agar. Danish agar has ash value 16.5 – 18.5%.
2. **Gelatin :** It can be deleted by addition of equal volume of 1% trinitrophenol and of agar solution, the solution produces turbidity or precipitate.

GUAR GUM

Synonyms

Guar flour, Jaguar gum

Biological Source

Guar gum is the powder of the endosperm of the seeds of *Cyamopsis tetragonolobus* Linn, belonging to family Leguminosae.

Geographical Source

It has been grown for centuries in India and Pakistan, and was introduced in 1900 in the USA. Its commercial production was started in 1953.

Preparation

Guar gum is industrially manufactured from the white, well developed seeds that are freed from foreign matter. The seeds are put into a grinder to get bifurcated guar seeds. The seeds are separated into husk and cotyledons containing embryo. The husk contains fibrous matter and the gum is located into endosperms. Guar seeds contain 14 - 17 per cent of hull, 35 - 40 per cent of endosperm and 45 - 50 per cent of germ. Cotyledons separated from the endosperm by winnowing and sifting fetch a very high price in the market as a cattle feed. The endosperms i.e. crude guar gum is pulverised by means of micropulverizer and grinding for 15 minutes.

The endosperm being harder is not affected by micropulverizer. The portion of cotyledons adhering to the endosperm is soft and is converted into fine powder which is separated by sifting. The crude guar gum is now free of cotyledons, the main impurity in the gum. The crude guar gum thus separated is put into pulverizer and grinding is continued for 3 - 4 hours followed by sifting. This process is repeated about 5 to 6 times for several hours to give white coloured guar gum. Finally, it is sifted through sieves of 40 - 60 mesh to give granular and powdered gum. In India, there are about 15 units producing guar gum on industrial scale.

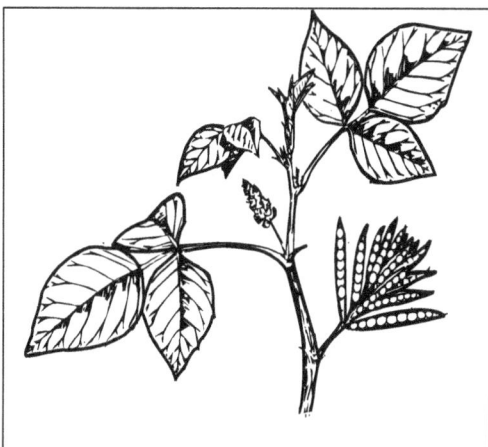

Fig. 3.1 : *Cyamopsis tetragonolobus plant*

Description

It is a colourless or pale yellowish-white coloured powder with characteristic odour and gummy taste. Guar gum swells rapidly in water with a translucent suspension. 0.5 per cent aqueous solution of gum is neutral to litmus.

Standards

Ash	- not more than 1 per cent
Acid-insoluble ash	- not more than 0.5 per cent
Loss on drying	- not more than 8 per cent

Chemical Constituents

The contents of guar gum are divided into water-soluble and water insoluble parts. The water soluble fraction constituting about 85 per cent of the gum is known as guaran, which is a high molecular weight hydro-colloidal polysaccharide. Guaran on hydrolysis yields 65 per cent galactose and 35 per cent of mannose, which is combined through glycosidic linkage. Guar gum also contains 5-7 per cent of proteins. The proposed structure of guaran is given here

Guaran

Identification

1. It does not acquire olive green colour with weak solution of iodine.

2. With solution of ruthenium red, the gummy solution does not acquire pink colour (distinct from agar and Sterculia gum).

3. About 2 per cent solution of lead acetate gives precipitate with the solution of guar gum.

4. Dissolve 0.5 g of guar gum in 20 ml of water by shaking. To it, add 0.5 ml hydrogen peroxide and 0.5 ml, 1 per cent solution of benzidine in alcohol. No blue colour is formed (distinction from gum acacia).

Uses

About 1 per cent mucilage of guar gum possesses similar viscosity to that of mucilage of acacia and a 3 per cent mucilage is similar to mucilage of tragacanth. It has 5 - 8 times thickening power than starch. It is used as a protective colloid, a binding and disintegrating agent, bulk laxative, appetite depressant and in peptic ulcer therapy. Guar gum is a good emulsifying agent. Industrially, this is used in paper manufacturing, printing, polishing, textiles and also in food and cosmetic industries.

It is extensively used as flocculent in ore-dressing and treatment of water.

Export of Guar gum during 2007 - 2008 was to the tune of ₹ 1125.25 crore.

ACACIA

Synonyms

Gum acacia, Gum arabica, Indian gum

Biological Source

Indian gum is the dried gummy exudation obtained from the stem and branches of wild *Acacia arabica* belonging to family Leguminosae.

Geographical Source

The plant is found in India, Sri Lanka, Sudan, Morocco and Africa. In India, it occurs in Punjab, Rajasthan and Western Ghats. About 85 per cent of world supply of gum acacia is from Sudan.

Cultivation and Collection

It is a common member of dry monsoon forests of India. It is an evergreen tree with short trunk. It is not cultivated on commercial scale. Gum is collected from wild grown plants, made free of bark and foreign organic matter, dried in sun, which also results in partial bleaching of gum. (*Fig. 8.1*)

Description

Colour	-	Tears are cream-brown to red in colour, while powder is light brown in colour.
Odour	-	Odourless
Taste	-	Bland and mucilaginous
Size and Shape	-	Irregular brown tears of varying size

Fig. 3.2 : Acacia tree

Extra Features

The tears are glossy and marked with minute fissures and are brittle in nature. The pieces of broken tears are with angular fragments and glistering surfaces, breaking with difficulty, and with conchoidal fracture.

Solubility

It is soluble in water; the watery solution is viscous and acidic. It is insoluble in alcohol.

Standard

It should contain not more than 15 per cent of moisture and 5 per cent of ash Indian gum should not contain tannin, starch and dextrin.

Chemical Constituents

It consists principally of arabin, which is a complex mixture of calcium, magnesium and potassium salts of Arabic acid. Arabic acid on hydrolysis gives L-arabinose, L-rhamnose, D-galactose and D-glucuronic acid. It also contains an enzyme oxidase and peroxidase.

Identification

1. Solution of lead sub acetate gelatinizes the aqueous solution of Indian gum.
2. It does not produce a pink colour with the solution of ruthenium red.
3. On addition of solutions of hydrogen peroxide and benzidine in alcohol to aqueous solution of gum, it turns blue in due to oxidase enzyme.
4. To 1 ml of gum solution add 4 ml of water and a few drops of lead acetate solution. No precipitate should be produced. (Gum ghatti, tragacanth and other gum produce ppt.).

Uses

Acacia is a demulcent. It is also administered intravenously in haemolysis. In the form of mucilage, it is used as a suspending agent, specifically in mixtures with resinous substance. Acacia is a-good emulsifying agent for fixed oils, volatile oils and also for liquid paraffin. It is a good binding agent and is used in the preparation of lozenges, pastilles and compressed tablets. It is a gum of choice, as it is compatible with other plant hydrocolloids, as well as, starches and carbohydrates. In combination with gelatin, it is used to form coacervates for microencapsulation of drugs.

Tests for Purity of Indian Acacia

1. Dilute 1 ml of the solution of gum with 10 ml of water and keep for a few hours. No sedimentation should take place.
2. To 1 ml of solution, add 4 ml. of water, boil, cool and add 2 drops of N/10 iodine. Brown colour indicates presence of dextrin, whereas blue colour is due to starch. This test should be negative with the authentic drug.
3. To the gum acacia solution, add a drop of hydrogen peroxide and tincture of guaiacum – colour changes to blue.
4. With a few drops of 0.1 per cent ferric chloride to 1 ml. of the solution, there is change in colour to blue or black (due to tannins).

Substitutes and Adulterants

The B.P. variety consists of gum obtained from wild *Acacia senegal* Wild, (Leguminosae), a plant of African origin and grown in Africa. The tears are rounded or ovoid and about 5 - 40 mm in diameter. Tears are yellowish white in colour. It can be used as a substitute to Indian gum.

Indian gum is adulterated with gum ghatti, obtained from *Anogeissus latifolia* (Combretaceae), which is distinguished from the genuine drug by the following characters. Its outer surface is dull and without fissures. It shows very slight precipitate with lead sub-acetate solution and its aqueous solution is highly viscous. Starch, tragacanth, dextrin and Sterculia gum are the other adulterants of acacia.

Storage

Acacia or powdered acacia should be stored in cool dry place in air-tight containers.

ISAPGOL

Synonyms

Ispaghula, Isabgul, Indian Psyllium, Isabgol.

The origin of the word isapgol is form the Persian words ISAP (the horse) and GHOL (the ear). Thus, the literal meaning of word isapgol is the ear of the horse. The seeds and the husk of the seeds are used in medicine since eighteenth-century. About 10 species of the plant are available in India. Seeds are very small in size. One thousand seeds weigh about 01.5 g. Isapgol has high export potential.

Biological Source

Isapgol consists of dried seeds of the plant known as *Plantago ovata* (Syn: *Plantago indica*; *Plantago afra*) Forskal, family Plantaginaceae. In the pharmaceutical field, the seeds and the dried seed coats — known as isapgol husk — are used.

Geographical Source

The plant is cultivated largely in Gujarat, Punjab and South Rajasthan. The factory for preparation of husk is located at Sidhpur in North Gujarat. In Maharashtra, it is found to be grown successfully near Pune. About 50 thousand hectares of area is said to be under cultivation for the drug in India.

Cultivation and Collection

Isapgol (Fig. 3.3) is a Rabi crop and needs well-drained loamy soil with a pH 7.5 to 8.5 and cool and dry weather. Heavy rains and cloudy weather at its maturity affect the yield adversely. The drug is cultivated by broadcasting method, in the month of November. About 6-12 kg seeds are needed per hectare. RI-87, RI-89, GI-1, GI-2, HI-1, HI-2, HI-5, MIB-121 are some of the species preferred for cultivation in Gujarat state. Irrigation is done 7-8 times at an interval of 8-10 days.

Ammonium sulphate is found to be a suitable fertiliser for the plant. 25 kg of nitrogenous fertilisers and 25 kg of 5.0% aldrin on the soil controls root-eaters per hectare is most suitable spray. Aerofungin is used to control mid-dew. The crop is harvested in March/April and the average yield of the seeds per hectare is 7.4 quintals. It is collected by cutting the plant just above the ground, converting it to sheaves and drying. Thrashing is done and the thrashed material is winnowed and sieved to maintain quality.

India is producing 48000 tones of seeds annually at present.

The world demand for psyllium and isapgol seeds and husk is increasing (approx. 50,000 tonnes) and the main markets are in U.S.A., France, West Germany, and U.K. The export of isapgol husk and seeds together during 1995-96 was ₹ 155 crores and during 1996-97 it was ₹ 137 crores.

Macroscopic Characters

Colour - Pinkish-grey to brown

Odour - None

Size - 10 - 35 mm in length and 1 - 1.75 mm in width

Shape - It is ovate cymbiform

Fig. 3.3 : Isapgol Plant

Seeds are hard, transparent and smooth with grey or reddish brown oval spot in the centre of the convex surface. Concave surface contains the hilum covered with thin membrane having two perforations. 1 gm accommodates 500 - 600 seeds.

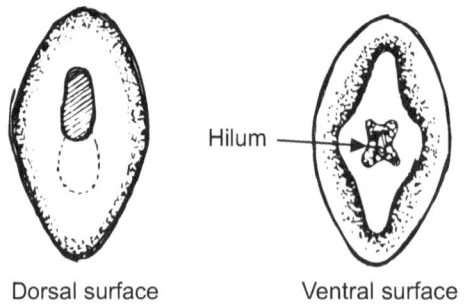

Dorsal surface   Ventral surface

Fig. 3.4 : Macroscopical Characters of Isapgol Seed

Isapgol Husk

Isapgol seeds are processed to take out seed coats, commercially known as husk. Husk makes up about 25 - 27 per cent of the seed. The seeds are thoroughly dried and sieved to get rid of foreign organic matter. Seeds are crushed in flat stone grinders by passing several times through them, so as to effect complete removal of the coating. The crushed material is then winnowed to separate the kernels and husk. Husk is sieved to get different grades and sizes. Thus, it consists only of the epidermis and its adjacent layers removed from the dried seeds of *Plantago ovata*.

Macroscopical Characters

It is in the form of pale buff ovate flakes with more or less lanceolate shape. The pieces are 1 - 2 mm in size; flakes are odourless, smooth and free flowing.

Indian psyllium or Isapgol seeds are preferred in the world market for the following reasons.

1. Indian psyllium seeds are available at a lower price.
2. The mucilage content of this species is more.
3. It yields practically colourless mucilage.
4. The husk of the Indian psyllium cracks off under slight mechanical pressure and even it can be easily separated from the seed.

Chemical Constituents of Seed and Husk

Isapgol husk and seeds contain mucilage which is present in the epidermis of the seeds. Chemically, it consists of pentosans and aldobionic acid. The products of hydrolysis are xylose, arabinose, galacturonic acid and rhamnose. Fixed oil and proteins are other important constituents of the isapgol seeds.

Chemical Tests

1. Swelling factor is the criterion for purity of the drug. Swelling factor of the drug is a quantitative swelling due to mucilage present in the drug. It is determined by putting 1 g of the drug in the measuring cylinder (25 ml capacity) in 20 ml water with occasional shaking. The volume occupied by the seeds after 24 hours of wetting is measured. Swelling factor for seeds is 10 - 14.

2. Being the mucilage chemically, isapgol gives pink colour with the solution of ruthenium red.

Uses

The seeds, as well as, husk are used as demulcent, laxative, emollient in the treatment of chronic constipation, amoebic and bacillary dysentery. Isapgol husk is preferred to the seeds as the husk contains more mucilage and seeds are said to be irritant as compared to the husk. Mucilage of the isapgol is used in the preparation of tablets and also as a stabilizer in the ice cream industry. The crushed seeds are, many a time, used in the form of poultice for rheumatic pain. Gujarat Drug Chemical Ltd. at Mehsana is engaged in manufacturing of isapgol formulations.

The product formed by removing cations from the mucilage by treatment with cation exchange resins followed by spray drying is an acid form of polysaccharide. This finds special pharmaceutical applications as enteric coating material, tablet disintegrator and also used in the sustained release drug formulations. The mucilage of isapgol has a property of glairiness or stringiness, which is desired in certain cosmetic formulations.

Substitutes

Several other species of *Plantago* have been investigated of which *Plantago rhodosperma* distributed in Missouri and Louisiana and *Plantago wrightiana* are important. The earlier variety contains 17.5 per cent of mucilage, while the latter contains about 23.0 per cent. In all respects, these two varieties favourably compare with the official drugs.

Plantago purshii and *Plantago aristata* are substitutes of official drug with good mucilage forming capacity. *Plantago asiatica*, found in Andhra Pradesh and Tamil Nadu is also used as a substitute for isapgol seeds.

Psyllium seeds (*Flea-seeds*)

These are the seeds of plant known as *Plantago psyllium*, grown in France and Spain, and has swelling factor of 12.5. They are used as a substitute for isapgol seed.

Adulterants

Isapgol seeds are adulterated with the seeds of *Plantago lanceolata*. These seeds are oblong, elliptical in shape and yellowish - brown in colour. The swelling factor of these seeds is about five.

GUM KARAYA

Synonyms

Indian tragacanth; Sterculia gum; Karaya gum

Biological Source

Gum karaya is a dried gummy exudate obtained from the tree *Sterculia urens* (Roxburgh); *Sterculia villosa* (Roxburgh), *Sterculia tragacantha* (Lindley) or other species of *Sterculia* (Sterculiaceae)

Geographical Source

Sterculia urens is wide spread in India, especially in north central parts.

Collection and Purification

The trees which have a girth of 1 metre are selected and blazes are made. The number of blazes per tree should not exceed two. Immediately after tapping, the exudation oozes out which is maximum during the first 24 hours. The large irregular tears which weigh in pounds are picked and sent to the collecting centres. Tapping is done during March-April up to June or till the commencement of monsoon.

During rainy season, the yield of gum is reduced. The plants are tapped again in September. The yield per tree is about 1 - 5 kg per year, and on an average the tree is tapped about five times during its lifetime. The large tears are broken into small pieces, which also enhance drying process. The pieces of bark, sand particles and foreign organic matter are removed. The size reduction and air flotation of loose bark ensure purification to a certain extent. Sand particles are removed by gravity. Granulated or crystal gum karaya has particle size between 6 and 30 mesh. Fine powdered variety usually passes through 150 mesh screen.

Fig. 3.5 : Karaya twig

Description

It is found in the form of irregular tears or vermiform pieces from white to brown in colour. It has slight acetous odour and bland mucilaginous taste. Wood fibres and small sand particles may be present in the drug. It is insoluble in water, but forms a translucent colloidal solution. Powdered gum swells in water.

Standards

Foreign organic matter   - Not more than 3.0 per cent

Acid insoluble ash   - Not more than 1.0 per cent

Chemical Constituents

Karaya gum contains about 8.0 per cent of acetyl group and more than 37% of uronic acid residues. On acid hydrolysis, it gives D-galactose, L-rhamnose, D-galacturonic acid, aldobiuronic acid and an acid trisaccharides. Gum karaya gives pink colour with solution of ruthenium red (not observed in tragacanth).

Uses

It swells about 60-100 times in water. It is neither digested nor absorbed by the body and hence, it is a good bulk laxative. It is also used as denture adhesive in dental treatment and in pharmaceuticals as emulsifier, thickener and stabiliser. Karaya gum is listed in the food chemical codex and hence, used on large scale in foods such as ice pops, cheese spread, sherbets, and ground meat products. It is also used in paper and textile industries.

During 1995-96 and 1996-97, India has exported Karaya gum of worth ₹ 675 lakh and ₹ 894 lakh respectively.

TRAGACANTH

Synonym

Gum Tragacanth, Tragacantha.

Biological Source

It is the dried gummy exudation obtained by incision from stems and branches of *Astragalus gummifer* Labill and other species of *Astragalus*, family Leguminosae.

Geographical Source

It is indigenous to Iran, Greece, Turkey, Iraq and Syria. In India, Garhwal, Kumaon and Central Punjab are the areas where few species of tragacanth are found. North Syria and Iran supply Persian tragacanth. Smyrna tragacanth is exported from Smyrna port in Asiatic Turkey.

(a)   (b)

Fig. 3.6 : (a) Tragacanth herb natural (b) Enlarged

Collection

Most of the shrubs from which tragacanth is collected grow at an altitude of 1000 - 3000 m. The shrubs are thorny. The mode of formation of tragacanth is entirely different from that of acacia, the gum exuding out immediately after an injury.

Most of the drug comes from Persian source only. Tragacanth gum is formed as a result of transformation of the cells of pith and medullary rays into gummy substance. Incisions are more on various parts of the stem and fluid which oozes out is collected after drying. Tragacanth is found as irregular flattened flakes with ribbon like appearance depending upon the incisions made on the plant. It is collected from April to November every year.

Description

Colour - The flakes are white or pale yellowish-white.

Odour - Odourless

Taste - Mucilaginous

Shape - Tragacanth occurs in the form of thin, flattened ribbon like flakes, more or less curved

Size - Flakes are approximately 25 × 12 × 2 mm in size.

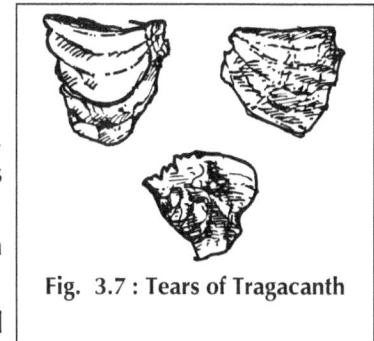

Fig. 3.7 : Tears of Tragacanth

The gum is horny, translucent with transverse and longitudinal ridges. Fracture of the drug is short.

It is partly soluble in water wherein it swells to a homogeneous, adhesive and gelatinous mass. It is insoluble in alcohol.

Chemical Constituents

Tragacanth contains two fractions of which one is soluble in water. The water-soluble portion of the tragacanth is known as tragacanthin, constituting about 8 - 10 per cent of the gum. Water-insoluble portion is known as bassorin (60 to 70%). Tragacanth contains about 15 per cent of methoxy group which swells in water. It is the constituent of the gum responsible for its high viscosity. Normally, 1.0 per cent solution of tragacanth has a viscosity of not less than 250 centipoises The products of hydrolysis of tragacanth are galactouronic acid, D-galactopyranose,   L-arabino-rhamnose and D-xylopyranose.

Standards

Foreign organic matter	-	Not more than 1.0 per cent
Sulphated ash	-	Not more than 4.0 per cent
Moisture content	-	Not more than 15.0 per cent

Identification tests

1. When solution of tragacanth is boiled with a few drops of 10 per cent aqueous ferric chloride solution, deep yellow precipitate is formed.

2. A stringy precipitate is formed by dissolving tragacanth and precipitated copper oxide in concentrated ammonium hydroxide.

3. When it is warmed with sodium hydroxide solution, canary yellow colour is developed. With strong iodine solution, it gives green colour.

Uses

It is used as a demulcent and as an emollient in cosmetics. Tragacanth is used as a thickening, suspending and as an emulsifying agent. It is used along with acacia as a suspending agent. Mucilage of tragacanth is used as a binding agent in the tablets and also as excipients in the pills. Tragacanth powder is used as an adhesive. It is also used in lotions for external use and also in spermicidal jellies, as a stabiliser for ice-cream in 0.2 - 0.3 per cent concentration and also in sauces.

OKRA MUCILAGE

Synonyms

Hibiscus esculentus, ladies' fingers, bhindi, gumbo.

Biological Source

Okra mucilage, obtained from fruits of Abelmoschus esculentus, family Malvaceae.

It is an annual and perennial plant, growing to 2 m height. The leaves are 10–20 cm long and broad, palmately lobed with 5–7 lobes. The flowers are 4–8 cm in diameter, with five white to yellow petals, often with a red or purple spot at the base of each petal. The fruit is a capsule up to 18 cm long with pentagonal cross-section, containing numerous seeds.

Fig. 3.8 : Okra fruits

Cultivation and Collection

Abelmoschus esculentus is cultivated throughout the tropical and warm temperate regions of the world. Okra plant grows very fast. Okra grows best on well-drained sandy loam soils. Okra prefers slightly acidic soils with a pH between 5.8 and 6.5. In cultivation, the seeds are soaked overnight prior to planting to a depth of 1–2 cm. Germination occurs between six days (soaked seeds) and three weeks. Seedlings require ample water. The seed pods rapidly become fibrous and woody, and, must be harvested when immature and eaten as a vegetable.

Chemical structure of polysaccharide of Okra mucilage

Extraction of Okra Gum

1. Collect okra fruits and carefully wash it.
2. Dry under shade for 24 h, further dry at 30–40°C until constant weight is obtained.
3. Pulverize through grinder. Pass through sieve no. #22 and store it in air tight container for further use.

Extraction of mucilage includes two steps.

Step 1: Extraction of mucilage:

Heat the powdered fruit in water approximately at 60°C for 4 hrs. Filter through muslin and concentrate. Store the concentrated solution at 4°C-6°C.

Step 2: Isolation of mucilage:

Add acetone to above solution to precipitate mucilage. Filter through muslin cloth. Wash with excess of acetone. Press the mucilage and further dry to constant weight at 35–45°C in hot air oven. Grind hard mucilage cake and pass through sieve # 22, stored in dessicator for further use.

Table 3.2 : Micromeritic study of mucilage

Sr. No.	Parameters	Values
1.	Angle of repose (^{0})	27 – 30
2.	Carr's index (%)	74-76
3.	True density (gm/ml)	2- 4
4.	Bulk density (gm/ml)	0.5-0.7
5.	Mean particle size (µ)	50-55

Table 3.3 : Physicochemical characterization of okra mucilage

Sr. No.	Parameters	Values
1.	Total Ash Value	7.53%
2.	Acid insoluble ash	0.93%
3.	Water soluble ash	4%
4.	pH	7.5
5.	Surface Tension of 0.25% w/v solution	0.0405
6.	Loss on drying	9.91

STARCH

Synonym

Amylum

Biological Source

Starch consists of polysaccharide granules obtained from the grains of maize (*Zea mays* Linn.); rice (*Oryza sativa* Linn.); or wheat (*Triticum aestivum* Linn.); belonging to family Gramineae or from the tubers of potato (*Solanum tuberosum* Linn.), family Solanaceae.

Geographical Source

Most of tropical, as well as, subtropical countries prepare starch commercially.

Preparation of Starch

Depending upon the raw material to be used for processing or type of the starch to be produced, different processes are used for the commercial manufacture of starch.

Potato Starch

The potatoes are washed to remove the earthy matter. They are crushed or cut and converted into a slurry. Slurry is filtered to remove the cellular matter. As potatoes do not contain gluten, they are very easy to process further. After filtration, the milky slurry containing starch is purified by centrifugation and washing. Then, it is dried and sent to the market.

Rice Starch

The broken pieces of rice sequel polishing are used for processing. The pieces of rice are- soaked in water with dilute sodium hydroxide solution (0.5 per cent), which causes softening and dissolution of the gluten. After this, the soaked rice pieces are crushed and starch prepared as described under potato starch.

Maize Starch (Corn Starch)

Maize grains are washed thoroughly with water to remove the adhered organic matter after which they are softened by keeping in warm water for 2 - 3 days. Sufficient sulphur dioxide is passed to the medium to prevent fermentation. The swollen kernels are passed through attrition mill to break the grains, so as to separate the endosperm and outermost coating of the grains. At this point, special attention is given to separate the germ (embryo). This is effected by addition of water, wherein germs float and are separated. The water which is used to soften the grains dissolves most of the minerals, soluble proteins and carbohydrates from the grains. The water, being rich in all these contents, is used as a culture medium for the production of antibiotics like penicillin (*corn steep liquor*). The separated germs are used to prepare the germ oil by expression method and are known as corn oil. The oil contains fatty acids like inoleic and linolenic acids and vitamin E. It is used commercially, for the preparation of soap. The starchy material contains gluten; most of this is removed by simple sieving and then by washing. Starch being heavier, settles at the bottom and is followed by gluten. Several treatments with cold water wash the starch effectively, which is then centrifuged or filter-pressed and finally, dried in flash dryers on a moving-belt dryer.

Wheat Starch

Wheat being the major article of food is restrictedly used for preparation of starch. In this process, the wheat flour is converted into dough and kept for a while. The gluten in the dough swells and the masses are taken to grooved rollers, wherein water is poured over them with constant shaking. The starchy liquid coming out of the rollers is processed conveniently to take out the starch, which is then dried and packed suitably.

Description

Starch occurs as fine powder or irregular, angular masses readily reducible to powder.

Colour   - Rice and starch grains are white, while wheat is cream coloured and potato is slightly yellowish.

Odour   - Odourless

Taste   - Mucilaginous

Size and Shape - Starch grains vary depending upon the types which can be described as under.

Microscopic Characters

1. Rice Starch: The granules are simple or compound. Simple granules are polyhedral, 2 - 12 microns in diameter. Compound granules are ovoid and 12 - 30 µ × 7 - 12 µ in size. They may contain 2 - 150 components.

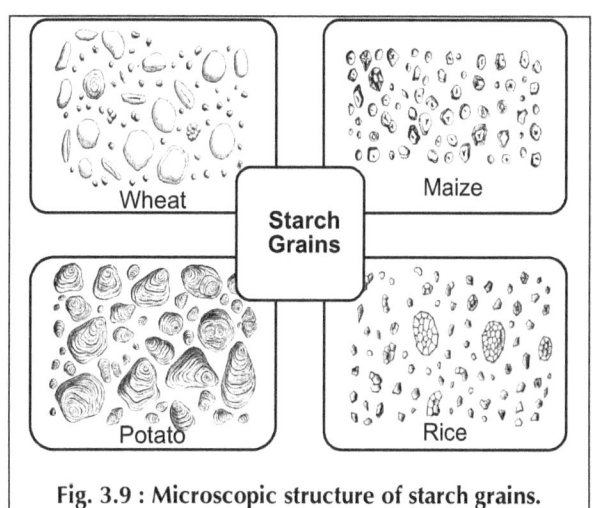

Fig. 3.9 : Microscopic structure of starch grains.

2. Wheat Starch: Simple lenticular granules which are circular or oval in shape and 5 - 50 µ in diameter. Granules contain hilum at the centre and concentrically faintly marked striations. Rarely, compound granules with 2 - 4 components are also observed.

3. Maize Starch: Granules are polyhedral or rounded, 5 - 31 in diameter, with distinct cavity in the centre or two to five rays cleft.

4. Potato Starch: Generally, found in the form of simple granules, which are sub-spherical, somewhat flattened irregularly ovoid in shape. Their sizes vary from 30 - 100µ. Hilum is present near the narrower end with well-marked concentric striations.

Starch is insoluble in cold water and also alcohol.

Standards

For pharmaceutical purpose, starch should have the following standards.

(a) Loss on drying - Not more than 15 per cent for rice, wheat and maize starches

                  - Not more than 20 per cent for potato starch.

(b) Ash   - Not more than 0.3 per cent for potato, wheat and maize starches

                  - Not more than 0.6 per cent in case of rice starch

Chemical Constituents

Starch contains chemically two different polysaccharides; Amylose (β-amylose) and amylopectin (α-amylose), in the proportion of 1 : 2. Amylose is water soluble and amylopectin is water-insoluble, but swells in water and is responsible for the gelatinising property of the starch. Amylose gives blue colour with iodine, while amylopectin yields bluish black colouration.

1, 4-linkage

Amylose

1, 6-linkage

1, 4-linkage

Amylopectin

Identification

1. Boil 1 g of starch with 15 ml of water and cool. The translucent viscous jelly is produced.
2. The above jelly turns deep blue by the addition of solution of iodine. The blue colour disappears on warming and reappears on cooling.

Uses

Starch is used as a nutritive, demulcent, protective and as an absorbent. Starch is used in the preparation of dusting talcum powder for application over the skin. It is used as antidote in iodine poisoning, as a disintegrating agent in pills and tablets, and as diluent in dry extracts of crude drug. It is a diagnostic aid in the identification of crude drugs. Glycerin of starch is used as an emollient and as a base for suppositories. Starch is also a starting material for the commercial manufacture of liquid glucose, dextrose and dextrin. Starch is industrially used for the sizing of paper and cloth.

Substitutes and Adulterants

Tapioca starch or Cassava or Brazilian arrowroot. This starch is obtained from *Manihot esculenta* (Euphorbiaceae) and is used as substitute for starch.

Soluble Starch

It is prepared from the potato or maize starch by chemical process, such as treatment with dilute hydrochloric acids so as to destroy the gelatinising property of the starch. Microscopically, it shows no change in its characters. It is soluble in water and forms a transparent mobile liquid. It may be sterilised by autoclaving.

Mucilage of starch is used as an emollient for skin and is also a base for some enemas.

Arrow Root Starch

There are several starches in the market known as arrow-root starch, their botanical identity is difficult. Very common in the field are cassava starch (*Manihot utilissima*) sweet potato starch (*Ipomoea batatas*), Convolvulaceae and canna starch *Canna edulis*, Cannaceae

In the pharmaceutical industry West Indian arrowroot and East Indian arrow-root varieties are well known.

Arrow Root Starch (West Indian)

Synonyms

Maranta starch, Natal arrowroot, Arrow root

Biological Source

It is obtained from rhizomes of *Maranta arundinaceae* Linn. family Marantaceae

Description

Shape	– Ovoid to ellipsoid
Size and aggregation	– 7 - 30 - 45 - 75 μm, simple
Hilum	– Cleft at broad end
Striations	– Faint and concentric
Appearance between crossed polarisers	– Well defined cross

Uses

West Indian arrowroot starch is used as a pharmaceutical aid.

Fig. 3.10 : Arrow-root starch (West-Indian)

ARROW ROOT STARCH (EAST INDIAN)

Synonyms

Curcuma starch

Biological Source

It is obtained from rhizomes of *Curcuma angustifolia* Roxburg or *C. leucorhiza* Roxburgh fam. Zingiberaceae

Description

Colour	– White
Shape	– Flattened avoid with slight terminal projection
Size and aggregation	– 15 - 30 - 60 µm; simple
Hilum	– Point in terminal projection
Striations	– Faint, numerous and transverse
Appearance between cross polarisers	– Well-marked cross

Fig. 3.11: Arrow-root starch (East-Indian)

Use

East Indian arrowroot is used as pharmaceutical aid.

PECTIN

Pectin is a complex carbohydrate component found in nature in the middle lamella of plant cells. Chemically, pectin is a neutral methoxy ester of pectic acid. Pectins are polyuronides and consist of a mixture of pectic substances like protopectin, pectin, pectinic acid and calcium pectate. They are obtained from the inner portion of the rind of citrus fruits or other vegetative matter, such as sun-flower, papaya etc. Pectin is a reversible colloid i.e. it may be dissolved in water, precipitated dried and redissolved, without altering its physical properties. Pectin, by addition of water, forms the lumps which on heating is converted into solution. The solution is clear to transmitted light and cloudy to reflected light. Under certain conditions, in presence of sugar and acid, it forms jelly like mass.

Pectin is available from a number of plants, belonging to different families. Following are a few important sources of pectin with content

Lemon peel	-	10 - 15 per cent
Orange peel	-	10 - 12 per cent
Apple pomace	-	10 - 15 per cent
Carrots	-	10.0 per cent
Sunflower-heads	-	05.0 per cent

Papaya, guavas and mangoes are also rich sources of pectin. Pectin has several industrial and pharmaceutical applications. Most of the requirement is met by import. In India, very a few units are manufacturing pectin on commercial scale. The USA, Switzerland and other European countries are producing pectin either from citrus peels or from apple pomace. Pectin is standardised on 'jelly grade' i.e. it's 'setting power' by the addition of sugar (100, 150 and 200 jelly grades are supposed to be standard grades for food and medicinal use).

Biological Source

Pectin is the purified carbohydrate product obtained by acid hydrolysis from inner portion of the rind of citrus peels i.e. *Citrus simon* or *Citrus aurantium*, family Rutaceae.

Method of Manufacture

Depending upon the raw material from which it is to be isolated the process of manufacture needs suitable modification. The type of pectin (i.e. low or high methoxy group) needed should also be considered. Following is the general process for isolation of pectin from citrus peels.

The preserved or fresh lemon peels are heated with 20 times their weight with water at 90°C for 30 minutes. The pH required for maximum extraction is 3.5 - 4.0. The pH can be adjusted by lactic, citric or tartaric acids. The peels after boiling are pressed and solution is cleared by settling or centrifugation. Starch and proteins are removed by suitable enzymic hydrolysis and the solution is heated to deactivate the enzymes and decolorised with active carbon or any other suitable agent. Pure pectin is precipitated out by using water soluble organic solvent, washed again and dried in vacuum. Pectin is incompatible with calcium, so necessary precaution should be taken to keep it away from its metallic salts throughout the process of extraction. It is packed in the containers or polyethylene bags for marketing.

Standards

Ash	-	not more than 4.0 per cent
Acid insoluble ash	-	not more than 0.4 per cent
Loss on drying	-	not more than 10.0 per cent
Microbial limit	-	1 g is free from *Salmonellae*

Description

Colour - Cream or yellowish-coloured powder

Odour - Odourless

Taste - Mucilaginous

Extra Features

It is coarse or fine light powder and hygroscopic in nature.

It is soluble in 20 parts of water, aqueous solution being viscous opalescent, colloidal and mobile. It is insoluble in alcohol and other organic solvents.

Chemical Constituents

Total hydrolysis of pectin yields D-galacturonic acid, methyl alcohol, small amount of galactose and arabinose.

Pectin

Pectin should not contain less than 7.0 per cent of methoxy groups and 78.0 per cent of galacturonic acid, calculated with reference to the ash-free and dried substance.

Identification Tests

1. 10 per cent aqueous solution forms stiff gel on cooling.

2. To 5 ml (1 per cent) solution add 1 ml (2 per cent) solution of potassium hydroxide and set aside at room temperature for 15 minutes. A transparent gel or semi-gel forms (distinction from tragacanth). Acidify gel with dilute hydrochloric acid and shake well. A voluminous, colourless, gelatinous precipitate forms which when boiled becomes white and flocculent.

Uses

Pectin is used as an adsorbent in the treatment of diarrhoea and as a haemostatic for internal or external haemorrhage. It is used as an emulsifying agent, a gelling agent in acid medium, and as a plasma substitute. In food industry, it is used as a thickening agent for sauces, jams, ketchups, etc. It is extensively used in cosmetic preparations.

Pectin is more stable in acidic medium. Pectin in combination with gelatin has been suggested for use as an encapsulating agent in pharmaceutical formulations to promote sustained release.

INULIN

Synonyms

Hydrous inulin, alant starch, Dehlia.

Biological Source

It is a polysaccharide from the bulbs of Dehlia, *Inula helenium* (Compositae), roots of Dendelion, *Taraxacum officinale*, (Compositae). Burdock root, *Saussurea lappa* (Compositae) or chicory roots, *Chichorium intybus* (Compositae).

(I)   *Inula* is the chief source and it contains 40 - 50 per cent of Inulin.

(II) Inulin is present to the extent of 20 - 50 per cent in these subterranean drugs.

Geographical Source

Inula is cultivated in Germany, France, and Belgium; chicory and dandelion in North America; while Saussurea in India.

Description

It is hygroscopic, amorphous, tasteless, colourless white powder with specific gravity of 1.35. Its molecular weight is 5000. It is soluble in hot water and insoluble in organic solvents.

It is not hydrolysed by mammalian enzymes and is excreted unchanged thus, it is useful for testing the renal efficiency.

It crystallises in the form of sphaerites (spherical crystals) in organic solvents.

Chemical Nature

It is a polymer consisting of 35-50, 1-2 linked fructo-furanose units, terminated with one glucose molecule.

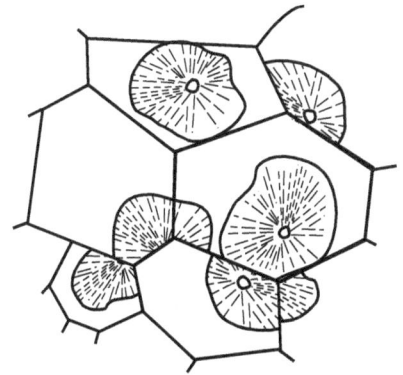

Fig. 3.12 : Sphaerites of Inulin

Inulin

Polysaccharide of Compositae family and is represented by formula

$(C_6H_{10}O_5)_n$ = 3 or 4.

Isolation

Commercially it is obtained from bulbs of the Dahlia plant. The bulbs are washed thoroughly to remove the earthy matter and vegetable debris and crushed. The pulp so obtained is heated to dissolve the inulin in large volume of purified water. The solution is filtered while hot to remove the impurities and then precipitated and purified by using water soluble organic solvent. Washed several times in organic solvent and dried.

Chemical Tests

To the test solution, add a solution of a-naphthol and sulphuric acid; brownish red colour is formed.

Uses

1. Used as diagnostic agent.
2. In preparation of culture media as fermentative identifying agent for certain bacteria.
3. Manufacture of fructose by using an enzyme inulase.
4. Ingredient of diabetic bread.

CHITOSAN

It is the polysaccharide derivative containing amino and acetyl groups and is the most abundant organic constituent in the skeletal material of the invertebrates. It is found in mollusks, annelids, arthropods and also, as a constituent of the mycelia and spores of many fungi.

During the canning of lobster, crab and shrimp, substantial quantities of crustacean waste material is formed. The waste mainly consists of shells and heads. Hard crustacean shells contain 15 - 20 per cent chitin while soft shells of shrimp are reported to have 15 - 30 per cent of chitin. Mycelia of *Penicillium* species contain about 20 per cent of chitin.

Deacetylated chitin is known as **chitosan**.

Preparation of Chitosan

The shells are pulverized to fine powder and treated with 5 per cent hydrochloric acid for about 24 hours to remove all calcium and other impurities of the shell (shells contain 60 - 75 per cent of calcium carbonate). The proteins of the shells are removed by subjecting the above extract with proteolytic enzymes like pepsin or trypsin. The product, thus obtained, is pink in colour. It is bleached by acidified hydrogen peroxide for 5 - 6 hours at ambient temperature. Bleached product obtained by this method is once again processed for deacetylation. Deacetylation is done at $120°C$ with two parts of potassium hydroxide, one part of ethyl alcohol and one part of ethylene glycol. It is tested to ascertain the acetyl content. When the acetyl content is low, the reaction is stopped. The deacetylated product is known as chitosan.

Description

It is an amorphous solid, practically insoluble in water, dilute acids and concentrated alkalis, alcohol and organic solvents; It is soluble in concentrated hydrochloric and sulphuric acids.

Properties

Good quality of chitosan with a concentration of 1.25 per cent in dilute acetic acid has very high viscosity, i.e. 120 cps. Its molecular weight is 1,43,000 - 2,10,000. It is a cationic polysaccharide. It contains approximately 6.5 per cent of nitrogen.

Chitin

Chemically, chitin is a 2-acetamido-2-deoxycellulose, because it is composed of N-acetyl - D-glucosaminyl units linked together by β - D (1 - 4) linkages.

Identification Tests

1. Soak chitosan in iodine solution and to it add 10 per cent sulphuric acid; a deep violet colour is developed.

2. Dissolve chitosan in 50 per cent nitric acid and allow it to crystallise the sphero-crystals of chitosan-nitrate are formed. If the crystals are examined by polarised light, using crossed nicols, a distinct cross is observed.

Uses

Due to cross linkages between glucose molecules in chitin, it is indigestible to humans like cellulose. Therapeutically, it is used in wound healing preparations. Chitin is used as a sizing agent for rayon, cotton, wool and even for synthetic fibres. It has great adhesiveness with glass and plastics. Industrially, chitin and chitosan are used in the process of water treatment.

CYCLODEXTRINS

Cyclodextrins are a group of structurally related natural products formed during bacterial digestion of cellulose. These cyclic oligosaccharides consist of (α-1,4)-linked α-D-glucopyranose units and contain a lipophilic central cavity and a hydrophilic outer surface. In the year 1891, French scientist A. Villiers first discovered cyclodextrins (CD) as degradation products of starch and named this dextrin "cellulosine". In 1903, the Austrian microbiologist Franz Schardinger, who is supposed to be founder of cyclodextrin chemistry, identified two crystalline compounds (A , B) similar to cellulosine from bacterial digest of potato starch and replaced the name "cellulosine" by α-dextrin and β-dextrin. These were later known as α-cyclodextrin and β-cyclodextrin. In 1935 Freudenberg and Cramer suggested the existence of larger cyclodextrin known as γ-cyclodextrin.

In the pharmaceutical industry they are used as complexing agents to increase the aqueous solubility of poorly soluble drugs and to increase their bioavailability and stability. In addition, cyclodextrins can be used to reduce gastrointestinal drug irritation, convert liquid drugs into microcrystalline or amorphous powder, and prevent drug–drug and drug–excipient interactions etc. Thus, the CDs are well known to form inclusion complexes with a variety of organic compounds, among them.

Properties of Cyclodextrins

Thus three well characterized and commercially available members of this family are α-, β-, and γ-CDs (with 6, 7 or 8 glucose units respectively). The α-cyclodextrin, also known as Schardinger's α-dextrin, α-CD, ACD, and C6A; β-cyclodextrin, also known as Schardinger's β-dextrin, β-CD, BCD, and C7A; γ-cyclodextrin, also known as Schardinger's γ-dextrin, γ-CD, GCD, and C8A. Due to the chair formation of the glucopyranose units, cyclodextrin molecules are shaped like cones with secondary hydroxyl groups extending from the wider edge and the primary groups from the narrow edge. This gives cyclodextrin

(a) α-cyclocextrin (α-DC)   (b) β-cyclodextrin (β-CD)

(c) γ-cyclodextrin (γ-CD)

molecules a hydrophilic outer surface, whereas the lipophilicity of their central cavity is comparable to an aqueous ethanolic solution. They have limited aqueous solubility due to the strong intermolecular hydrogen bonding in the crystal state. The natural α-CD and β-CD, unlike γ-CD cannot be hydrolysed by human salivary and pancreatic amylases.

Importance of cyclodextrins (CDs):

1. **Enhancement of solubility**: CDs increase the aqueous solubility of many poorly soluble drugs by forming inclusion complexes with their apolar molecules or functional groups.

2. **Enhancement of bioavailability**: When poor bioavailability is due to low solubility, CDs play an important role to improve solubility. When drug is complexed with CD, dissolution rate and, consequently, absorption are enhanced.

3. **Improvement of stability**: CD complexation improves the chemical, physical and thermal stability of drugs. When a molecule is entrapped within the CD cavity, it is difficult for the reactants to diffuse into the cavity and react with the protected drug molecule.

4. **Reduction of irritation**: Drug substances that irritate the stomach, skin or eye can be encapsulated within a CD cavity to reduce their irritancy. As the complex gradually dissociates and the free drug is released, it gets absorbed into the body

and its local free concentration always remains below the levels that might be irritating to the mucosa.

5. **Odour and taste masking**: Unpleasant odour and bitter taste of drugs can be masked by complexation with CDs.

6. **Prevention of incompatibility**: Drugs are often incompatible with each other or with other inactive ingredients present in a formulation. Encapsulation of the incompatible ingredients within a CD molecule stabilises the formulation and prevent drug-drug or drug additive interaction.

Uses:

Hydrophilic cyclodextrins are considered nontoxic at low to moderate oral dosages. The natural cyclodextrin and its derivatives are used in topical and oral formulations, but only α-cyclodextrin and the hydrophilic derivatives of β- and γ-cyclodextrin can be used in parenteral formulations.

Table 3.4 : Cyclodextrins that are found in marketed pharmaceutical products

Cyclodextrin	Molecular weight (Da)	Solubility in water (mg/ml)	Applications
α-Cyclodextrin	972 145	145	Oral, topical, parenteral
β-Cyclodextrin	1135	18.5	Oral, topical
2-Hydroxypropyl-β-cyclodextrin	1400	> 600	Oral, topical, parenteral
Randomly methylated β-cyclodextrin	1312	> 500	Oral, topical
β-Cyclodextrin sulfobutyl ether sodium salt	2163	> 500	Oral, topical, parenteral
γ-Cyclodextrin	1297	232	Oral, topical, parenteral
2-Hydroxypropyl-γ-cyclodextrin	156	> 500	Oral, topical, parenteral

B. LIPIDS

The term lipids include fixed oils, fats and waxes. These are esters of long-chain fatty acids and alcohols or other closely related derivatives. The main difference between these substances is the type of alcohol involved in ester formation e.g. in case of fixed oils and fats, glycerol is involved in ester linkage with the fatty acids while in waxes high molecular weight alcohols like cetyl alcohol combines with fatty acids. Fixed oils and fats differ in melting point. The fixed or fatty oils are liquid at ordinary temperature whereas fats are semi-solid or solid at room temperature.

The primary function of lipids is storage of energy or as food reserve. The fats, fixed oils and waxes are obtained from plants or animals. Lipids are separated from crude vegetable drugs by expression or from animal drugs by extraction methods which are further refined and used.

Lipids are important pharmaceutically, industrially and nutritionally.

Fixed oils posses the following properties.

1. Fixed oils are thick-viscous liquids with characteristic odour.

2. They are insoluble in water and ethanol but soluble in semi-polar to non-polar organic solvents like solvent ether, petroleum ether, benzene, chloroform etc.

3. They are non-volatile.

4. They undergo auto-oxidation upon storage and turn rancid.

5. They can not be distilled.

6. They are an important source of energy and posses food value.

Fixed oils and fats of vegetable origin obtained by expression in hydraulic press. If such expression is carried out in cold, the obtained oil is known as "cold-press oil" or "virgin oil" and if expression is carried out in heat, the oil is known as "hot-pressed oil". The oils can also be obtained by solvent extraction method. They may be further refined by filtration and bleached with ozone.

Various parts of plants show presence of fixed oils and fats but seeds contain larger quantities of fats and oils than other plant parts.

e.g. sesame seed, linseed, castor seeds, cotton seed etc.

In case of oil, pericarp yields considerable quantities of fixed oil.

Some fungi like ergot, fat serves as reserve food material.

Chemically, fats, and oils are esters of glycerol and various straight chained monocarboxylic acids, known as fatty acids. Fatty acids have 4 – 24 carbon atoms. they may be saturated, monounsaturated, polyunsaturated or cyclic unsaturated.

General chemical formula for fatty acid-ester.

$$CH_2 - O - CO - R$$
$$|$$
$$CH - O - CO - R'$$
$$|$$
$$CH_2 - O - CO - R''$$

where R, R', R'' may be same (e.g. triolein, tripalmitin) or different.

Table 3.5 : Common saturated fatty acids

Fatty acid and source	Structural formula	No. of carbon atoms present
Butyric acid in butter fat	$CH_3(CH_2)_2COOH$	4
Caproic acid in palm kernel oil	$CH_3(CH_2)_4)COOH$	6
Caprylic acid in coconut oil	$CH_3(CH_2)_6COOH$	8
Capric acid in palm oil	$CH_3(CH_2)_8COOH$	10
Lauric acid in coconut oil	$CH_3(CH_2)_{10}COOH$	12
Myristic acid in palm oil	$CH_3(CH_2)_{12}COOH$	14
Palmitic acid in Arachis and sesame oil	$CH_3(CH_2)_{14}COOH$	16
Stearic acid in Arachis and sesame oil	$CH_3(CH_2)_{16}COOH$	18
Arachidic acid in mustard oil and peanut oil	$CH_3(CH_2)_{18}COOH$	

Table 3.6 : Some unsaturated fatty acids

Fatty acid and source	Structural formula	No. of carbon atoms present
Palmitoleic acid in cotton seed oil	$CH_3(CH_2)_5CH = CH(CH_2)_7COOH$	16
Oleic acid in safflower oil and corn oil	$CH_3(CH_2)_7CH=CH(CH_2)_7COOH$	18
Linolenic acid in linseed oil and soyabean oil	$CH_3CH_2CH = CHCH_2CH = CHCH_2CH = CH (CH_2)_7 COOH$	18
Linolenic acid in sesame oil and sunflower oil	$CH_3(CH_2)_4CH = CHCH_2CH = CH (CH_2)_7 COOH$	18

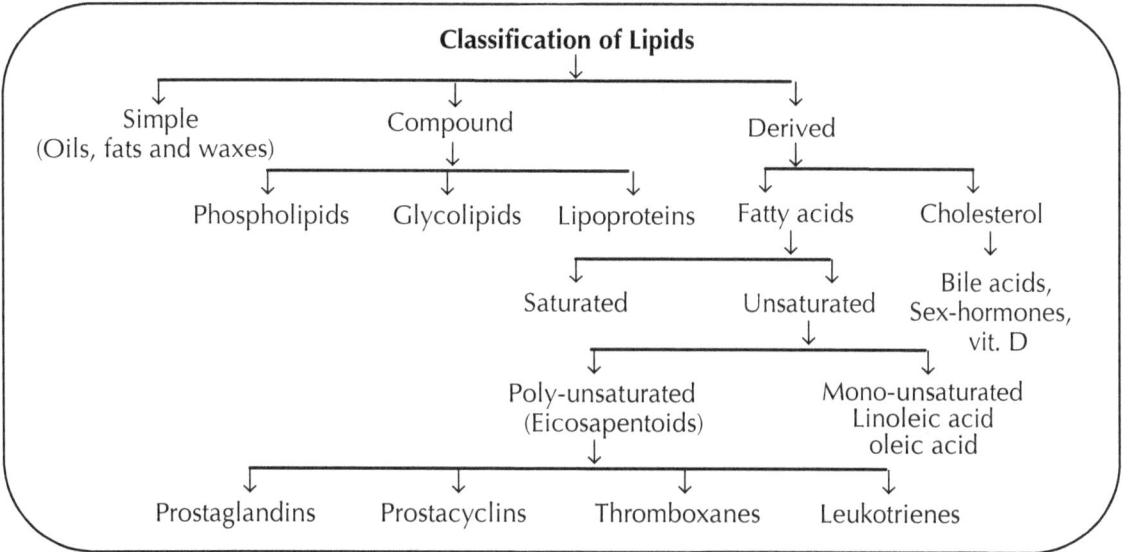

The fixed oils and fats can be obtained from vegetable or plant source and animals source hence classified as follows:

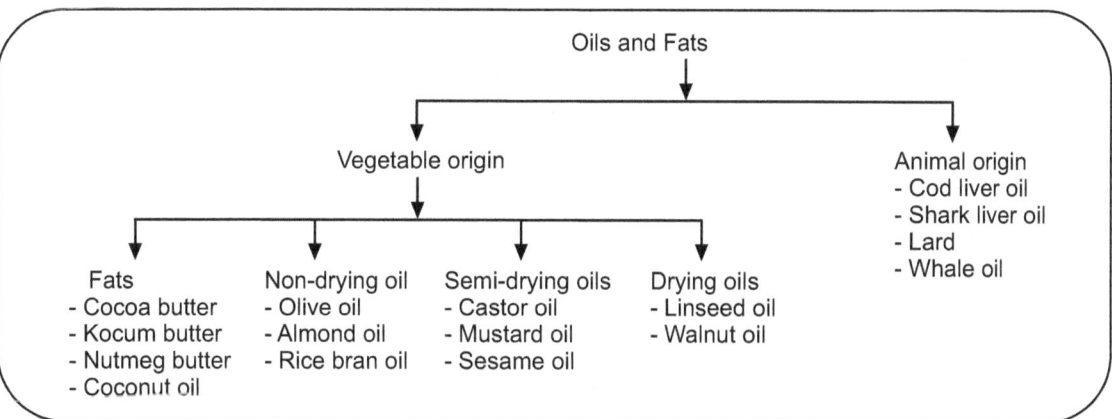

Classification of Waxes:

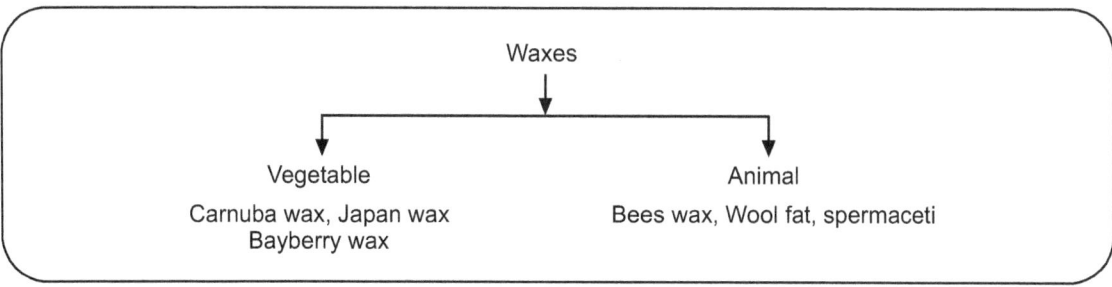

Analytical parameters for oils and fats

Several tests that determine the identity, quality and purity of fixed oil are described as follows:

1. **Iodine value:** It is defined as the weight of iodine absorbed by 100 parts by weight of the sample of fat or oil. Iodine value is a measure of the extent of unsaturation. Susceptibility to rancidity increases for the oil or fat having higher iodine values.

2. **Saponification value:** It is defined as the number of milligrams of potassium hydroxide required to neutralise the fatty acids resulting from complete hydrolysis of 1 g of the sample of oil or fat. Saponification value occurs in an inverse proportion to the average molecular weights of fatty acid present in the oil. This value is normally applied for butterfat, coconut oil in which lower fatty acids glycerides occur in high content.

3. **Hydroxyl value:** It is defined as the number of milligrams of potassium hydroxide required to neutralise the acetic acid capable of combining by acetylation with 1 g sample of fat or oil.

4. **Acetyl value:** It is the number of milligrams of potassium hydroxide required to neutralize the acetic acid obtained when 1 g of sample acetylated oil is saponified. Except castor oil (acetyl value 150), most of the oils and fats have low acetyl value (3 - 15).

5. **Unsaponifiable matter:** It is the matter present in fats and oil, which after saponification by caustic alkali and subsequent extraction with an organic solvent, remains non-volatile on drying at 80°C. It includes sterols (phytosterol and cholesterol), oil soluble vitamins, hydrocarbons and higher alcohols. Paraffin hydrocarbons can be detected by this method as adulterants.

6. **Acid value:** It is defined as the number of milligrams of potassium hydroxide required to neutralise the free acids present in 1 g sample of fat or oil. Generally, rancidity causes free fatty acids liberation, hence acid value is used as an indication of rancid state.

7. **Peroxide value:** It is a measure of peroxides present in oil. A peroxide value is generally less than 10 mEq/kg in fresh samples of oil. Due to temperature or storage, rancidity occurs causing increase in peroxide values.

8. **Kreis test (rancidity index):** Due to rancidity, epihydrin aldehyde or malonaldehyde are increased which are detected by Kreis test using phloroglucinol which produces red colour with the oxidised fat.

9. **Ester value:** It is defined as the number of milligrams of potassium hydroxide required to combine with fatty acids which are present in glyceride form in 1 g sample of oil or fat. Difference between saponification value and acid value is ester value.

10. **Reichert Meissle Value:** This value is a measure of volatile water soluble acid contents of the fat. It is defined as number of millilitres N/10 potassium hydroxide

solution required to neutralise the volatile water soluble fatty acids obtained by 5 g fat.

11. **Polenski value:** It is defined as the number of millilitres of N/10 potassium hydroxide solution required to neutralise water-insoluble, steam - distillable acids liberated by hydrolysis of 5 gm of fat.

CASTOR OIL

Synonym

Oleum Ricini

Biological Source

Caster oil is the fixed oil obtained by the cold expression of the kernels of seeds of *Ricinus communis*. Family : Euphorbiaceae

Fig. 3.13 : Castor Plant (Flowering)

Geographical Distribution

Castor seeds are produced in almost all tropical and sub-tropical countries. In India, castor is one of the major oil seed crops and India is the second largest producer of castor seeds in the world, producing about 2.8 lakhs tonnes per annum. Brazil, U.S.S.R. Thailand, U.S.A., and Romania are other countries producing drug on large scale. In India, it is largely grown in Andhra Pradesh, Gujarat and Karnataka. Andhra Pradesh is producing about 60 % of the total crop in India.

Castor seeds are rich in phosphorous contents and most of it is in thesphytin. Hull is rich in mineral and also contains an alkaloid ricinine, resin, pigment etc. The oil content of the kernel varies from 36 to 60 %. Amongst different varieties, Hyderabad muggelai variety is supposed to be the richest (about 48 %) in oil content. Castor seeds contain several enzymes including lipase, maltase and invertase. The toxic principle ricin, constituting about 3 % of the whole seeds, is poisonous.

Preparation of Castor Oil

Castor oil can be prepared by two different methods : the first being the crushing of whole or decorticated seeds in power driven hydraulic presses and the second one known as *Ghani*, which consists of manually operated screw press driven by bullocks. For commercial scale of extraction, the first method is adopted. The oil, thus produced, is a non-medicinal castor oil.

In other method, decorticated seeds are pressed under the hydraulic press with a pressure of 2 tonnes per square inch, which helps in extracting out 30 % of the oil present in the seeds at room temperature. The oil is known as *cold pressed oil*. Rest of the oil from the seeds is removed by further increasing pressure, and sometimes by hot pressing or even by solvent extraction process. The oil, thus processed, is not suitable for medicinal purposes. The cold drawn oil is then steamed at 80°C, to destroy the enzyme lipase and ricin (toxic protein). It is then bleached and deacidified with sodium carbonate to remove free fatty acid. If necessary, oil is washed with hot water before steaming to remove mucilaginous matter present in oil. Finally, it is treated with activated earth or animal charcoal to remove final impurities by adsorption and filled into the containers.

Organoleptic Characters

Colour   : Pale yellow or almost colourless, transparent, viscid liquid.

Odour   : Nauseating.

Taste   : First it is bland, but afterward slightly acrid, and usually nauseating.

Solubility

It is soluble in alcohol, (an exception to the category of fixed oils), miscible in chloroform, solvent ether, glacial acetic acid and petroleum ether.

Standards

1. Weight per ml   : 0.945 to 0.965
2. Acid value   : Not more than 2
3. Acetyl value   : Not less than 143
4. Iodine value   : 82 to 90
5. Sap value   : 177 to 185
6. Optical rotation : Not less than + 3.5°

Chemical Constituents

Castor seeds contain 46 – 53% of fixed oil which chiefly contains triglyceride of ricinoleic acid (about 80 %). Other glycerides are also present in the drug, where the fatty acids are represented by isoricinoleic, linoleic, stearic and isostearic acids. The viscosity of the castor oil is due to ricinoleic acid.

Ricinoleic acid : $CH_3(CH_2)_5CHOH\ CH_2\ CH = CH\ (CH_2)_7\ COOH$

Triricinolein is hydrolysed in the duodenum by lipase enzyme to release ricinoleic acid that exerts cathertic effect.

Identification

1. It mixes with half its volume of light petroleum either (40 - 60°) and partly soluble in its 2 volumes.

2. Add to the oil an equal volume of alcohol; clear liquid is obtained. On cooling at 0°C and on storage for three hours; the liquid remains clear.

Uses

Castor oil is used as a cathartic, the usual dose is 15 – 60 ml. It is also used for lubrication commercially. Several other forms of the castor oil like dehydrogenated castor oil (DCO) and hydrogenated castor oil (HC) are used industrially for several other purposes. The fatty acids like ricinoleic; heptaldehyde and undecenoic acid are the other substances commercially prepared out of castor oil. Turkey red oil and soap are other commercial products, extensively used in textile industry. The castor oil is used in the preparation of paints, enamel, varnishes, grease, polishes, printing ink, hydraulic and brake spirit with little modifications.

The cathartic property of castor oil is due to irritant action of ricinoleic acid. Castor oil is often given orally or as aromatic castor oil or in the form of capsules. It is used in abortificient paste and ricinolic acid is used in contraceptive creams and jellies. Atropine and cocaine for opthalmic purposes are suspended in castor oil. It is also used as an emollient in preparation of lip-stick and as sulphorecinolate in tooth formulation being strong bactericide. Other cosmetic purpose for which the oil is used include perfumed hair oil and hair fixers.

The following castor oil derivatives are included in BP/EP as pharmaceutical aid :

a) **Hydrogenated castor oil :** Fine, almost white to pale yellow powder, M.P. 83-88°C. Practically insoluble in water. It contains 12 hydroxystearic acid.

b) **Polyoxyl castor oil :** A clear viscous yellow liquid freely soluble in water.

c) **Hydrogenated polyoxyl castor oil.**

Allied drugs: Croton seed oil obtained from *Croton tiglium* family : Euphorbiaceae. The seed contain 50% fixed oil, resin and diesters of diterpenes.

LINSEED OIL

Biological Source

It consists of fixed oil obtained from the dried fully ripe seeds of *Linum usitatissimum*, Linn., (Family : Linaceae).

Geographical Source

It's origin is uncertain, but it is regarded as indigenous to India. It is cultivated at present extensively as a source of fibres in Egypt, Algeria, Spain, Italy and Greece, while as a source of oil in Turkey, Afghanistan and India. In Russia, it is cultivated for both oil and fibre.

Method of Preparation

The variety yielding high percentage of oil is selected for extraction of oil. Seeds are sieved to make free of earthy matter and other materials.

Commercially, linseed oil is produced by use of expellers. Before the seeds are subjected to the expellers, they are rolled into meal, then moistened and heated by means of steam-jacketed troughs filled over the expellers. An average yield of oil is 30 - 35 %. The expressed oil is tanked for a long period to settle colouring matter and mucilage. The oil is then treated with alkali immediately after filtration. Alkali treatment helps to remove free fatty acids. Bleaching of the oil is done by using either charcoal or fueller's earth at elevated temperature. The refined oil produced as above, is chilled to separate wax.

Description

Colour : Yellow coloured clear liquid.

Odour : Characteristic.

Taste   : Pleasant.

Linseed oil gradually thickens on exposure to air forming thin transparent film.

Solubility

It is slightly soluble in alcohol, insoluble in water and miscible with ether, petroleum ether and chloroform.

Fig. 3.14 (a) : A Twig of Linseed

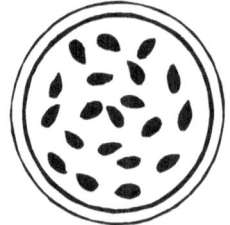

Fig. 3.14 (b): Linseed Seeds

Standards

Specific gravity	:	0.927 to 0.931
Refractive index	:	1.4786 to 1.4815
Sap. value	:	188 -195
Iodine value	:	160 - 200
Acid value	:	Not more than 4
Unsaponifiable matter	:	Not more than 1.5

Chemical Constituents

It contains glycerides of palmitic, stearic, oleic, linoleic and linolenic acids. The unsaponifiable matter of oil contains considerable quantities of sterols, tocopherol and squalene. Linseed seeds contain a cyanogenetic glycoside **linamarin** and mucilage (5 %) and 25% protein, in addition to fixed oil (20 - 40%). The other constitutents are phenylpropanoid glycosides, falvonoids etc.

$$Glu - O - \underset{\underset{CN}{|}}{\overset{\overset{CH_3}{|}}{C}} - CH_3$$

Linamarin

Uses

Medicinally, it is mainly recommended for external applications like lotions and liniments. It is used in treatment of scabies and other skin diseases alongwith sulphur. Since, it has very high iodine value, it is used in the preparation of non-staining iodine ointment **(Iodex)** and other products like cresol with soap **(Lysol)**. It is nutritive and emollient, too.

Industrially, it is an important oil used for various purposes such as in manufacture of soap, linoleum, greases, polishes, plasticizers, polymers etc. It is most important drying oil and hence, considerably large quantities are used for paints and varnishes.

Caution

To meet requirements of various industries, different grades and types of linseed oil are available in the market. Boiled linseed oil dries at a faster rate and forms smooth and lustrous film. Thus, linseed oil that has been boiled or treated in dryers such as linoleates or resinates of lead, manganese, cobalt or zinc should not be used in medicine.

Adulterants

Linseed oil is adulterated with boiled linseed oil, cotton seed oil, sunflower oil, rosin, mineral fish oils and mustard oil. Fish oil is detected by odour and rosin and mineral oils are detected by studying the composition of unsaponifiable matter.

NEEM OIL

Synonym

Margosa oil

Biological Source

It is a non-edible fixed oil obtained from fully matured seeds of *Azadirachta indica* Juss, family Meliaceae, collected late in summer.

Geographical Source

The plant is found throughout India, Myanmar and other tropical countries. In India, it is very common in Maharashtra, Rajasthan, MP, UP and Tamil Nadu.

The present estimated production of the oil is about 6,00,000 tones per annum. The seeds contain about 20 per cent oil.

The export of neem oil was approximately ₹ 263 Lakhs during 1996-97.

Description

It is a yellow coloured oil with specific odour and bitter taste. It is soluble in ether and chloroform.

Fig. 3.15 : Neem plant

Standards

Specific gravity	:	0.913 - 0.918
Refractive index	:	1.417 - 1.4627
Saponification value	:	195 - 205
Iodine value	:	68 - 75
Unsaponifiable matter	:	0.7 - 1.0 per cent
Acid value	:	not more than 2.0

Preparation

The oils can be obtained through pressing (crushing) of seed kernel both by cold pressing or by solvent extraction using hexane.

Chemical Constituents

It contains glycerides of saturated and unsaturated fatty acids. The main fatty acids are oleic (50 per cent) and stearic (20 per cent) acids. The oil contains 2.0 per cent of bitters, which are sulphur containing compounds, nimbidin, nimbin, nimbinin and nimbidol. The unsaponifiable part contains nimbosterol (0.03 per cent).

Use

Nimbin, nimbidin and related compounds possess anti-viral activity. As non-edible oil, it is used for soap making and for manufacture of oleic and stearic acids. It is indicated in rheumatism and also as a pesticide and in medicated soaps for skin diseases. It is also spermicidal.

India has exported neem oil during 1994-95 and 95-96 to the tune of ₹ 356 lakhs and 217 lakhs respectively.

CHAULMOOGRA OIL

Synonyms

Hydnocarpus oil, Gynocardia oil

Biological Source

Hydnocarpus oil is fixed oil obtained from ripe seeds of the plants *Hydnocarpus anthelminitica* Pierre, Taraktogenos kurzil king. *Hydnocarpus heterophylla* Kurz and other species of the *Hydnocarpus*, (Family : Flacourtiaceae, Syn: Achariaceae) prepared by cold expression method.

Geographical Distribution

Chaulmoogra plant is native of Myanmar, Thailand and Eastern India. It is also found in Bangladesh. In India, it is grown in Assam and Tripura.

Method of Preparation

Chaulmoogra seeds contain 40-45 % fixed oil. Seeds are decorticated by machine after grading. The kernels are pressed with hydraulic press and oil is filtered.

Organoleptic Characters

Colour   :   Yellow to brownish-yellow coloured liquid.

Odour   :   Characteristic.

Taste   :   Somewhat acrid.

Solubility :   Slightly soluble in alcohol, soluble in chloroform, ether, benzene and carbon disulphide.

It is white solid below 25°C and soft.

Standards

Weight per ml   :   0.935 to 0.960 g

Acid value   :   Not more than 10

Sap. value   :   195 to 213

Iodine value   :   93 to 104

Specific rotation :   Not less than + 48° and not more than + 60°

Refractive index :   1.472   to   1.476   specific gravity   at   25°C : 0.950 – 0.960.

Fig. 3.16 : *Hydnocarpus wightiana*
(Chaulmoogra)

Chemical Constituents

It contains esters of cyclic unsaturated fatty acids, viz. chaulmoogric acid (27 %) and hydnocarpic acid (48 %) and glycerides of palmitic acid.

$(CH_2)_{12}COOH$ $(CH_2)_{10}COOH$

Chaulmoogric acid   **Hydnocarpic acid**

Uses

The cyclic unsaturated fatty acids of chaulmoorgra oil possess strong bactericidal effect, against *Mycobacterium leprae.*, and *Mycobacterium tuberculosis*. It is found useful in the treatment of T.B., leprosy, psoriasis and rheumatism eczema. It is also used as counter irritant for bruises, sprains etc. Some times it is applied to open wounds. The oils is also used to make soaps with must - like odour. **It is intended only for external use**.

The oil was used intravenously or intramuscularly in early part of 20th century against Leprosy.

Storage

It is stored in closed containers away from light and in cool place.

Substitutes

The plant is substituted in India by *Hydnocarpus wightiana* (Fig. 3.16) found abundantly in West Bengal, Kerala and Western ghats and also by Hydnocarpus alpine occurring in Karnataka, Kerala and Tamil Nadu.

COD LIVER OIL

Synonym

Oleum morrhi

Biological Source

It is processed from fresh liver of cod fish, *Gadus morrhua* and other species of *Gadus;* Family - Gadidae.

Geographical Source

Large quantities of oil consignments are prepared in coastal regions of Norway, Scotland, Iceland, Germany, Denmark and Britain.

Method of Preparation

The fishes are caught by nets, opened, and livers are separated. The healthy livers free from gall bladders are washed, minced, steamed in steam jacketed vessels or 'kars' at a temperature not exceeding 85°C for half an hour, cooled and buried in snow for several days. Special barrels are used for this cooling process, which results in separation of stearin. The steaming of oil destrsoys enzyme lipase. The medicinal oil after filtration is kept in well-closed air tight containers in a cool place protected from light.

Description

Cod liver oil is a pale yellow thin liquid with slightly fishy taste and odour, disagreeable on exposure to air and light.

Solubility

It is freely soluble in chloroform, ether, carbon disulphide, petroleum ether, and slightly soluble in alcohol.

Five major steps involved in refining of medicinal cod-liver oil are (a) removal of impurities, (b) drying, (c) winterization, (d) deodorisation, (e) standardisation for vitamin content. The vitamin A content of the oil is determined spectrophotometrically.

Standards

Specific gravity - 0.918 - 0.927

Refractive index - 1.4705 - 1.4745

Acid value   - less than 2

Sap. value   - 180 - 190

Iodine value   - 145 - 180

Fig. 3.17 : Cod fish (*Gadus morrhua*)

Chemical Constituents

The medicinal value of oil is due to vitamin A and vitamin D. About 1 g of oil contains not less than 255 mcg. of vitamin A and 2.125 mcg. of vitamin D. The oil contains glyceryl esters of oleic, linoleic, gadoleic, myristic, palmitic and other acids. Cod liver oil also contains 7 per cent eicosapentaenoic acid (EPA) and 7 per cent docesahexanoic acid (DHA)s. (Both of them are omega-3 fatty acids).

Vitamin D3 (Cholecalciferol)

Uses

The oil is used as source of vitamins, as a nutritive and in treatment of rickets and TB.

As a result of competition from vitamin concentrates, the consumption of medicinal oil has substantially decreased in developed countries of Europe and the USA. The renewed interest in fish liver oils, particularly cod liver oil resulting from nutritional requirements for polyunsaturates in diet, coupled with blood cholesterol reducing property the vistas of trade seem to open ahead for commerce and industry of fish liver oil.

Non-destearinated cod liver oil is the entire oil that has not been chilled to separate stearin. The oil contains not more than 0.5 per cent by volume of water and liver tissues and it deposits stearin upon chilling.

Storage

In order to avoid loss of vitamins during storage, the oil should be kept in well-filled airtight containers, protected from light and in a cool place. The addition of small quantities of certain antioxidants (e.g. dodecyl gallate) is permitted. It may be bottled in containers from which air has been expelled by production of vacuum or by an inert gas like nitrogen.

SHARK LIVER OIL

Synonyms

Oleum Selachoids

Biological Source

Shark liver oil is the fixed oil obtained from the fresh and carefully preserved livers of various species of the shark, mainly *Hypoprion brevirostris*. In India, *Scoliodon*, *Carcharias* and *Sphyrna* are abundant among the species, and are generally utilised for the extraction purpose. According to I. P., one gram of oil should not contain less than 6000 International Units of vitamin A activity.

Geographical Source

In India, the sharks are processed and oil is obtained on commercial scale in Tamil Nadu, Maharashtra and Kerala. Most of the European countries also produce shark liver oil on large scale.

Method of Preparation

With a little variation, the principle involved in extraction of the oil from the livers is uniform in almost all cases. Government factories in Tamil Nadu and Maharashtra process livers for extracting the oil. The livers are cleaned and minced. The minced mass is taken to a boiling pot, where the temperature of 80°C is maintained. The oil extracted is treated with a dehydrating agent to remove traces of water.

Fig. 3.18 : Shark Fish (Carcharias Species)

The oil is then taken to a vacuum still for dehydration and chilled to separate stearin. Centrifuges are used to separate the suspended materials in oil. The clear oil is manipulated to adjust the desired strength. The oil being sensitive to light and air, all the while, care is taken to minimise its exposure to sunlight and air. Many a times, the livers are stored at very low temperature, until they are taken for processing.

Description

Colour :Pale yellow to brownish-yellow.

Odour :Characteristic fishy, but not rancid.

Taste   :Bland or fishy.

Solubility

Shark liver oil is soluble in solvent ether, chloroform and light petroleum. However, it is insoluble in water and slightly soluble in ethyl alcohol.

Standards

The pharmaceutical grade of shark liver oil should comply with the following standards.

Specific gravity   :   0.912 to 0.9l6

Refractive index   :   1.459 to 1.477 at 40°

Acid value   :   Not more than 2

Iodine value   :   Not less than 90

Chemical Constituents

Shark liver oil contains vitamin A. The concentration of vitamin A in the oil varies from 15000 to 30000 International Units of vit. A activity per gram. Other constituents of the oil are the glycerides of saturated and unsaturated fatty acids.

Vitamin A

Identification

1. Dissolve one gram of shark liver oil in 1 ml of chloroform and treat with 0.5 ml of sulphuric acid. It acquires light violet colour, changing to purple and finally to brown (due to vitamin A).

2. Dissolve 1.0 ml of shark liver oil in 10 ml of chloroform and treat with saturated solution of antimony trichloride in chloroform. Shake it well. Blue colour develops (due to vitamin A).

Uses

It is used for treating deficiency of vitamin A. It is also known as antixeropthalmic factor. (However, it should be noted that shark liver oil is free of vitamin D and is required to be fortified when necessary. Due to the absence of vitamin D, shark liver oil is not a vitamin substitute for cod liver oil). It is also nutritive. Pharmaceutically, it is used in the preparation of dilute shark liver oil, shark liver oil emulsion (Indian N.F.) and shark liver oil with vitamin D. It is used in burn and sunburn ointments. The shark liver oil is used along with usual cancer drugs to treat lukemia, to prevent radiation illness from cancer X-ray therapy.

Storage

Shark liver oil is preserved in well-filled and well-closed containers protected from light and in cool place.

RICE BRAN OIL

Synonym

Rice oil.

Biological Source

Rice bran is the cuticle existing between the rice and the husk of the paddy and consists of embryo (germ) and endosperm of the seeds of *Oryza sativa*, family Gramineae. It is obtained as a byproduct in rice mill during polishing of rice obtained after dehiscing of paddy.

Rice bran contains about 15 per cent of fixed oil and is obtained by solvent extraction method.

Method of Preparation

The quality of rice bran oil depends upon the time which elapses between milling of the rice and removal of oil from the bran. Rice bran contains an active enzyme lipase, which raises the free fatty acid content on storage. The oil obtained from fresh bran is of good quality and has good flavour and low free fatty acid content. Therefore solvent extraction plant for rice bran oil should be set as nearer as possible to the rice milling so as to process out the rice bran oil quickly.

Rice bran is found in extremely small pieces. It is impermeable to solvents. Before solvent extraction, it is subjected to drying, cooking and flaking operations. The normal percolation method of solvent extraction does not serve the purpose with this type of material, but it is pressed and then extracted with solvent special continuous immersion extractors.

Description

It is a golden yellow oil difficult to bleach, not affected by temporary heating to 160°C. It is insoluble in water but soluble in common fat solvents.

Standards

Acid value	- 04	- 05	Total unsaturated fats	75%	
Saponification value	- 181	- 189	Mono unsaturated fats	38%	
Iodine value	- 99	- 108	Oleic acid	38%	
Thiocyanogen value	- 69	- 76	Poly unsaturated	37%	
Hydroxyl value	- 05	- 14	Omega 3 – fatty acids	2%	
Refractive index	- 1.470	- 1.473	Omega 6 – fatty acids	34%	
Specific gravity	- 0.916	- 0.921			
Smoke point	- 232°C				
Unsaponifiable matter	- 3 - 5				

Chemical Constituents

Rice bran oil contains 20 - 25 % of saturated and 80 - 85 % of unsaturated fatty acids as glycerides. Main fatty acids are oleic (40 - 50 %), linoleic (30 - 40 %) and palmitic acids (12 -18 %). The oil contains squalene and antioxidants like tocopherols.

Uses

It is superior salad, cooking and frying oil. The high smoke point prevents fatty acid breakdown at high temperature. Oryzanol is most effective antioxidant found in rice bran oil (about 2,000 ppm).

Since it contains antioxidants, its keeping quality is very good. It is used in the manufacture of cosmetics as it is very effective skin protecting moisturizer and as an emollient. It is an edible oil and used in preparation of vegetable ghee. It is preferably used in cosmetic baby formulations, hair and skin products.

COCOA BUTTER

Synonyms

Theobroma oil; Cacao butter.

Biological Source

It is a fat obtained from roasted seeds of *Theobroma cacao* L, family Sterculiaceae.

Geographical Source

Cocoa is cultivated in most of the tropical and sub-tropical countries, especially Sri Lanka, Philippines, Brazil; Curacao, Mexico, Ecuador; West Africa and parts of India.

Cocoa has been used by Mexicans since long time and even was known to Columbus and Cortez. Cocoa butter was prepared as early as 1695 A. D.

Cultivation of Cocoa

Cocoa is cultivated up to an altitude of 1000 metres above sea level. It needs well-drained good quality soil, with a capacity to hold moisture. About 15 - 30 cm of top soil should have sufficient organic matter. Cocoa plant can withstand a rainfall of 150 - 500 cm per annum, provided it is properly distributed. Proper irrigation is essential at least for the first two years of cultivation to enable taproot of the plant to penetrate particular depth in the soil. Cocoa plant is sun loving, but cannot bear direct sunlight. Hence, permanent ever-green forest trees are grown to provide shade, well in advance before cocoa plants are planted. Inter-planting can be done successfully by raising coconut or arecanut trees between. Cocoa plants survive for 60 - 70 years and start bearing fruits after three years of planting. Fruits are about 15 – 20 cm long containing 40 – 50 fleshy seeds embedded in mucilaginous pulp. Hindustan Cocoa Products Limited in India has undertaken extensive cultivation of cocoa in Kerala.

Cocao seed

Shape :   Irregualrly ellipsoidal or ovoicl.

Length :   15 – 30 mm.

Colour :   Reddish - brown

Preparation of Cocoa butter

Cocoa seeds contain about 50 per cent of cocoa butter. The seeds are separated from pods and are allowed to ferment wherein the seeds change their colour from white to dark reddish-brown due to enzymatic reaction. The fermentation process takes place at 30 - 40°C. The process of fermentation is carried out in tubes, boxes or in the cavities made in the earth for 3 - 6 days. After fermentation, the seeds are roasted at 100 - 140°C, resulting in loss of water and acetic acid from the seeds and facilitates removal of seed coat. The seeds are then cooled immediately and are fed to nibbling machine to remove the shells followed by winnowing. The kernels are then fed to hot rollers which yield a pasty mass containing cocoa butter. This is further purified to give cocoa butter. The cocoa shells are processed further to yield an alkaloid.

Description

Cocoa butter is yellowish-white solid and brittle below 25°C. It has pleasant chocolate odour and taste.

It is insoluble in water, but soluble in ether, chloroform, benzene and petroleum ether.

Cocoa butter exhibit polymorphism α_1 γ, β' and β with melting point 17, 23, 26 and 35 – 37°C respectively.

Fig. 3.19 : *Cacao* Plant (Fruiting)

Standards

Specific gravity	-	0.858 - 0.864
Melting point	-	30 - 35°C
Refractive index	-	1.4637 - 1.4578
Saponification value	-	188 – 195
Iodine value	-	35 - 40
Total unsaturated fats	-	36 - 43%
Monosaturated	-	29 - 43%
Polyunsaturated	-	0 - 5 %

Chemical Constituents

It consists of glycerides of stearic (34 %), palmitic (25 %), oleic (37 %) arachidic (1 %), lauric (1%), acids and small amounts of arachidic and linoleic acids. The non-greasiness of product is due to its glyceride structure. The seeds also contain 15% starch, 15% proteins, 1-4% theobrobmine and 0.05 – 0.5% caffeine. The red colour of seed is due to cacao – red which is formed by enzymatic action.

A triglyceride derived from palmitic, stearic and oleic acid.

Chemical test

Dissolve 1 gm of theobroma oil in 3 ml of ether in a test-tube at a temp of 17°C and immerse the tube in water having the temp of melting ice. The solution does not become turbid or deposit white flexes in less than three minutes after congealing raise the temp to 15 °C, a clear liquid is gradually formed.

Uses

It is used as a base for suppositories and ointments, manufacture of creams and toilet soaps.

It is high in fatty acids and hydrates the skin deeply. It is useful in skin irritations such in eczema and dermititis.

Substitute

Mango kernel oil, which is a solid fat at room temperature and has a melting point of 35°C, is used as substitute for cocoa butter.

KOKUM BUTTER

Synonyms

Goa butter, Kokum oil, Mangosteen oil, Amsul, Red mangosteen.

Biological Source

It is the fat expressed from the seeds of *Garcinia indica* Chois, belonging to family Guttiferae. Commercial kokum butter from the market is melted; its free acidity is neutralised on treatment with sodium carbonate solution and washed in hot water. It is decolourized, if necessary, by using suitable adsorbent.

Geographical Source

The tree is indigenous to Thailand, Cambodia, and China. It is also found in India. It is a wild plant that grows in Konkan, Western Ghats, Coorg dist and Nilgiri Hills. It is cultivated in Maharashtra and in Mauritius. Nearly, 1200 hectares of land is under cultivation in India producing 10,500 tones of drug per annum.

Method of Preparation

The kernels from the seeds are churned and boiled in water. The melted fat is separated by skimming, washed twice with hot water and decolourised with animal charcoal or fueller's earth.

Fig. 3.20: Garcinia gambogia herb

Description

Colour - Light grey or yellowish.

Odour - Slight and characteristic.

Taste - Characteristic.

Shape - It is marketed in the form of egg-shaped lumps.

Standards

Weight per ml	-	0.895 - 0.899 g	Moisture :	0.25
Melting point	-	39 - 42°C	Peroxide value:	4.0 maximum
Acid value	-	not more than 3		
Sap. value	-	185 to 190		
Iodine value	-	35 - 37		
Refractive index	-	1.4565 - 1.4575		
Unsaponifiable matter	-	2 - 3 per cent		

Chemical Constituents

Kokum butter contains glycerides of stearic (55 per cent), oleic (40 per cent), hydroxy capric acid (10 per cent), palmitic (2.5 per cent), and linoleic acids (1.5 per cent). The fat is slightly bitter.

Uses

It is used as a nutritive, demulcent, astringent and emollient. Locally, it is used in fissures of lips and hands. Cake, left after the extraction of the oil, is manure. The antioxidants in butter helps in regeneration of cells and regular use helps prevent wrinkles. It is employed in the sizing of cotton yarn.

It is used in the preparation of ointments and suppositories. The dried rind of the fruit is called *amsul* and used as a substitute for tamarind.

HYDROUS WOOL FAT (LANOLIN)

Synonyms

Lanolin, Adeps Lanae

Biological Source

Lanolin fat is the purified fat-like substance obtained from the wool of the sheeps *Ovis aries* Linn. (Family : Bovidae). It contains between 25 % to 30 % of water and therefore is commonly called as hydrous wool fat.

Geographical Source

Commercially, lanolin is manufactured in Australia, U.S.A. and to some extent in India.

Method of Preparation

Raw wool contains about 31% wool fibres, suint or wool sweat (chemically potassium salts of fatty acids), about 32% earthy matter and about 25% wool grease or crude-lanolin. Crude lanolin is separated by washing with sulphuric acid or suitable organic solvent or soap solution. It is further purified and bleached. The product is known as anhydrous lanolin or wool fat. The hydrous wool fat is produced by intimately mixing wool fat with 30.0 % of water.

Description

Colour : Whitish yellow.

Odour : Faint and characteristic.

Taste   : Bland.

Extra Features

It is found in the form of ointment-like mass and on heating in water bath, it separates into two layers.

Solubility

It is practically insoluble in water and soluble in chloroform and solvent ether with separation of water.

Standards

Anhydrous lanolin (wool fat) has the following standards.

Melting point   :   34 to 40°

Acid value   :   Not more than 1.0

Iodine value   :   18 to 32

Sap. value   :   92 to 105

Ash   :   Not more than 0.15 %

Cholesterol

Chemical Constituents

Hydrous wool fat contains esters of cholesterol and isocholesterol with carnaubic, oleic, myristic, palmitic, lanoceric and lanopalmitic acids.

Chemical Tests

Dissolve 0.5 g of hydrous wool fat in chloroform and to it add 1 ml of acetic anhydride and two drops of sulphuric acid. A deep green colour is produced indicating the presence of cholesterol.

Uses

The lanolin is mainly used as water absorbable ointment base. It is a very common ingredient and base for several water soluble creams and cosmetic preparations. It may also be allergic.

Anhydrous Lanolin

Anhydrous lanolin contains NMT 0.25% of water. After lanolin has been purified and bleached, it is dehydrated. It is also referred as wool fat.

It is more readily absorbed through skin and is therefore important base for most of the therapeutic agents.

Lanolin Alcohols

A mixture of sterols, triterpenoid alcohols and aliphatic alcohols is known as lanolin alcohols. It contains NLT 30% of cholesterol and is used an rectifying agent.

YELLOW BEESWAX

Synonyms

Beeswax; Cera-flava

Biological Source

Yellow beeswax is purified wax and obtained from honey-comb of the bees *Apis dorsata, Apis mellifica* and other species of *Apis*, belonging to family Apidae.

Geographical Distribution

It is processed and commercially prepared in France, Italy, West Africa, Jamaica and India.

Processing and Preparation for Market

The combs and capping of honey-comb are broken and boiled in soft water. These are then enclosed in a porous bag weighted to keep it under water. The boiling causes oozing of the wax, which collects outside of the bag and forms a cake after cooling. The debris on the outer surface is removed by scraping. Bees wax is purified by heating in boiling water or dilute sulphuric acid and settling. The process is repeated several times and finally wax is skimmed off. Various techniques are adopted to bleach wax, such as treatment with hydrogen peroxide; chromic acid, ozone etc. Sometimes, treatment with charcoal, chlorine or potassium permanganate is also given to bleach the wax. Natural bleaching by exposing the wax to the sun-light in thin layers is also preferred.

Description

Colour : Yellow to yellowish-brown mass.

Odour : Agreeable and honey like.

Fig. 3.21 : Honey-bee

Extra Features

Yellow bees-wax is non-crystalline solid. It is soft to touch and crumbles under the pressure of fingers to plastic mass. Under molten condition, it can be given any desired shape. It breaks with a granular fracture.

Solubility

It is insoluble in water, soluble in hot alcohol, ether, chloroform, carbon tetrachloride, fixed and volatile oils.

Standards

Melting point	:	60 to 65° C
Specific gravity	:	0.958 to 0.967
Acid value	:	5 to 8
Sap. value	:	90 to 103
Ester value	:	80 to 95

Chemical Constituents

The wax consists of mainly alkyl esters of fatty and wax acids (about 72%). The chief constituent of beeswax is myricin i.e. myricyl palmitate (about 80 %). Free cerotic acid (about 15 %), small quantities of melissic acid and aromatic substance cerolein are the other constituents. It also contains hydrocarbons (12%), moisture and pollens. Indian beeswax has the acid value of 17 to 22.

Uses

Beeswax is used in preparation of ointments, plasters and polishes. It is used in ointment for hardening purposes in the manufacture of the candles, moulds and in dental and electronic industries. It is also used in the cosmetics for the preparation of lipsticks and face creams. Pharmaceutically, it is an ingredient of paraffin ointment I.P.

White bees wax : Obtained by bleaching yellow bees wax, should not be used for ophthalmic purposes. It is used in ointments and cold creams.

Adulterants

Very frequently, beeswax is adulterated with colophony, hard paraffin, stearic acid, Japan wax, spermaceti, carnauba wax and several other substances. Adulteration can be detected on the basis of solubility and melting points. The genuine wax should not give turbidity when 0.5 g of wax is boiled with 20 ml of aqueous caustic soda for 10 minutes and cooled.

LECITHIN

Synonyms

Vitellin, Lecithol, Phosphatidylcholine is synonymous with Lecithin.

Source

Commercial lecithin consists of acetone-insoluble phosphates of phosphatidyl choline, phosphatidyl ethanolamine (Cephalin), phosphatidyl serine and triglycerides, fatty acids. It should contain not less than 50.0 per cent of acetone insoluble matter.

$$\alpha CH_2 - O - \overset{\overset{\displaystyle O}{\|}}{C} - R_1$$
$$\beta CH - O - \overset{\overset{\displaystyle O}{\|}}{C} - R_2$$
$$\alpha CH_2 - O - \overset{\overset{\displaystyle O}{\|}}{\underset{\underset{\displaystyle OH}{|}}{P}} - O - CH_2 - CH_2 - N \overset{CH_3}{\underset{CH_3}{\overset{}{<}}} CH_3$$

Choline

Lecithin

It is mainly obtained from soybean oil. It is also available in several vegetable seeds, egg-yolk, corn and from animal brain and nervous tissue.

Description

Lecithins are waxy, white substances which become brown on exposure to air. They may also be thick pourable fluids depending upon acid value; characteristic in smell; insoluble in acetone, and soluble in other organic solvents. Lecithins swell in water forming colloidal solution, soluble in mineral oils and fatty acids. Lecithins decompose on heating.

Properties

When treated with sulphuric acid, choline separates forming phosphatidic acid. If boiled with alkalis or acids glycerophosphoric acid, choline and fatty acids are formed.

Chemical Nature

Chemically, lecithin contains glycerol, fatty acids, phosphoric acid and choline. Normally lecithins contain a saturated fatty acid at α-position and an unsaturated fatty acid at β-position.

Uses

With the combination of proteins it forms lipoproteins of plasma and cells; acetylcholine formed from choline part has very important role in transmission of nervous impulses across the synapses. It is a very important lipotropic agent and can prevent formations of fatty liver and lower the surface tension of lung alveoli.

It is an emulsifying agent of natural origin, dispersing agent, wetting agent, penetrating agent and also an antioxidant. It is used in the manufacture of cosmetics, soaps, candies, chocolates. It is industrially used as a lubricant for textile fibres, petroleum industry and printing inks.

POLYUNSATURATED FATTY ACIDS (PUFAS)

Unsaturated fatty acids contain one or more double/triple carbon-carbon bonds in the carbon chain. On this basis they can be divided into three classes:

- **Monounsaturated** fatty acids (MUFA), when only one double bond is present in their structure.
- **Polyunsaturated** fatty acids (PUFA), when at least two double bonds are present in their chemical structure.
- **Acetylenic** fatty acids, when one or more triple bonds are present in their structure.

Polyunsaturated fatty acids (PUFAs) are saturated fatty acid (i.e., an alkyl-chain fatty acid) with two or more ethylenic carbon–carbon double bonds. Depending on the relative positions of the double bonds, PUFA are divided in three categories:

- **Conjugated**, when double-bonds are alternate with single bonds (– C = C – C = C –); most common ones are trienes, but they are present in small amount in animal fats and are abundant in only a few seed oils.

- **Unconjugated**, when the double bonds are separated by carbon atoms bonded with single bonds, usually in a methylene-interrupted arrangement (– C = C – C – C = C–); These are most important PUFA and are subdivided depending on the position of the double bond closest to the methyl side. They are categorized in 12 omega (designated as 'n' or 'ω') families.

  For human nutrition, the most important omega families are **omega-3**, **omega-6**, and omega-9 fatty acids.

- The third group, in which double bonds are not entirely in a **methylene-interrupted arrangement** (present in certain microorganisms, marine lipids and some seed oils).

Classification of Fatty Acids

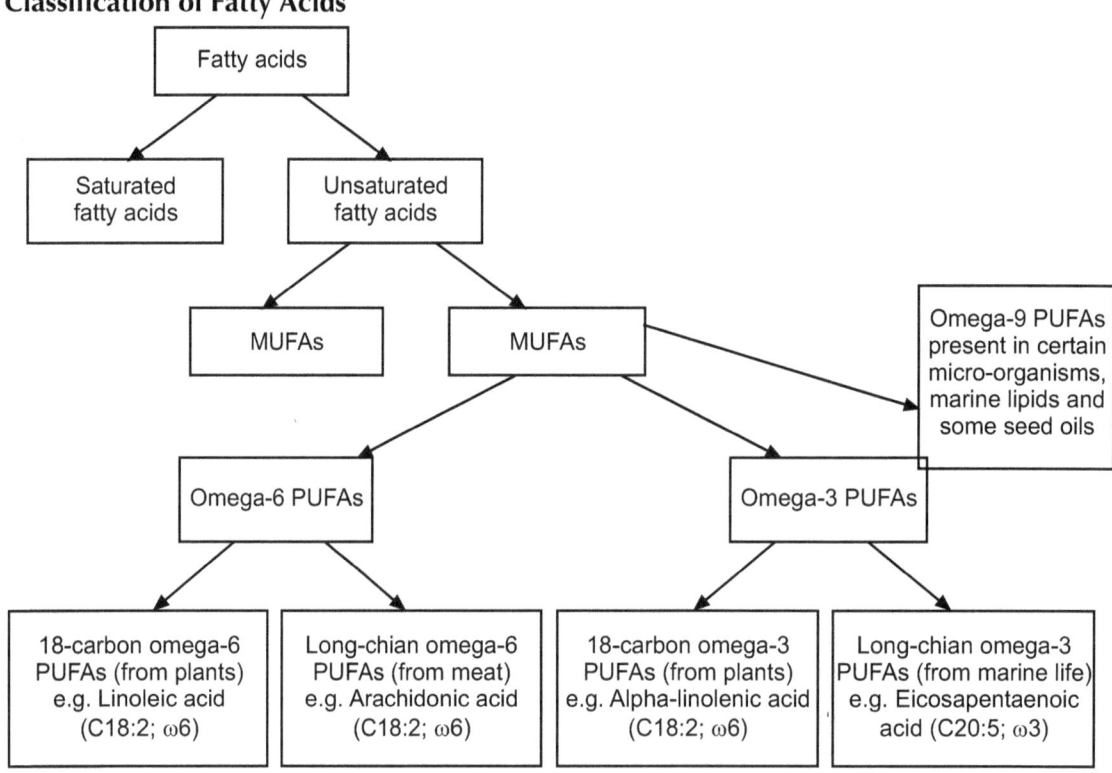

Table 3.7 : Polyunsaturated fatty acids (PUFAs)

Name	Type	Number of carbon atom	Number of double bonds	Symbol
Palmitic acid	Saturated	16	0	16 : 0
Stearic acid	Saturated	18	0	18 : 0
Oleic acid	Monounsaturated	18	1	18 : 1n - 9

Contd...

α-linolenic acid (ALA)	ω-3 polyunsaturated	18	3	18 : 3n - 3
Eicosapentaenoic acid (EPA)	ω-3 polyunsaturated	20	5	20 : 5n - 3
Docosapentaenoic acid (DPA) n-3	ω-3 polyunsaturated	22	5	22 : 5n - 3
Docosahexaenoic acid (DHA)	ω-3 polyunsaturated	22	6	22 : 6n - 3
Linoleic acid (LNA)	ω-6 polyunsaturated	18	2	18 : 2n - 6
DPA n-6	ω-6 polyunsaturated	22	5	22 : 5n - 6
Arachidonic acid (ARA)	ω-6 polyunsaturated	20	4	20 : 4n - 6

The most important PUFAs are the unconjugated and methylene-interrupted PUFA. Within **omega-3 (ω-3) polyunsaturated fatty acid** family alpha-linolenic acid (ALA), eicosapentaenoic acid (EPA), docosahexaenoic acid (DHA) are important fatty acids.

Omega-3 fatty acids: It is also called ω-3 fatty acids or *n*-3 fatty acids. The double bond (C=C) is located at the third carbon atom from the end of the carbon chain. Omega-3 fatty acids are important for normal metabolism. Common sources of plant oils containing the omega-3 ALA fatty acid include walnut, edible seeds, clary sage seed oil, algal oil, flaxseed oil, and hemp oil, while sources of animal omega-3 EPA and DHA fatty acids include fish oils and egg oil.

(a) Alpha- Linoleic acid (ALA)

(b) Eicosapentaenoic acid (EPA)

(c) Docosahexaenoic acid (DHA)

Structures of Omega-3-PUFA's

Omega-6 fatty acids: These are also referred to as ω-6 fatty acids or *n*-6 fatty acids that have in common a final carbon-carbon double bond in the *n*-6 position, that is, the sixth bond, counting from the methyl end. These are pro-inflammatory and anti-inflammatory polyunsaturated fatty acids. Linoleic acid is the shortest-chained omega–6 fatty acid and is one of many essential fatty acids. It is categorized as an essential fatty acid because the human body cannot synthesize it.

Linoleic acid

Table 3.8 : Food rich in PUFA

Omega-3 (ω-3) polyunsaturated fatty acid (n-3 PUFAs):
Alpha-linolenic acid (LNA)
Flax, hemp, soybean, and walnut oils, green leafy vegetables (low levels)
Eicosapentaenoic acid and Docosahexaenoic acid (EPA and DHA)
fatty marine fish from colder waters: bluefish, eel, halibut, salmon, sturgeon, and tuna; som fish from warmer marine waters: bream, menhaden, and sardines; freshwater fish
Omega-6 (ω-6) polyunsaturated fatty acid (n-6 PUFAs)
Linoleic acid (LA)
corn, cottonseed, flax, hemp, peanut, rice bran, safflower, sesame, soybean, sunflower, an wheat germ oils, tree nuts (almonds, pecans, and pistachios)
Gamma-linolenic acid (GLA)
black currant seed, borage, evening primrose, hemp
Arachidonic acid (AA)
dairy products, eggs, meat, shellfish, freshwater fish and marine fish from sub-tropical and tropical environments

CAROTENOIDS

Plants play an important aesthetic function by providing flowers with a broad spectrum of colors. Plant pigments are physiologically important. They are also involved in protective mechanisms, both photo-protective and anti-oxidative and are nutritionally important.

Definition and distribution of carotenoids:

Carotenoids are naturally occurring pigments synthesized as hydrocarbons (carotenes) and their oxygenated derivatives (xanthophylls) by plants and microorganisms but not animals.

Carotenoids are responsible for many of the red, orange, and yellow colour of plant leaves, fruits, and flowers, as well as the colours of some birds, insects, fish etc. play important role in defining the quality of fruit and vegetables. They are found principally in plants, algae, and photosynthetic bacteria, where they play a critical role in the photosynthetic process. They also occur in some non-photosynthetic bacteria, yeasts, and molds where they may carry out a protective function against damage by light and Oxygen. More than 600 carotenoids have so far been identified in nature. However, only about 40 are present in a typical human diet. Of these carotenoids, only 14 and some of their metabolites have been identified in blood and tissues. E.g. β carotein, α carotein, lycopene, lutein and cryptoxanthin.

Role of Carotenoids in plants

1. In plants, they contribute to the photosynthetic machinery. Thus, these pigments are important in signalling, as in attracting pollinating and dispersal agent in plants.
2. They are also involved in protection against oxidative damage by quenching photosensitizers, interacting with singlet oxygen and scavenging peroxy radicals, thus preventing the accumulation of harmful oxygen species.
3. They also perform the function of protection by repelling herbivores.

Role of Carotenoids in Human Health

1. Carotenoids are thought to be responsible for the beneficial in preventing human diseases including cardiovascular diseases, cancer and other chronic diseases.
2. They are important dietary sources of vitamin A.
3. They also exhibit antioxidant properties.

Chemistry and Dietary Sources

They consist of eight isoprenoid units. All carotenoids may be formally derived from the acyclic $C_{40}H_{56}$ structure, having a long central chain of conjugated double bonds, by

(I) hydrogenation,

(II) dehydrogenation,

(III) cyclization, or

(IV) oxidation or any combination of these processes

Due to the presence of the conjugated double bonds, carotenoids can undergo isomerisation to cis-trans isomers. The trans isomers are more common in foods and are more stable.

β carotene

α- carotene

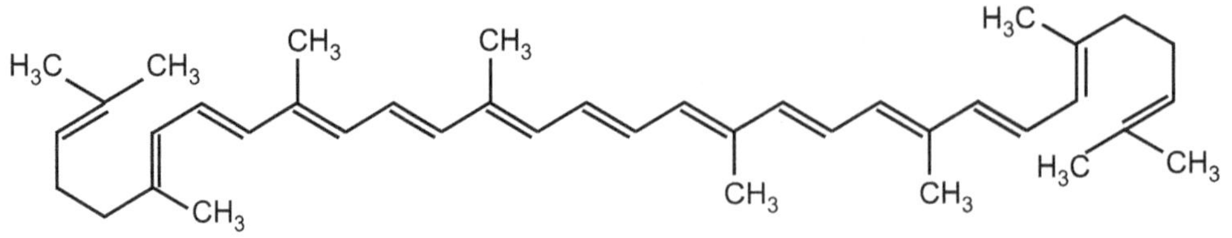

Lycopene

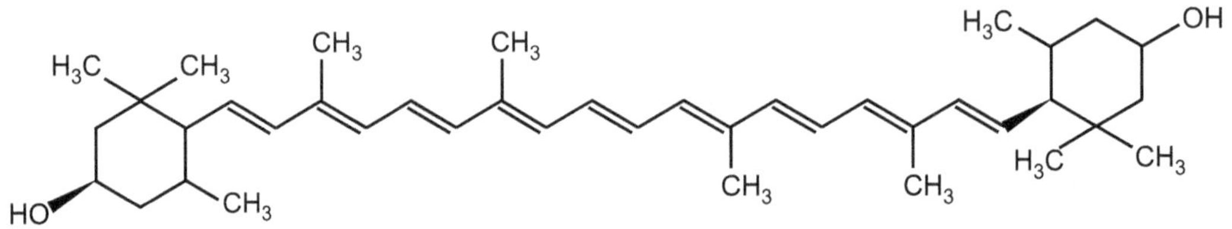

Lutein

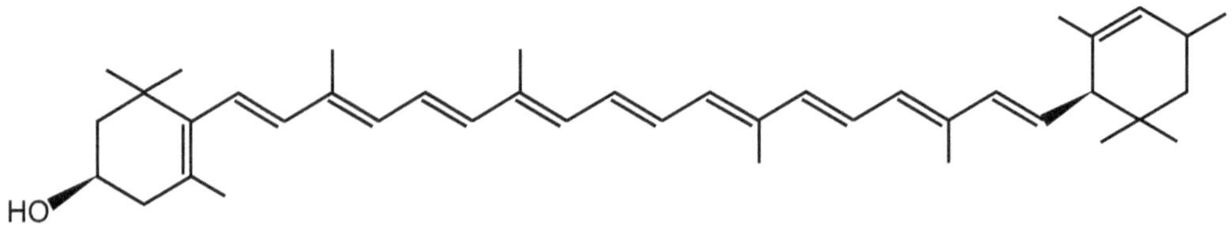

β -Cryptoxanthin

Some of the examples of types of Carotinoids

Carotenoids are present in many common human foods, deeply pigmented fruits, juices and vegetables. Due to the unsaturated nature of the carotenoids they are subject to changes due mainly to oxidation. In general carotenoid content of foods is not altered to a great extent by common household cooking methods such as microwave cooking, steaming and boiling but extreme heat can result in oxidative destruction of carotenoids

Table 3.9 : Some Important Source of Carotenoids

Sr. No.	Type of Carotenoid	Food source
1.	β carotene	Apricot, Carrots, Spinach, Beet root, Green Broccoli, Tomato
2.	α-carotene	Carrots and most green plants
3.	Lycopene	Tomatoes as raw, in form of juice, paste, sauce, ketchup
4.	Lutein	Spinach, Beet root, Green Broccoli, Green peas.
5.	β-Cryptoxanthin	Papaya
6.	γ-Carotene	Present in many plants, often with β-carotene
7.	ε-Carotene	Present in most green plants

C. PROTEINS AND ENZYMES

Enzymes are proteins produced by living organisms. They act as biological catalysts. They can be isolated from living organisms isolated enzymes also exert catalytic effect. They vary in chemical compositions but exhibit common properties like.

1) They are soluble in water and in dilute alcohol but get precipitated by concentrated alcohol.

2) They show maximum activity at temperatures between 35°C – 40°C. They get destroyed above 65°C, whereas they activity is negligible at 0°C.

3) Their activity is reduced by formaldehyde, free iodine, heavy metals and tannins while pH of medium also affect their activity.

4) They catalyse specific reactions. Thus, they are highly selective in their action.

Six major classes are recognised by commission on Enzymes of International union of biochemistry. The major classes are

1) **Oxidoreductases :** Catalysing oxidation and reduction reactions.

2) **Transferases:** Catalysing transfer of group from one molecule to another.

3) **Hydrolases :** Catalysing hydrolytic reactions of esters, peptides, glycosyl etc.

4) **Lyases:** Catalysing removal of group from substrate by other mechanism than hydrolysis.

5) **Isomerases:** Catalysing inter conversion of different isomers. It may be geometric, optical or positional isomers.

6) **Ligases or synthetases :** Catalysing linkage of two compounds coupled to the cleavage of pyrophosphate bond ATP or same triphosphate.

Enzymes can also be categorised as under.

A) **Esterases:** including phospholipase, acetyl cholinesterase etc.

B) **Nucleases:** including ribonucleases, deoxyribonucleases etc.

C) **Prototytic enzymes:** including pepsintrypsin, chymotripsin, papain etc.

D) **Amidase:** including urease, arginase etc.

Further on the basis of site of action enzymes can be grouped as

a) **Endo-enzymes:** Those enzymes that act only inside the cell.

   e.g. isomerase, phosphorylases, synthetases catalysing intracellular reactions.

b) **Exo-enzymes:** Enzymes that act extracellularly.

   e.g. proteases, lipases, etc.

   Many enzymes are coupled with non-protein component. Such non-protein component is known as prosthetic group while enzyme moiety is known as apoenzyme. Prosthetic group act as a co-factor or co-enzyme. Certain vitamins and metals act as co-enzymes.

Table 3.10 : Summary of enzymes and their applications

Sr. No.	Name of enzyme	Biological source	Type	Application
1.	Thaumatin	Fruits of *Thaumatococcus danielli* family : Marantaceae.	Plant proteins	Sweetner
2.	Papain	Latex of unripe fruit of *Carica papaya*, family: Caricaceae.	Proteolytic enzyme	Meat tenderizer and clarification of beverages and Anti-inflammatory
3.	Bromelin	Stems of *Ananas comosus* family : Bromeliaceae.	Mixture of protcolytic enzymes	Treatment of tissue inflammation
4.	Gelatin	Animal collagenous tissue	Animal protein	Used in manufacturing of hard and soft gelatin capsule shells

THAUMATIN

Synonym

Talin

Biological Source

Thaumatin is a highly potent sweetener obtained from the fruits of the plant known as *Thaumatococcus danielli* family: Marantaceae. It is composed of thaumatins I, II, IIII, b and c. It is 100,000 times sweeter than sucrose.

Geographical Source

The plant is found in Africa, especially in Ghana, Ivory Coast, Sierra Leone and Togo.

Macroscopic Characters

The plant bears reddish trigonal fruits with 2-3 seeds. Seeds of the plant are covered with fleshy aril. Arils contain active constituents and are sweet in taste.

Chemical Constituents

The aqueous extract of the arils is a mixture of two water soluble proteins thaumatin I and thaumatin II. These proteins are quite stable and their sweet taste is not lost by heating, it is stable at pH 2.7 to 3.0.

Sweet taste of the thaumatin can be detected even in concentration of 10^{-8}. Thaumatin is non-toxic and non-carcinogenic. It gives flavour even at low concentration.

Properties of Thaumatin

(1) It has a sweet taste with distinct after taste.

(2) It is strongly cataionic

(3) It looses sweetness upon heating

Uses

Thaumatin is used as a sweetening agent for consumer products such as chewing gums and branch fresheners.

Market Products

Under patented name TALIN, it is commercially available in the USA and Japan.

Important Nutraceuticals

Preparations: Rejoov capsules – Rhone – Poulenc. Mumbai.

PAPAIN

Synonym

Vegetable pepsin.

Biological Source

It is a mixture of proteolytic enzymes derived from the latex of unripe fruit of tropical melon tree, *Carica papaya,* belonging to family Caricaceae. It is indigenous to tropical America and cultivated in India, Shri Lanka, Hawai etc.

Method of Preparation

For processing of papain, the latex of these fruits is collected in aluminium trays. Incisions and collections are made weekly intervals as long as the fruit exudates the latex. To the collected latex, potassium metabisulphite (5 g/kg of latex) is added. The extraneous matter is cleared out by passing through sieves and latex is dried in vacuum shelf drier at 55 - 60°C. It is also processed by spray-drying method. This dried latex is called papain.

Description

Papain is available as light brown or white coloured amorphous powder with typical odour and taste. It is soluble in water and glycerine. Papain acts in acid, neutral and alkaline media, similar to pepsin.

Chemical Nature

The different proteolytic enzymes present in papain are a mixture of papain and chymopapain, proteolytic enzymes that act on polypeptides and amides. The proteolytic enzymes are peptides. It also contains coagulating enzymes. Papain can digest about 35 times its own weight of lean meat, therefore used to tenderize meat.

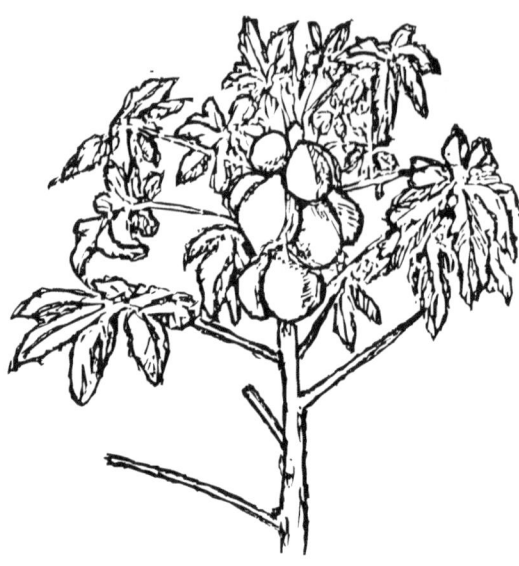

Fig. 3.22 : Papaya tree with fruits

Identification

1. It decolourises aqueous potassium permanganate solutions.
2. It causes curdling of milk (Proteolytic activity).

Uses

It is used in clarification of beverages and as a meat tenderiser. It is employed in cheese manufacture as a substitute of rennin. It is also used for degumming of silk fabrics in textile industry and in leather industry for removing hairs of skins and hides. It is used as an ingredient in cleansing solutions for soft contact lenses.

Medicinally, it is used as an anti-inflammatory agent. It has shown relieving symptoms in episiotomy.

One NF unit of papain represents the activity which releases equivalent of 1 µg of tyrosine from a standard casein substrate.

In 1995-96 and 96-97, India has exported pure papain of ₹ 132 lakhs & ₹ 143 lakhs respectively.

BROMELAIN (BROMELIN)

Biological Source

Bromelain is a mixture of proteolytic and milk clotting enzymes from the stem and ripened fruits of pineapple plant *Ananas comosus,* belonging to family Bromeliaceae. It differs from papain because it is obtained from both ripe and unripe fruits.

Description

It is available as odourless to slightly putrid buff coloured powder with irritating taste.

Fig. 3.23 : Pineapple Fruit

Solubility

It has slight solubility in water. It is insoluble in organic solvents like ether, chloroform, alcohol etc.

Uses

It is used in treatment of soft tissue inflammation and oedema due to surgery and injury. It is mainly used as adjunctive therapy, to accelerate tissue repair. It is also used in production of protein hydrolysates, in tenderizing meats and in leather industry.

STREPTOKINASE

This bacterial protein is supplied as lyophilized powder.

It is an enzyme obtained from culture filtrates of β-hemolytic *Streptococci* group C. Plasmin degrades fibrin, fibrinogen and other plasma proteins. This enzyme has the property of activating human plasminogen to plasmin.

It is available as a sterile, friable solid or white powder. It is soluble in water with maximum activity at pH 7. The solution at higher concentrations is stable for 6 hours at 4°C, otherwise dilute solutions are unstable. It is used in the treatment of thromboembolic disorders for the lysis of pulmonary emboli, arterial thrombus, deep vein thrombus and acute coronary artery thrombosis. The route of administration, dosage, duration of treatment vary for different thrombo embolic disorders. It is marketed in sterile vials containing 250,000 to 750,000 IU.

GELATIN

Synonyms

Gelatina, Gel foam, puragel.

Biological Source

Gelatin is a protein extracted by partial hydrolysis of animal collagenous tissue like skins, tendons, ligaments and bones with in boiling water. Commercially it is prepared from by products of slaughtered cattle, sheep and hogs.

Description

This protein product is available in the form of flakes, sheets, shreds or a coarse or fine powder. It has a characteristic odour and faintly yellow to amber colour.

Commercially, gelatin is available in two types : Type A and B.

Type (A) : It is incompatible with anionic compounds like acacia, tragacanth, agar.

Type (B) : It is compatible with anionic compounds.

Solubility

It is insoluble in cold water, but soluble in hot water. In cold water, it swells, softens and absorbs about 5 - 10 times its weight of water. With hot water, it forms a jelly on cooling. It is soluble in a mixture of glycerine and water, but insoluble in fixed and volatile oils, alcohol, chloroform and ether.

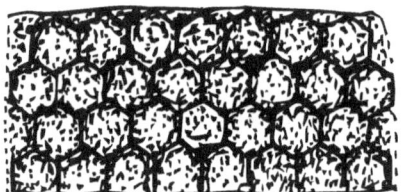

Fig. 3.24 : Gelatin Sheet

In dried condition, gelatin remains stable in air, but when moist may be degraded due to microbial attack.

The quality of gelatin is expressed as 'bloom strength'. It is the weight in gramme, which when applied to a plunger, 11.7 mm in diameter, under controlled conditions shall produce a depression exactly 4 mm deep in a jelly matured at 10°C and containing 6.66 per cent w/w gelatin in water. The jelly strength of not less than 150 blooms is recommended by British Pharmacopoeia for pharmaceutical uses such as coating of pills, as vehicle for suppositories and as an emulsifying agent. But gelatin for capsule manufacture and microbial culture media, higher jelly strengths are used. The jelly strength is designated by bloom gelometer number.

Preparation of Gelatin

For the manufacture of gelatin, the bones are to be defatted and decalcified with organic solvent and mineral acid respectively. The material obtained by this treatment is treated with water at 85°C in successive quantities, due to which collagen dissolves into gelatin. It is further bleached and concentrated under reduced pressure to specific gelatin content and allowed to set in shallow trays. Such moulded gelatin is dried in drying room to eliminate moisture.

Chemical Constituents

As a protein, chemically, it contains different amino acids out of which the major component is lysine, an essential amino acid, but does not contain tryptophan. Gelatin is composed of gluten protein (adhesive substance). The gelatinizing constitutent is chondrin.

Standards

Ash	:	Not more than 3.2 per cent
Gel strength	:	150 - 250
L.O.D.	:	Not more than 15 per cent
pH of 1.0 per cent soln.	:	3.6 - 7.6

Microbial limits   :   19 should comply for absence of *E.coli* and 109 for *Salmonella*. Total bacterial count should be less than 1000 per g.

Solubility

For confirming the identity of gelatin, the following chemical tests are applied.

Identification

1. It evolves ammonia when heated with soda lime.
2. It is precipitated by trinitrophenol and solution of tannic acid, but not with alum, lead acetate or acids which indicates that it does not contain chondrin.
3. It gives a white precipitate with mercuric nitrate and on warming turns to brick red colour.

Uses

Gelatin is mainly used in manufacture of hard and flexible capsule shells. It is also used for preparing pessaries, pastes, pastiles and suppositories. Gelatin in the form of absorbable gelatin sponge is used as haemostatic. Sometimes, it is also recommended for treatment of brittle finger nails and non-mycotic defects of the nails. Gelatin is employed for microencapsulation of drugs, perfumes, flavours and some industrial materials. It is used as a vehicle for certain injections, like heparin in the form of Pitkin's menstrum which contains gelatin, dextrose, acetic acid and water. Gelatin is also used in preparation of bacteriological culture media, absorbable gelatin sponge and gelatin film.

Absorbable Gelatin Sponge

Absorbable gelatin sponge is a sterile, white, tough and finely porous spongy material, which is absorbable and water insoluble.

For the preparation of this material, the warm solution of gelatin is whisked to form a foam of uniform porosity and then it is dried, cut into pieces of specific size and finally, sterilised at 150°C for one hour.

Though, it is insoluble in water, it is absorbed in body fluids. It takes up not less than 30 times its weight of water. About 9 gm of absorbable gelatin sponge takes upto 45 times its weight of well agitated oxalate whole blood.

It is used as a haemostatic. It is moistened with sterile sodium chloride solution and put within a surgical incision where it gets absorbed in 4-6 weeks. It is also used as a local anti-coagulant and haemostatic.

Absorbable Gelatin Film

It is sterile, light amber, pliable, non antigenic gelatin film obtained from a specially prepared gelatin formaldehyde solution by drying, followed by sterilisation.

Description

It is a transparent film which becomes rubbery on moistening, but it is insoluble in water. It is used in the form of saline soaked sheets in surgical repair of defects in membranes like, pleura and dura mater, where it serves as mechanical protective, replacement matrix and temporary supportive structure.

D. NATURAL FIBRES

The tissue composed of elongated cells with pointed ends is known as prosenchyma, while such elongated or spindle shaped cells are with thick walls, they are known as fibres. The cell wall composed of cellulose or may contain various degrees of lignification.

Fibres are developed from single cell, that grow in axial direction. In plants, fibres are differentiated on the basis of the tissue in which they occur e.g. pericycle fibres, xylem and phloem fibres.

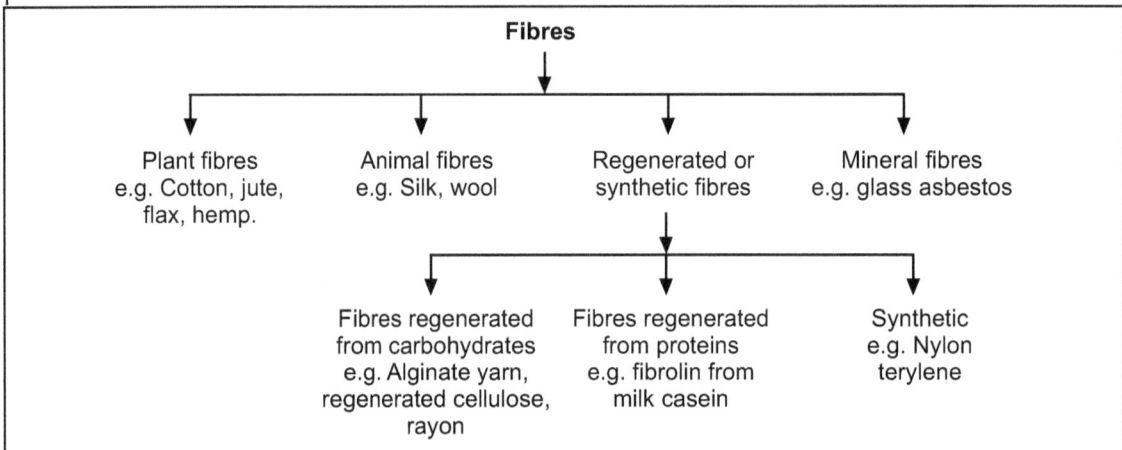

Fibres are not only used in textile industries but also posses pharmaceutical applications like in surgical dressings, as filteration media and also for insulation purpose.

COTTON

Synonyms

Cotton wool, Purified cotton, Absorbent cotton, Surgical cotton.

Biological Source

Cotton consists of the epidermal trichomes or hairs of the seeds of cultivated species of the *Gossypium* (*Gossypium herbaceum,. Gossypium barbadense*), belonging to family Malvaceae. Purified cotton or absorbent cotton consists of the trichomes as mentioned above, but freed from fatty matter and adhering impurities. It is also bleached and sterilized.

Geographical Source

Cotton is produced commercially in U.S.A., Egypt and India. It is also cultivated in various parts of Africa and South America.

Preparation of Absorbent Cotton

Cotton is commonly grown for the purpose of fibres in the tropical countries. The plant after flowering, bears fruits known as capsules. The fruits are 3 to 5 celled. Each capsule contains numerous seeds. The seeds covered with hairs are known as bolls. The bolls are collected, dried and taken to the ginning press, wherein the trichomes are separated from the seeds. Various devices are used to separate short and long hairs.

The hairs with short length are known as linters and are used in the manufacture of absorbent cotton, while long hairs are used for the preparation of cloth. The raw cotton obtained by this way is full of impurities, like wax, fat, colouring matter, vegetable debris etc. It is processed to get rid of most of the impurities. It is taken to the machine known as cotton opener and followed by treatment with dilute soda solution or soda ash solution under pressure for about 10 to 15 hours. The wax, fatty material and colouring matter are removed by this treatment. It is then washed with water and treated with suitable bleaching agent. It is again washed with water, dried and carded into flat sheets. It is finally packed in wrappers and sterilised.

Fig. 3.25 : Cotton herb with Fruit

Organoleptic Characters

Colour -   White (due to bleaching)

Odour -   Odourless

Taste   -   Tasteless

Size   -   2.5 to 4.5 cm in length and 25 to 35 micron in diameter.

Extra Features

It is free from pieces of leaves, seed coat, foreign matter and dust. It may be slightly off-white in colour, if sterilized.

Standards

Absorbent cotton wool I.P. has the following standards

1. Length of staples   - not less than 15 cm.

2. Water soluble extractive   - not more than 0.5 %

3. Ash   - not more than 0.5 %

It should comply with the test for the following as mentioned in the monograph.

1. Neps,
2. Fluorescence,
3. Acidity,
4. Absorbency and
5. Oxidising substances.

Microscopic Characters

The trichomes are unicellular, flattened and ribbon-like with slightly thickened edges and rounded apex. They are tubular and hollow. The cotton hair is cylindrical when young, but becomes flattened and twisted as matures. The mature fibers show larger lumen which contains protoplasm. The cellulose wall of hair is covered with a waxy cuticle may be stained with ruthenium red. The bleached cotton and absorbent cotton wool are readily wetted by water.

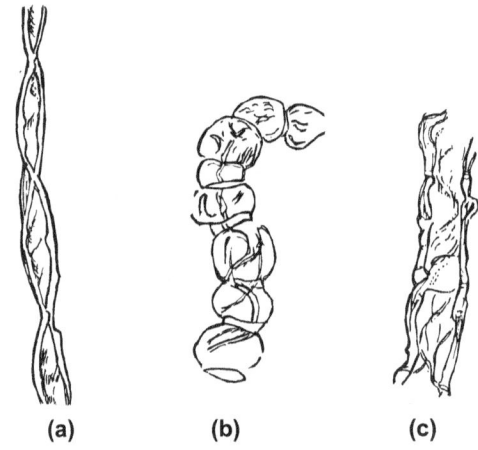

(a)   (b)   (c)

Fig. 3.26 : Cotton Fibres
(a) Raw Cotton (b) Raw cotton mounted in cuoxam reagent
(c) Absorbent cotton mounted in cuoxam reagent

Chemical Constituents

Raw cotton contains about 90 % of cellulose, 7 to 8 % of moisture, wax, fat and remains of wax and fat. Purified cotton or absorbent cotton is entirely cellulose, with 6 to 7 % of moisture. The cellulose molecule made up of glucose residues linked by 1 – 4 β-glucosidic linkage.

This unit is "cellobiose unit" many of which are united in polysaccharide cellulose molecule.

Chemical Tests

(1) Soak cotton fibres in iodine water and dry. Add a few ml of 80 % sulphuric acid-trichomes assume purplish-blue or bluish-green colour (distinction from jute, hemp, wool, silk, nylon, alginate yarn and acetate rayon).

(2) Ammoniacal copper oxide solution (cuoxam reagent) dissolves raw cotton fibres with the formation of balloons, while absorbent cotton dissolves completely with uniform swelling.

(3) Cotton is insoluble in dilute sodium hydroxide solution and hydrochloric acid (distinction from silk). It is soluble in 66 % of sulphuric acid.

(4) With iodinated zinc chloride solution, it becomes violet coloured.

(5) To 0.1 g add 10 ml of zinc chloride solution, heat to 40°C, fibres do not dissolve.

(6) On ignition, cotton burns with flame, gives very little odour or fumes, leaves small white ash (distinction from wool, silk, acetate rayon, nylon).

(7) Gives no red stain with phloroglucinol and hydrochloric acid (distinction from jute, hemp).

Uses

Cotton is used as a filtering medium and in surgical dressings. Absorbent cotton absorbs blood, mucus, pus and prevents the wounds from infection of micro-organisms.

It is also used as an insulating material.

Absorbent cotton wool

Cotton wool is mainly prepared from linters, card strips and comber waste. In this, fibers are long, twisted and offer appreciable resistance when pulled.

The comber waste is loosened and heated with dilute caustic soda and soda ash solution, this removes fatty cuticle. Then it is washed with water and bleached with dilute sodium hypochlorite solutions and very diluted hydrochlonic acid. It is then washed and dried and finally converted into continuous sheet of even thickness.

Storage

Absorbent cotton should be stored in cool place. Bacterial contamination makes the cotton friable and brittle. The absorbent cotton should be packed in wrappers so as to prevent from the dust and microbial contamination. Heat and long storage make absorbent cotton non-absorbent.

JUTE

Synonyms

Gunny

Biological Source

It consists of phloem fibres of the stem bark of various species of the *Corchorus* (*Corchorus olitorius* and *Corchorus capsularis* Linn.), family : Tiliaceae.

Cultivation and Collection

The plants producing jute are cultivated in West Bengal, in the basins of Ganges and in Assam. It needs damp and warm climatic conditions with alluvial soil. The plants are annual and about 1.5 to 3.5 m in height.

Preparation of Jute

Normally, during the month of July when plant is in flowering stage, the straight unbranched stems are cut, formed into bundles and put into stagnant water for 10 - 12 days. During this period, disintegration takes place and phloem and parenchymatous tissue of the bark get separated. Stripping is done and the fibres are cleaned and washed several times with water. The fibres, thus obtained, are bleached and dried by exposing them to sunlight. After drying, the jute fibres are graded according to colour, length and glossiness. The jute fibres constitute about 5 - 7 % of the total green weight of the plant. The prepared fibres are made into bales of 175 – 200 kg and sent to market.

Organoleptic Characters

Colour   :   yellowish - brown

Length   :   0.8 to 5.0 mm

Diameter :   10 - 25 μm

Commercial fibres are, however, 1 to 3.0 metres in length.

Chemical Constituents

Chemically, jute contains true cellulose (53%), hemicellulose (20%) and lignin (10%). It also contains 13 % of moisture. The middle lamella is highly lignified and gives red colour with phloroglucinol and hydrochloric acid.

Preparation

The middle lamella constitutes phloem fibers. It is destroyed by oxidising agents. This distintegrates the bundles into individual fibers.

Uses

It is used in the manufacture of tows (stupa)[*], padding splints, filtering and straining medium. Jute fibres are used for the preparation of coarse bags.

Storage

It needs to be stored in cool place, the dryness makes the jute fibres brittle and dusty. Exposure to light causes its darkening and bleaching reduces its tensile strength.

Substitute

The fibres obtained from *Hibiscus cannabinus* (Malvaceae) are used as a substitute for jute.

---

[*]   Stupa : These are the unmedicated tows, tow consists of jute fibres in cheese rolls free from woody tissues.

SILK

Biological Source

These are the fibres obtained from the cocoons of *Bombyx mori* (Mulberry silkworm) and other species of *Bombyx* and also from *Antheraea* species, family : Bombycidae (Order : Lepidoptera).

Geographical Source

Fine quality of silk is manufactured in Japan, Italy, China and France. Now-a-days, a large quantity of silk is also produced in India.

Preparation of Silk

The larvae of the silkworm (Fig. 3.27) produce silk fibroin fibres from the glands in their mouth. This fibroin gets united with a gum-like secretion known as sericin and forms cocoon. These cocoons are not allowed to grow further into an insect, but are heated to 60 - 80°C by exposing them to steam. The exposed cocoons are put into hot water to dissolve the gum and to separate the fibres.

Silk fibres are 5 to 25 microns in diameter. Silk threads are very fine, solid, smooth and usually yellow in colour.

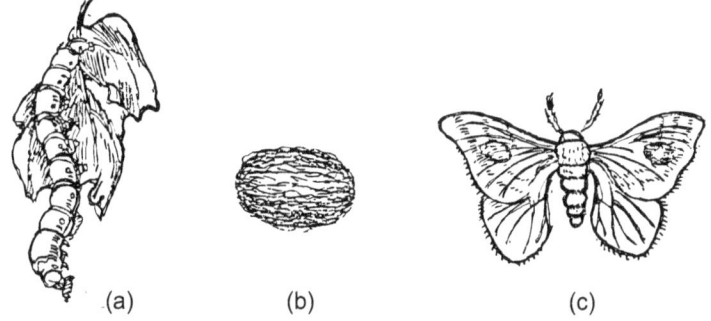

(a) (b) (c)

Fig. 3.27 : Silk Worm Moth *Bombyx mori* Linn.

(a) Larve, (b) Cocoon, (c) Moth

Chemical Constituents

Silk contains a protein known as fibroin. Fibroin on hydrolysis yields amino-acids glycine, alanine and small amount of serine, tyrosine and other amino acids.

Silk is soluble in cuoxam, sulphuric acid (66 %) and concentrated hydrochloric acid (distinction from wool).

Chemical Tests

(1) When flammed it gives smell of burnt hair.

(2) It does not contain sulphur and hence, the test with lead acetate does not form black precipitate (distinction from wool).

(3) Silk is soluble in ammonical copper oxide solution.

Uses

Special types of non-absorbable sutures, sieves and ligatures are prepared from the silk.

WOOL

Biological Source

Wool or wool fibres are obtained from the fleece of sheep *Ovis aries*, family : Bovidae, Order : Ungulata (Fig. 10.4) by cleansing and washing.

The length and quality of hair varies not only from animal to animal but also in different part of same fleece.

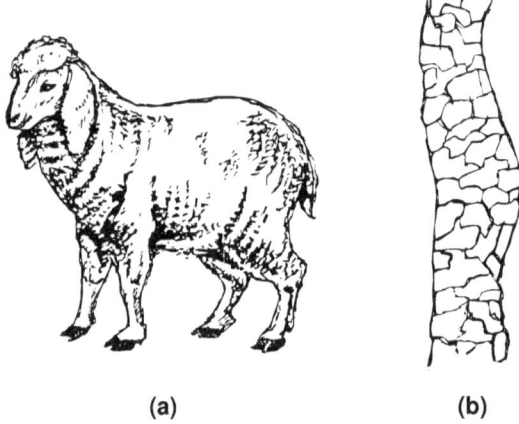

(a)   (b)

Fig. 3.28 : (a) The Sheep , (b) Wool fibre

Geographical Source

Large quantities of wool are manufactured in Australia, Russia, Argentina, U.S.A. and also in India.

Preparation of Wool Fibres

The hairs, forming the fleece of the sheep are removed at shearing time. They are then processed to remove the wool fat and dirt. The clean and defatted wool is subjected to bleaching, washed again and dried.

Description

Wool hairs are smooth, elastic, lustrous, curly, hygroscopic and slippery to touch. Wool hairs have tendency to cling together. When observed under high power, wool shows cuticle, cortex and medulla. The composition of raw wool includes – wool fiber (31%), Suint or wool sweat (potassium salt of fatty acids – 32%), earthy matter 26% and wool grease. This when purified known as wool fat or lanolin.

Chemical Constituents

Chemically, wool contains sulphur containing protein known as keratin. Keratin is rich in amino-acid cystine. The keratin is present in both the forms α and β. β-keratin is unstable while α-keratin is stable. Both these components are responsible for wool elasticity.

Chemical Tests

1. Wool is insoluble in cold concentrated sulphuric acid, (distinction from cotton) concentrated hydrochloric acid (distinction from silk).

2. When lead acetate is added to a solution of wool in caustic soda, a black precipitate is formed owing to high sulphur content (distinction from silk).

3. Wool hair are soluble in 1.25 M sodium hydroxide solution.

4. Wool hair are stained blue with ammoniacal copper oxide solution.

Uses

Wool is used as filtering and straining medium and in the manufacture of dressings like domette and crepe bandages and flannel.

Chapter 4

GLYCOSIDES

Glycosides are the organic compounds obtained from plants or animals, that yield one or more sugar moieties along with non-sugar moieties upon acid or enzymatic hydrolysis. The most commonly occurring sugar is β-D glucose, although rhamnose, galactose, digitoxose, cymarose and other sugars are also found in plants. When the sugar obtained on hydroglysis is glucose, the compound is known as "glucoside".

Chemically, they are acetals or sugar-ethers in which hydroxyl group of sugar is condesned with hydroxyl group of non-sugar, with loss of water molecule. The hydroxyl group of non-sugar may be alcoholic, phenolic, sulf hydryl or amines. The non-sugar component is known as aglycone while sugars are glycone which are linked together through *glycosidic linkage*. Depending upon the stereoconfiguration of glycosidic linkage, both *alpha* and *beta* glycosides are possible. This may be the theoretical aspect as plants contains only *beta* glycosides.

The sugar moieties facilitate absorption of glycoride and also help in transportation of aglycone to the site of action.

Though exact role of glycosides in plants is not known, they are significantly important as they are involved in regulatory, protective and excretory functions. Many glycosides are therapeutically active agents. They are cardiotonic, analgesic, anti-rheumatic, purgative, demulcent agents.

Some glycosides contain more than one sugar, may be di or trisaccharides along with another organic compound (aglycones). The glycosides when boiled with mineral acids undergo hydrolysis. They can also be hydrolysed by enzymatic hydrolysis. Such enzymes are also present in same plant but in different cells from those that contain glycosides. A large number of enzymes have been found in plants. e.g. emulsin in almond kernels and myrosin in black mustard.

The glycosides, that contain rhamnose sugar require rhamnase enzyme for hydrolysis.

Classification of Glycosides

Phytochemical classification of glycosides is based on chemical nature of aglycone part, while they can also be classified based on therapeutic activity exhibited by aglycone part. Another mode of classification is based on type of glycosidic linkage.

According to chemical nature of aglycone moiety, glycosides are classified as follows -

1. Anthraquinone or anthracene glycosides,
2. Sterols or cardiac glycosides,

3. Saponin glycosides,

4. Cyanogenetic or cyanophoric glycosides,

5. Isothiocynate glycosides,

6. Flavonoids or Flavonol glycosides,

7. Coumarins and Furanocoumarin glycosides,

8. Aldehyde glycosides,

9. Phenol glycosides,

10. Steroidal glycolkaloids

11. Glycosidal bitters or miscellaneous glycosides.

The glycosides may be classified, according to their therapeutic activity into different groups like cathartics, cardiotonics, analgesics, anti-rheumatics, anti-ulcer etc.

Sometimes glycosides are also classified on the basis of type of sugar or the glycone part of their structure. Accordingly, there are glucosides with glucose, rhamnosides with rhamnose, pentosides with pentose like ribose, etc.

The sugars involved in the structure are normally the common type of sugars. Only in few cases, deoxy-sugars like digitoxose, cymarose are present.

Another approach for their classification is by considering the linkage across glycone and aglycone part. Basically, all types of glycosidal linkages have occurred by interaction of – OH group of glycone and hydrogen coming through any of the radicals like CH, – OH, – SH and – NH present on aglycones part. Hence, by elimination of one water molecule, linkage or a bridge is formed and the type of glycoside formed is named by putting the element as prefix like C-glycoside, N-glycoside, O-glycoside or S-glycoside.

To illustrate the individual pattern, brief account of such glycosides is given below.

(1) C-glycosides (when sugar moiety is linked to carbon atom): Some of the anthraquinone glycosides such as cascarosides from cascara and aloin from aloe, as well as, some members of flavone type of glycosides show the presence of C-glycosides.

Glycone —$\boxed{\text{OH} + \text{H}}$ C — aglycones $\longrightarrow$ glycone - C - aglycones + H_2O

C - glycosides, which are also called as aloin-type glycosides, are mainly present in members of Liliaceae, e.g. Aloe. They are not hydrolysed by heating with dilute acids/alkalies, but by oxidative hydrolysis with ferric chloride. Cochineal contains C-glycoside in the form of a colouring matter called carminic acid.

(2) O - glycosides (when sugar moiety is attached to oxygen atom): They are very common in higher plants e.g. senna, rhubarb frangula, etc. They are hydrolysed by treatment of acid or alkali into aglycones and sugar, i.e. glucoranillin, amygdaling.

Glycone - O$\boxed{\text{H} + \text{HO}}$ — aglycones $\longrightarrow$ glycone O - aglycones + H_2O.

(3) S - glycosides (when sugar is linked to sulphur atom): Their occurrence is restricted to isothiocynate glycosides like sinigrin from black mustard.

$$C_3 H_5 \ - \ C - S - C_6 H_{11} O_5$$
$$\|$$
$$N - O - SO_3 \, K$$

They are formed by interaction of sulfhydryl group of aglycones and hydroxyl group of glycone.

Glycone - $\boxed{OH + H}$ S - aglycones $\longrightarrow$ glycone - S - aglycones + H_2O

(4) N - glycosides: The most typical representative example of N - glycosides is nucleosides, where the amino group of base reacts with - OH group of ribose/deoxyribose and ultimately gives N - glycosidic form.

Glycone - $\boxed{OH + H}$ N - Glycone $\longrightarrow$ Glycone - N - aglycones + H_2O

The glycosides contain sugars but still the physical, chemical and therapeutic properties are dictated by aglycone part. The sugar moiety facilitates absorption of glycosides and helps in transportation of aglycone portion at the site of action.

Properties of glycosides

1) They are crystalline or amorphous substances.
2) They are soluble in water or alcohol except resin glycosides, but are insoluble in chloroform and ether.
3) The aglycone part is soluble in benzene or ether.
4) They are optically active compounds.
5) Glycosides do not reduce Fehling's solution, until they are hydrolysed.

They are believed to participate in growth regulation and protection of the plant.

Biosynthesis of glycosides

The principal pathway of glycoside formation involves the transfer of uridylyl group from uridine triphospahte to sugar 1- phosphate. This reaction is catalysed by enzyme uridylyl transferase. This is then followed by transfer of sugar from uridine diphosphate to suitable acceptor (aglycone). This reaction is mediated by glycosyl transferases.

The reaction is summerised below -

$$\text{UTP + Sugar -1-P} \quad \underset{\text{Transferase}}{\overset{\text{Uridylyl}}{\rightleftharpoons}} \quad \text{UDP – Sugar + PPi}$$

$$\text{UDP – Sugar + Acceptor} \quad \underset{\text{Transferase}}{\overset{\text{Uridylyl}}{\rightleftharpoons}} \quad \underset{\text{(Glycoside)}}{\text{Acceptor – Sugar + UDP}}$$

Acceptor is aglycone part

Once such glycoside is formed, other enzymes may transfer another sugar unit to the monosaccharides and convert it to disaccharides.

E.g. cardio-active glycoside formation. The aglycone of cardioactive glycosides are steroidal in nature. They contain cyclopentanoperhydrophenanthrene ring containing an unsaturated lactone ring at C-17. The steroidal biosynthesis is derived from cholesterol through acetate mevalonate pathway followed by cyclization of aliphatic triterpene squalene.

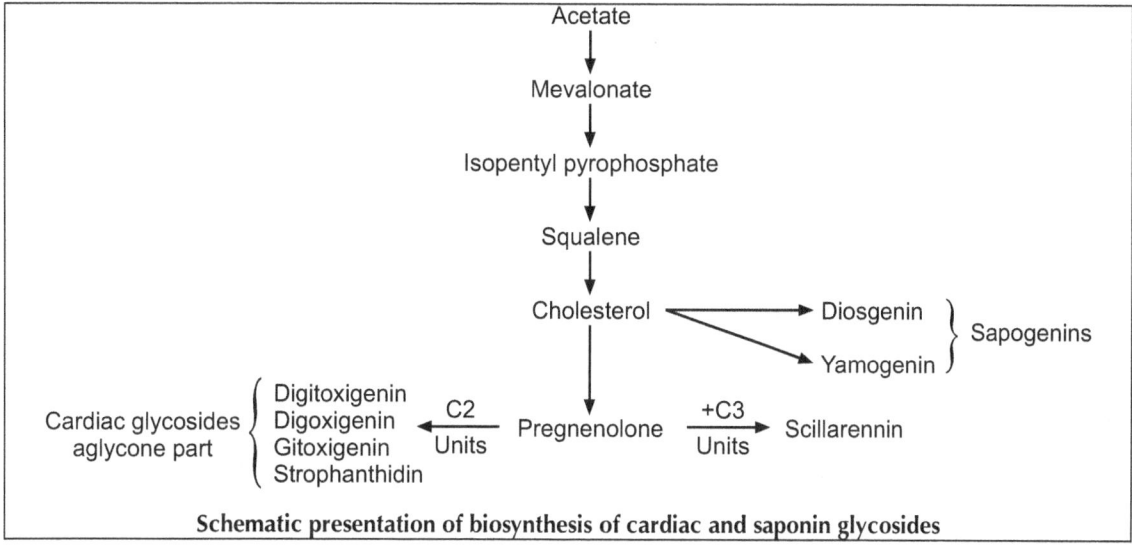

Schematic presentation of biosynthesis of cardiac and saponin glycosides

In case of saponin glycosides, they are the derivatives of steroids that posses triterpenoid structure. The squalene formation is followed by cholesterol and various other steroidal compounds.

The biosynthesis of anthracene aglycones has been studied with *Penicillium islandium*. The acetate unit undergoes condensation to form anthraquinones.

Poly - β - keto methylene acid - intermediate   Emodin and other related anthraquinone derivatives

Biosynthsis of anthraquinone derivatives

A. SAPONIN GLYCOSIDES

Most of the plants containing saponin glycosides are medicinally and commercially important. As the name indicates, the aglycone part of these glycosides has soap like action. They exhibit some physical properties like foaming action on shaking with water and yielding colloidal solutions. They are generally considered as haemotoxic, because they cause haemolysis of erythrocytes. Due to this activity, some of them are used as fish poisons. Saponins have a bitter and acrid taste. They cause irritation of mucous membrane.

They are mostly non-crystalline substances soluble in water and alcohol, but insoluble in non-polar organic solvents.

Chemically, they contain aglycone called as sapogenin. Sapogenins are high molecular weight substances which by acetylation give crystalline forms. The harmful sapogenins are called as sapotoxins. Depending on the nature of aglycone, saponins are categorised into 2 groups viz.

Steroid Pattern of Saponins
(Tetracyclic Triterpenoids)

Pentacyclic Triterpenoids

(i) Steroidal saponins (Tetracyclic triterpenoid saponins)

(ii) Pentacyclic triterpenoid saponins

Both types of aglycones are linked with different types of sugars and uronic acids.

1. Steroidal Saponins

Commercially, steroidal saponins are more important, as they are used as raw material for the synthesis of various medicinally useful steroids like vitamin D, cardiac glycosides, corticoids like betamethasone and cortisone acetate, sex hormones like progesterone, testosterone and oestradiol, oral contraceptives such as mestranol and norethisterone; and spironolactone which is a diuretic steroid. Steroidal sapogenins viz. diosgenin and hecogenin can be considered as representative – ex. of this group of saponins. Due to their pharmaceutical importance, many plants have been screened for detection of steroidal saponins. Their distribution is limited to plant kingdom. In dicot plants, important sources are from Leguminosae, Solanaceae, Apocynaceae, etc. They are mainly obtained from monocot plants like Liliaceae, Dioscoreaceae and Amaryllidaceae.

2. Pentacyclic Triterpenoid Saponins

α–amyrin   β–amyrin   Lupeol

This group contains the sapogenin with pentacyclic triterpenoid nucleus, which is linked with sugars or uronic acids. The sapogenin is further differentiated into

(a) α - amyrin type; (b) β - amyrin type; and (c) Lupeol.

An important derivative of this group is triterpenoid acids. These acids are present in various drugs formed by substitution of carboxylic group at C_4, C_{17} and C_{20}.

	R'	R"
Gypsogenin	CHO	H
Hederagenin	$CH_{20}H$	H
Oleanolic acid	CH_3	H
Quillaic acid	CHO	OH

Triterpenoid acids

Besides the chemical structure, these types of saponins differ from steroidal saponins by way of their distribution. Pentacyclic triterpenoid saponins are available from various families of dicot plants like Polygalaceae, Caryophyllaceae, Berberidaceae, Umbelliferae, Rubiaceae, Compositae, Primulaceae, Rutaceae, Chenopodiaceae, etc. They are however scarcely found in monocot plants.

LIQUORICE

Synonyms

Liquorice root; Glycyrrhiza, Mulethi.

Biological Source

Liquorice consists of dried peeled or unpeeled roots and stolons of the plant known as *Glycyrrhiza glabra* Linn. belonging to family Leguminosae. It should contain not less than 3.0% of Glycyrrhinic acid.

BP 2007 included the dried unpeeled roots and rhizomes of *G.uralensis*, *G.inflata* or *G.glabra* in their monograph.

Geographical Source

It is commercially cultivated and collected in various countries. It is grown in Russia, Iran, Italy, Spain, China, France, Iraq and Greece.

Varieties of Glycyrrhiza glabra

1. *G. glabra* var *typica* (Spanish liquorice). Plant is grown in Spain, Italy, England, France, Germany and USA. It has purplish papilionaceous flowers and gives off a large number of stolons.

2. *G. glabra* var. *glandulifera* (Russian liquorice) : It is abundant in the wild in central and South Russia. It bears large roots but no stolons.

3. *G. glabra* var. *β-violacea* (Persian liquorice) : It is collected in Iran and Iraq. It bears violet flowers.

Cultivation and Collection

Liquorice requires deep moist soil, particularly on the banks of the rivers and dry sunny climate. For cultivation, soil should be well prepared and liberally manured. Root cuttings with 2 to 3 aerial buds are planted at a distance of 60 cm, the distance being maintained in two rows is about a metre. Manuring and irrigation are done at intervals. The crop is kept free of weeds. Alternative crop like carrot or cabbage may be grown alongwith liquorice. The roots are ready for harvesting 3 to 4 years after planting. Rhizomes and roots are dug up in the autumn, preferably from the plants which have born the fruits. Buds and rootlets are removed and the drug is washed properly. It is dried slowly under cover. The drug is decorticated before drying to produce peeled liquorice. Liquorice looses about 50 % of its weight on drying.

Organoleptic Characters

Colour	:	Unpeeled-yellowish brown or dark brown externally, and yellowish internally, while the peeled liquorice is pale yellow in colour.
Odour	:	Faint and characteristic.
Taste	:	Sweet.
Size	:	Length 20 to 50 cm and 2 cm in diameter.
Shape	:	Cylindrical pieces which are straight may be peeled or unpeeled. Peeled liquorice is angular.
Fracture	:	It is fibrous in bark and splintery in wood.

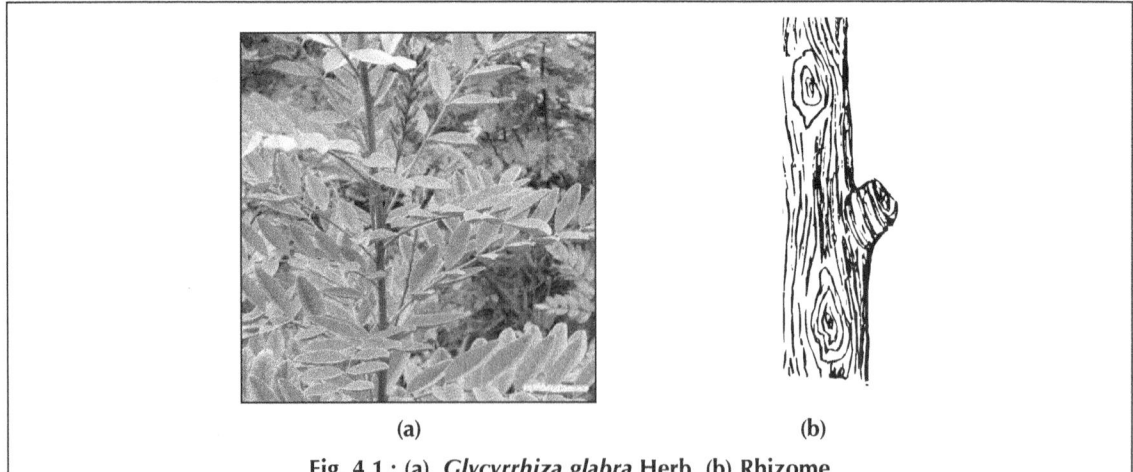

(a)   (b)

Fig. 4.1 : (a) *Glycyrrhiza glabra* Herb (b) Rhizome

Extra Features

Unpeeled pieces show presence of small buds encircling scale leaves and longitudinally the drug is wrinkled, while peeled drug is fibrous without wrinkles.

Microscopic Characters

The important histological characters of liquorice are given below.

Unpeeled drug shows presence of polyhedral tabular; brownish cork cells within the cork phellderm or secondary cortex is present which is parenchymatous in nature.

Fibres are thick, lignified or partially lignified, in the group of 10 to 15 in phloem and xylem. Vessels are large and closely arranged with bordered pits. Starch and prisms of calcium oxalate crystals are present in parenchyma. In case of stolons, the pith is present and is parenchymatous. The root is characterised by presence of tetrarch xylem and absence of pith. The secondary xylem is composed of large vessels, wood fibers and wood parenchyma. The vessels show reticulate or pitted walls.

Chemical Constituents

The chief constituent of liquorice is triterpenoid saponin known as glycyrrhizin (glycyrrhizic acid), which is a potassium and calcium salt of glycyrrhizinic acid. Glycyrrhizinic acid is a glycoside and on hydrolysis yields glycyrrhetinic acid (glycyrrhetic acid), which has a triterpenoid structure. The different varieties are found to contain varying amount of glycyrrhizin (from 6 to 13 %). Spanish liquorice contains 5 to 10 %, Russian variety contains about 20 %, while Persian liquorice contains 7.5 to 13 % of glycyrrhizin. The yellow colour of liquorice is due to flavonoids like liquiritin, iso liquiritin, liquiritigenin, isoliquiritigenin. Other constituents of liquorice include polysaccharides bitter principles (glycyramarin), resins as paragine (amide of aspartic acid 1-2%) 0.04 – 0.06 % volatile compounds, β-sitosterol.

Chemical Test

When moistened with 80 % sulphuric acid, liquorice develops a deep yellow colour due to change of flavone glycoside liquiritin to chalcone glycoside.

Standards

Ash value   :   Peeled drug not more than 6%

                              Unpeeled drug not more than 10%

Acid insoluble ash   :   Peeled drug not more than 0.5%

                              Unpeeled drug not more than 2%

Liquiritin - R = Glucosyl
Liquiritigenin R = H

Glycyrrhetinic acid

Chemical constituents of *Glycyrrhiza glabra*

Uses

Glycyrrhiza is used as demulcent and mild expectorant. It is used as a sweetening agent, an antispasmodic, anti-inflammatory and antiulcer drug. It is used as a flavouring agent and for improving taste of bitter medicines like quinine, cascara etc. It is also used in cough-lozenges, cough-pastilles and also as an absorbent pill excipient in the form of powder. Glycyrrhiza does not exhibit laxative property as described many a times, but it potentiates laxative action of senna. One of the constituents of glycyrrhizin, i.e. Glycyrrhetinic acid in the form of disodium salt is used as an anti-inflammatory agent in gastric ulcers. Glycyrrhetinic acid is used in the treatment of Addison's disease. Residual matter produced in the preparation of liquorice extract is reported to have been used as a foam stabilizer in foam type of fire extinguisher. Liquorice is used as a flavouring agent. Ammoniated glycyrrhiza is used as a flavouring agent in beverages, confectionary and pharmaceuticals. Ammoniated glycyrrhiza is 50 times sweeter than sucrose. However, it cannot be used as a flavouring agent in acidic medium. Liquorice in the form of sticks or rolls is used for manufacture of confectionaries. Liquid extract of liquorice, granulated and spray dried liquid are supposed to be ideal for this purpose.

Carbenoxolone is an oleandane derivative prepared from glycyrrhiza and possesses significant minerelocoticoid activity. It is used as an anti-ulcer drug. It changes the composition of mucous and increases mucosal barrier for the diffusion of acid. It is postulated that carbenoxolone inhibits the enzymes which inactivate prostaglandins and suppresses the activation of pepsinogen. This drug has marked anti-inflammatory effects. It is employed in treatment of gastric and duodenal ulcers. It is also used along with antacids for treatment of gastric reflux and reflux oesophagitis. It has also application in the form of gel for mouthwash in treatment of oral ulcers.

GINSENG

Synonyms

Ninjin, Pannag, Panax.

Biological Source

Ginseng is the dried root of various species of *Panax*, like *P. ginseng* (Korean ginseng), *P. japonica* (Japanese ginseng), *P. notoginseng* (Chinese ginseng) and *P. quinquefolium* (American ginseng), belonging to family Araliaceae. It contains not less than 0.4% of ginesenosides calculated on dried baris.

Geographical Source

It grows widely in Korea, China and Russia. Presently, ginseng is commercially cultivated in Korea, China, Japan, Russia, Canada and United States of America. In India at present it is cultivated in Kohima, Tunsang district of Nagoland.

The term *Panax* indicates cure all (*Pan and axos*), while *ginseng* is derived from Chinese words *shen sang*, which stands for manroot, because the shape of the root resembles the human body. The references about ginseng are found in ancient Chinese literature, stating its medicinal properties. Now-a-days, ginseng is considered as adaptogen. It increases non-specific resistance and defence mechanism of the body.

Cultivation and Collection

The cultivation technology adopted in Korea is briefly described.

Ginseng is propagated by means of seeds in nursery beds and then transplanted into open fields i.e. permanent beds. The ripe seeds are collected from four year old plants. They are sown in November in nursery beds. There are 3 types of nursery beds viz. Yang-Jik, To-Jik and Ban-Yang-Jik. The first type gives high quality seedlings. After attaining sufficient growth, the seedlings are dug up in the following May and transplanted to permanent beds for next 3 - 5 years. Ginseng requires clay loam or sandy loam soil. It grows at altitudes from 100 - 800 metres. The soil with high amount of potassium gives better results. About 7 -10 days after transplantation, shades are provided to plants to protect them from excessive sunlight. Generally, use of fertilizers is avoided, but before transplantation, the soil is mixed with large amount of green grass. Periodically, weeding is done. The plants are harvested 3 - 5 years after transplantation. Generally, they are harvested between July to October. White ginseng is obtained by removing the outer layers of the roots. Red ginseng is obtained by first steaming the roots and after that they are dried. But, removal of outer layers may lead to loss of active constituents, as saponins are located outside the root cambium.

White ginseng show humerous rootters on the lower surface whereas rootlets are absent in red ginseng. The roots are graded and packed. They are wrapped in cotton, silk or paper.

Macroscopic Characters

Ginseng roots are tuberous corpulent roots. They are yellowish brown, white or red in colour depending on type. They are translucent and possess the stem scars.

Chemical Constituents

Ginseng contains complex mixture of triterpenoid saponin glycosides, belonging to triterpenoid group. They are grouped as follows -

(1) Ginsenosides;

(2) Panaxosides; and

(3) Chikusetsusaponin

Ginsenosides contain aglycone dammarol while panaxosides have oleanolic acid as aglycone. About 13 ginsenosides have been identified. Panaxosides give oleanolic acid, panaxadiol and panaxatriol on decomposition.

(a)   (b)

Fig. 4.2 : Ginseng plant (Panax ginseng) with Root (b) Ginseng root enlarged

Oleanolic acid   *Panaxadiol*   Panaxatriol

Ginseng glycosides

Standards

Foreign organic matter	≯	2.0 %
Total ash	≯	7.0 %
Acid insoluble ash	≯	1.0 %
Sulfated ash	≯	12.0 %
Alcohol soluble extractive	≮	22.0 %
Water soluble extractive	≮	27.0 %
Loss of drying	≮	10.0 % at 105° with 1.0 gm drug

Uses

It is important in Chinese medicine as it hasimmunomodulatory property. It shows a wide range of activities. It increases the natural resistance (non-specific resistance) and enhances the power to overcome the illness or exhaustion. It is used as aphrodisiac.

It has tonic, stimulant, diuretic and carminative properties. It is also used in the treatments of anemia, insomnia, gastritis, etc. It reduces blood sugar level and improves cellular uptake of glucose and hence used in diabetes. Ginseng is a good adaptogen as it helps the body to adapt stress and correct adrenal and thyroid dysfunctions.

Although, ginseng shows a low toxicity, long term use leads to poisoning, similar to that of corticosteroids.

Ginseng extracts are also used externally in cosmetics.

Allied species:

1) *Panax pseudoginseng* (himalayan ginseng) : The roots contain ginsenosides and chickusetsusaponins.

2) *Panax japonicum* var. major : contains chikusetsusaponins and glycans.

3) *Panax vietamensis* (vietnamese ginseng) : Roots contain a number of new ginsenosides.

DIOSCOREA

Synonyms

Yam, Rheumatism root

Biological Source

It consists of dried tubers of the plants, *Dioscorea deltoidea*, *D. composita*, and other species of *Dioscorea*, (Family : Dioscoreaceae).

Geographical Distribution

D. deltoidea is found growing in North Western Himalayas from Kashmir and Punjab to Nepal and China upto an altitude of 1000 to 3000 m. It is cultivated in Jammu and Kashmir and in parts of Himachal Pradesh. *D. deltoidea* is also found in U.S.A. and Mexico.

Table 4.1 : *Dioscorea species* and their sources

Species	Location
D. deltoidea	India
D. mexicana and D. eomposita	Mexico and Central America
D. flouribundo	Central America, India
D. tolcord	Japan
D. nipponica	China

Cultivation and Collection

In view of the pharmaceutical significance of the drug, it has been tried and successfully grown in various parts of India. Commercially, it is grown in Tamil Nadu, West Bengal, Maharashtra, Karnataka and Jammu and Kashmir. Both wild and cultivated plants are used.

The crop can be raised from seeds. Healthy tubers of about 70 - 80 g in weight, with crown are selected for cultivation. For checking the tuber-rot, they are treated with fungicide and sown in nursery beds. It takes about 30 to 40 days for. After 2 to 3 months of growth, tubers are transplanted in the field, which them to sprout has been treated with insecticides earlier. While planting, the tubers are placed at a distance of 30 × 60 cm. Since the tubers are very exhaustive, a high dose of farmyard manure to the extent of 5-10 tonnes per hectare is applied in the beginning. According to the species tubers reach maturity in 3 – 5 years and on an average yield 1 – 8% of total sapogenin. Organic fertilisers should be applied subsequently in equal doses at an interval of one month. Irrigation should be done after every 10 days.

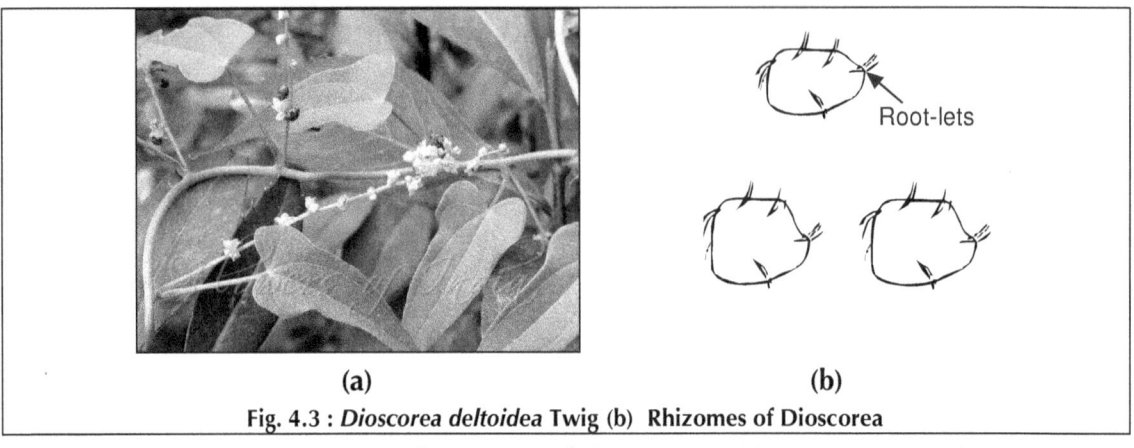

(a)   **(b)**

Fig. 4.3 : *Dioscorea deltoidea* Twig (b) Rhizomes of Dioscorea

No major pests are reported in case of Dioscorea. However preventive measures should be observed against white-grubs and mites. Harvesting is done by deep ploughing in the dormant season, as during this period the diosgenin content is found to be high as compared to other seasons. Tubers lose about 50 % of their weight after drying.

Organoleptic Characters

Colour : Slightly brown.

Odour : Odourless.

Taste : Bitter.

Size : Varies depending upon age of rhizomes, 3 to 4 cm.

Shape : Oval

Extra Features

It is a climber with alternative leaves. Tubers are soft, horizontally arranged and are borne very close to the soil. Drug is covered with scattered roots. They weigh about 50-200 g.

Microscopic Characters

Epidermis is normally absent in the transverse section of the drug. The cork consists of only a few layers, followed by thin walled cortical parenchymatous tissue. Stele forms the major part of the drug and consists of several close collateral fibro-vascular bundles. Endodermis and pericycle are indistinguishable.

Chemical Constituents

Dioscorea tubers contain 75 % of starch. They are non-edible, since they are very bitter in taste. The chief active constituent of dioscorea is diosgenin, a steroidal sapogenin (4 to 6 %). Tubers are also found to contain an enzyme sapogenase. Tubers are also rich in glycosides, and phenolic compounds. Diosgenin is the hydrolytic product of saponin-dioscin.

Diosgenin

Isolation

The tubers are dried, powdered and hydrolysis of dioscin is done by mineral acids. The liberated diosgenin is extracted with the help of non-polar solvents like benzene or solvent ether.

After isolation, diosgenin is degraded to 16-dehydropregnenelone acetate. This latter substance is used as precursor for synthesis of :

1. Corticosteroids like cortisone, hydrocortisone, prednisolone.

2. Pregnenes like progesterone, 17 - α - hydroxy progesterone.

3. Androstanes like testosterone, methyl testosterone, etc. and

4. 19 - NOR steroids like estrone, 17 - α - ethynyl estradiol and norethisterone acetate, mestranol.

The conversions are done with the help of microbial transformations.

Uses

Pharmaceutically, the tubers are used as rich source of diosgenin. Diosgenin being steroidal in structure is used as precursor for synthesis of several corticosteroids, sex-hormones and oral-contraceptives. Dioscorea is used in the treatment of rheumatic arthritis.

Allied Species

Dioscorea flouribunda is cultivated in Central America and India (Karnataka State). It contains 3 to 5 % of diosgenin. *D. villosa* Linne mainly from Virginia and Corolina in U.S.A. is also very rich in diosgenin content. *D. villosa* is a twining perennial with beautiful yellow flowers and triangular capsules *D. sikkimensis* Prain and Burkill (syn. *D. deltoidea* wall var. *sikkimensis* Prain) occurs in Eastern Himalayas, Nepal, Sikkim, Bhutan, Assam, Bihar and Bengal upto an altitude of 1600 - 2000 m. It contains 2 to 2.8 per cent of diosgenin.

Costus speciosus is an alternative potential source for diosgenin (1.5 %) and can be used as a substitute for the genuine drug.

B. STEROIDAL GLYCOSIDES OR CARDIAC GLYCOSIDES

The occurrence, chemistry and pharmacology of natural compounds with cardiac actions have been widely studied. Though, few plants are used in therapeutics their presence in varied concentrations has been reported in number of plants.

Cardenolide   **Bufadienolide**

Chemically, the aglycone part of cardiac glycosides is a steroidal moiety. They are either C_{23} or C_{24} steroids, because of either five members or six members lactone ring respectively.

Those with five membered lactone ring are called as cardenolides, while with six members lactone ring are termed as bufadienolides. The lactone of cardenolide contains only one double bond and is attached to steroidal nucleus through C - 17 position. In bufadienolide, the lactone ring contains 2 double bonds and is attached to steroidal nucleus through 17 β position. The presence and attachment through a specific position to steroidal nucleus of the lactone is essential for proper cardiac activity. The term bufadienolide has been derived from bufalin, obtained from skin of toads.

The sugar part is attached through C - 3, β - linkage. Various types of sugars have been reported to be present in cardiac glycosides, such as glucose, fucose, rhamnose, digitoxose, digitalose, cymarose, sarmentose, thevatose, etc. Though, the sugars do not potentiate the medicinal activity of aglycone part, they are useful in solubilisation of aglycone thereby, beneficial in absorption and distribution in the body. At a time upto three sugar molecules are attached to aglycone. It has been also shown that increase in number of OH groups on aglycone leads to quicker onset of action and enhanced metabolism.

The occurrence of cardenolides from nature is quite high as compared to those of bufadienolides.

Though, a number of plants contain cardiac glycosides, they are broadly restricted to angiosperms. Leguminosae, Sterculiaceae, Cruciferae, Scrophulariaceae, Euphorbiaceae etc. show the presence of cardenolides. Very few families like Liliaceae and Ranunculaceae contain bufadienolides. The toad poison present on its dorsal part is a bufadienolide.

Congestive Cardiac Failure (CCF), which is a consequence of different diseases, is treated by cardiac glycosides. They act as cardiotonic by increasing the force of systolic contractions. The cardiac glycosides have a significant position in modern therapeutics, because of their utility and also because they have not yet been synthesized satisfactorily.

DIGITALIS

Synonyms

Digitalis leaves, Foxglove leaves.

Biological Source

Digitalis consists of dried leaves of *Digitalis purpurea*. (Scrophulariaceae), dried at a temperature below 60°C, immediately after collecting the leaves. It should contain not less than 0.3% of total cardenolides calculated as digitoxin.

Geographical Distribution

It is cultivated and collected in England, other parts of Europe, United States and India. In India, it is cultivated to a limited extent in Kashmir .

Cultivation and Collection

It is biennial or perennial herb of about 1 to 2 metres in height. It is propagated by seeds of selected strain, containing high glycosidal content. It needs calcarious, sandy, light soil with traces of manganese. Therefore this element is always found in the ash. The soil is sterilised by steam before sowing. It grows suitably in sandy situation, luxuriantly at an altitude of 1600 to 3000 m. The seeds of digitalis are very small in size, i.e. 100 seeds weigh 40 to 70 mg. They are mixed with fine sand and sown in the nursery beds in March/April. The young seedlings are transplanted in September and November. The crop is manured properly and kept free of weeds. The plantation is done twice a year. In the first year, the plant bears rosette leaves and in the second year sessile leaves. The plant bears purple colour flowers in the month of April and is followed by fruiting.

The leaves are picked in the afternoon during August and September in the first and the second year, when 2/3 rd of the flowers are fully developed. The basal leaves and the leaves at top are collected at the end. The discoloured leaves are rejected. While collecting the leaves, dry weather is specifically selected. After collection, the leaves should be immediately dried at a temperature of about 60°C. It curtails the exposure of fresh leaves to atmospheric conditions. The dried leaves (containing not more than 6 % of moisture) are packed into air-tight containers, containing suitable dehydrating agents.

The activity of the leaves is due to glycosides. The presence of moisture and the enzymes (i.e. digipurpuridase and oxidase) cause hydrolysis of glycosides of leaves. If the leaves are dried above 60°, it they lose their potency due to chemical degradation.

Organoleptic Characters

Colour : Dark greyish-green

Odour : No marked odour

Taste : Bitter

Size : 10 to 40 cm long and 4 to 20 cm wide

Shape : Ovate-lanceolate to broadly ovate; with irregularly crenate or serrate or occasionally dentate margin.

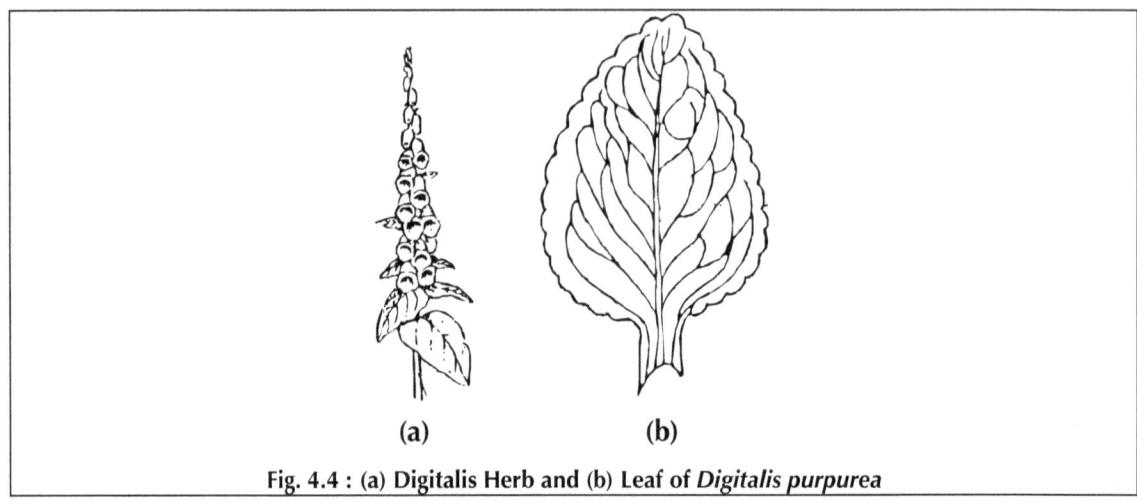

Fig. 4.4 : (a) Digitalis Herb and (b) Leaf of *Digitalis purpurea*

Extra Features

The leaves are slightly pubescent on both the surfaces with pinnate venation and prominent veinlets on the lower surface. Generally, the leaves are broken and crumbled.

Microscopic Characters

A transverse section shows bifecial structure and a midrib convex on the lower surface. Digitalis is a dorsiventral leaf. It has anomocytic stomata on both surfaces and water pores at the apex of most of the marginal teeth. The trichomes are uniseriate multicellular (3 to 5 cells) and bluntly pointed. There are glandular trichomes with unicellular stalk and unicellular or bicellular head. The glandular trichomes are generally located over the veins. Collapsed cells covering trichomes are one of the important characteristics of digitalis. Digitalis is free of calcium oxalate and sclerenchyma. Starch grains are present in the endodermis. There is collenchyma at 3 different places i.e. at the upper epidermis, lower epidermis, and pericyclic part, which is also characteristic of digitalis. The cuticle of the hairs and epidermal cells may be stained red with a solution of sudan red.

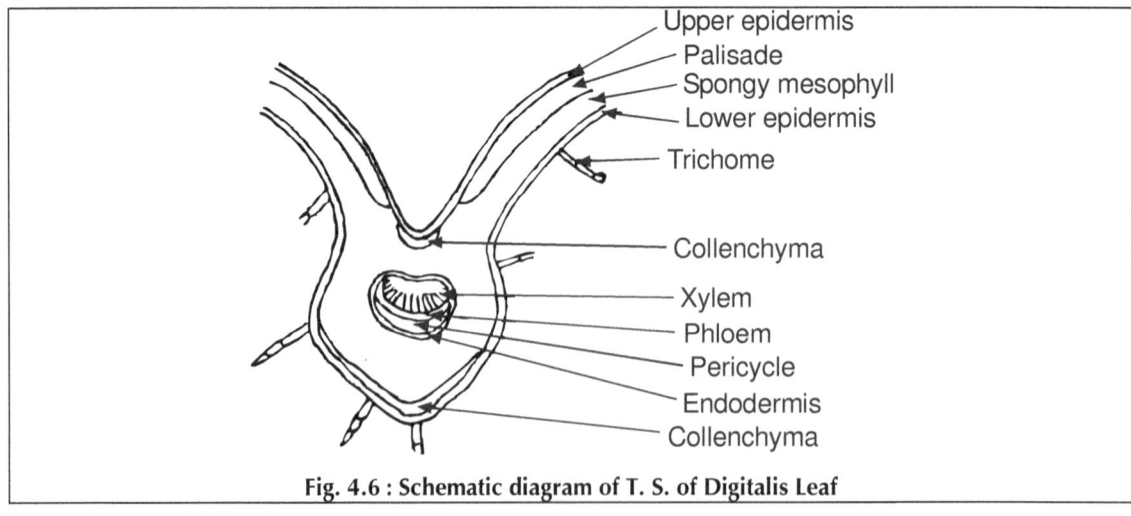

Fig. 4.6 : Schematic diagram of T. S. of Digitalis Leaf

Chemical Constituents

Important contributions to studies pertaining to chemical composition of the drug were made by Nativelle (1868), Killiani (1891) and Stoll (1938).

Digitalis contains 0.2 to 0.45 % mixture of cardiac glycosides (cardenolides), purpurea glycosides A and B. which are primary glycosides. All posses at C-3 of genin a linear chain of a 3 digitoxose sugar moieties terminated by glucose. In addition, digitalis also contains several other glycosides such as odoroside H, glucogitaloxin, gitaloxin, verodoxin, and glucoverodoxin. The products of hydrolysis of purpurea glycoside A and purpurea glycoside B. the chief active constituents of the drug, are as under.

Purpurea glycoside A	Purpurea glycoside B
↓ enzymatic hydrolysis	↓ enzymatic hydrolysis
digitoxin + glucose	gitoxin + glucose
↓ hydrolysis	↓ hydrolysis
digitoxigenin + digitoxose	gitoxigenin + digitoxose

Fig. 4.7: Schematic presentation of hydrolysis of purpura glycosides

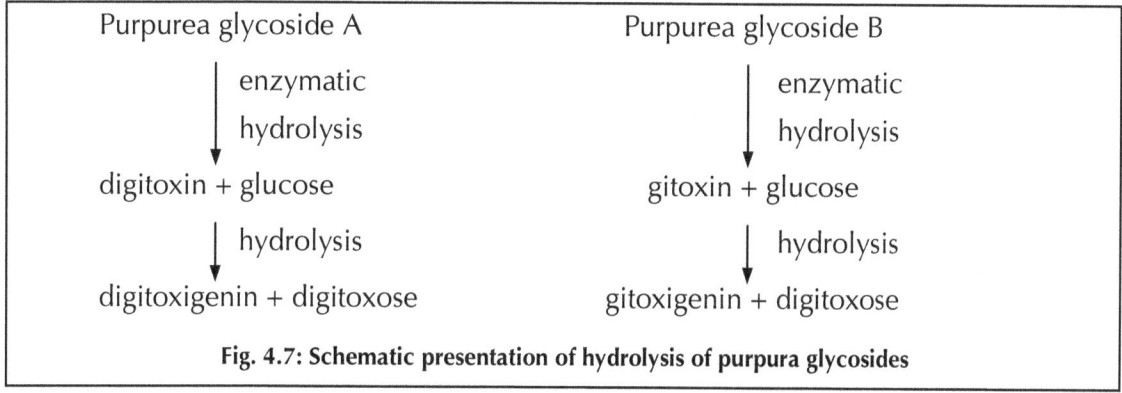

Structures of a few Cardenolide aglycones from Digitalis

Additionally, it contains 2 saponin glycosides, viz. digitonin and gitonin. The total number of glycosides reported in drug is about 30. Purpurea glycoside A is the major component (about 50% of total glycoside mixture). Apart from glycosides, leaves also contain hydrolytic enzymes. The leaves also contain anthraquinone derivatives and flavonoids.

Digitalis and its official preparations like prepared digitalis, digitalis tablets, digitalis tincture etc. are assayed biologically. Several animals like guinea-pigs, frogs, cats, pigeons etc., are used for standardisation. One unit activity of drug is equal to 76 mg of the digitalis or one mg is equivalent to 0.00310 units in pigeon. Since exact chemical nature of the glycoside is known, the glycosides content can also be estimated chemically.

Chemical Test

Keller-Killiani test for digitoxose : The test consists of boiling about one gram finely powdered digitalis with 10 ml of 70 % alcohol for 3 minutes. The extract is filtered. To the filtrate is added, 5 ml of water and 0.5 ml of strong solution of lead acetate, filtered and filtrate is treated with equal volume of chloroform and evaporated to yield the extract. The extract is dissolved in glacial acetic acid and after cooling, 2 drops of ferric chloride solution are added to it. These contents are transferred to a test tube containing 2 ml of concentrated sulphuric acid. A reddish-brown layer acquiring bluish-green colour after standing is observed due to presence of digitoxose.

Uses

Digitalis increases excitability of cardiac muscles and produces more powerful contractions. It is effective in congestive cardiac failure to increase cardiac output and to relieve venous congestion. Hence, it is described as a cardiac tonic. The improvement of circulation through kidney results in diuresis and loss of oedema. The major disadvantage of digitalis is that it has cumulative effect and therefore, in prolonged treatment one has to watch the patient carefully.

Prepared Digitalis

Powdered digitalis leaves are adjusted to standard strength in prepared digitalis. It is an official preparation alongwith digitalis tablets, digitalis tincture and digitoxin injection.

Storage

Digitalis should be stored in a well-closed, well-filled container in cool place away from light. While storing care must be taken to ensure that, leaves do not contain more than 5 % of moisture, because it causes destruction of the glycosides and ultimately loss of cardiac activity on storage. Therefore, digitalis powder is stored in containers, with dehydrating agents like calcium chloride or silica gel to absorb excess of water present in the drug or atmosphere.

Substitutes and Adulterants

Digitalis leaves are adulterated with the following -

1. The leaves of *Verbascum thapsus* (Scrophulariaceae) are mixed with genuine drug and can be distinguished microscopically by the presence of large woolly branched candelabra trichomes.

2. The primrose leaves : The leaves of *Primula vulgaris* (Primulaceae) are added to digitalis. They can be detected microscopically by presence of uniseriate covering trichomes, which are 8 to 9 celled long. The lateral veins of the leaves of primrose are straight.

3. Comfrey leaves : These are the leaves of *Symphyfum officinale* (Boraginaceae) and can be detected by the presence of multicellular trichomes forming hook at the top.

Allied Drugs -

1. *Digitalis lanata* **:** The leaves are also known as Grecian or Woolly foxglove leaves. These are the dried leaves of *Digitalis lanata* Ehrhart (Scrophulariaceae) found in England, Holland and U.S.A. The leaves are oblong, lanceolate, sessile with entire margin and about 21×6 cm in dimensions. The half basal part of these leaves is covered with cilia and hence are known as woolly leaves. The potency of these leaves is four times the potency of *Digitalis purpurea*. Chemically, leaves contain digitoxin, gitoxin, digoxin, lanatosides A, B and C. By loss of a glucose and acetyl group, lanatoside A, B and C yield digitoxin, gitoxin and digoxin respectively. The leaves are commercially used for preparation of digoxin and lanatoside.

2. *Digitalis lutea* **or Straw foxglove :** These are the dried leaves of *Digitalis lutea* (Scrophulariaceae) grown in U.S.A. and Europe. Leaves are sessile, oblanceolate with serrate or dentate margin. The size of the leaves is 28×6 cm, but most of the leaves reach only 50 % of their size. The drug is as potent as *Digitalis purpurea*. It is used for the same purpose, but, is supposed to have less irritation. The chemical constituents of drug are not thoroughly known, but it is free of calcium oxalate. It is used as a common substitute for official drug.

3. *Digitalis thapsi* **or Spanish foxglove :** It is found in Spain and Italy. The leaves of the drug are small (i.e. 5 to 10×1.5 to 5 cm) in size. The leaves are yellowish-green in colour and lanceolate with crenate margin and decurrent lamina. Histologically, leaves can be identified by absence of non-glandular trichomes and also due to presence of very strongly striated cuticle. The leaves show two types of glandular hairs, some consisting of bicellular head and unicellular stalk and other type is unicellular head with 3-4 celled stalk. It contains calcium oxalate crystals. The drug is 2 to 3 times more potent than *Digitalis purpurea*.

4. *Digitalis ferruginia* **:** It is one of the most widespread spices of digitalis, grown in Turkey.

DIGITALIS LANATA

Synonyms

Woolly fox glove leaf, Austrial Digitalis.

Biological Source

These are the dried leaves of *Digitalis lanata* Ehrhart, belonging to family Scrophulariaceae, and contain 1 to 1.4 per cent of a mixture of cardiac glycosides.

This drug is indigenous to Southern and Central Europe and currently it is cultivated in U.S.A., Holland and Equiddor.

Macroscopic Characters

The leaves are oblong, lanceolate and sessile with entire margin. It is about 21 cm in length and 6 cm in width. The plant is a biennial herb about one metre in height.

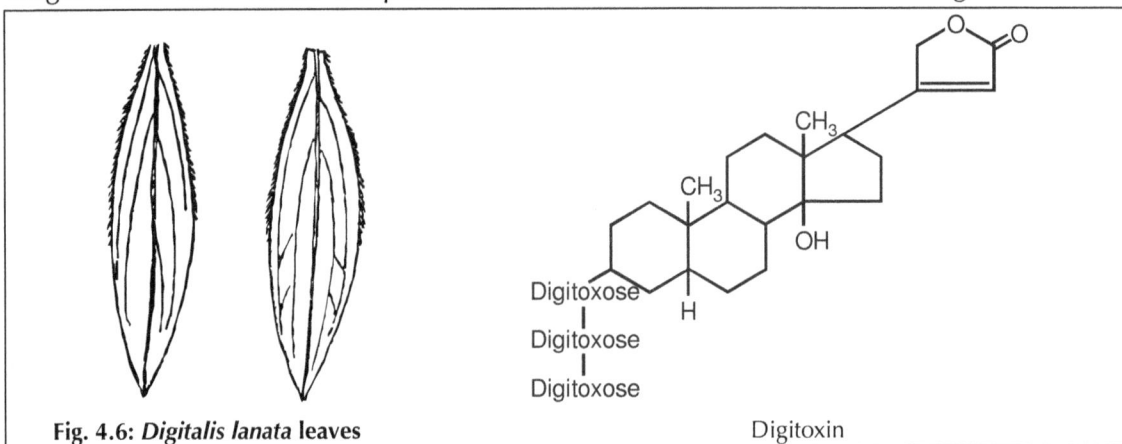

Fig. 4.6: *Digitalis lanata* leaves   Digitoxin

Digitoxose
|
Digitoxose
|
Digitoxose

Gitoxigenin R = H
Gitaloxigenin R = CHO

Digoxin

(Digitoxose)$_3$

Chemical Constituents

It contains five primary glycosides and in all about 70 cardiac glycosides. The primary glycosides are identified as lanatosides A, B, C, D and E. It should be noted that glycone digitoxose and not aglycone, is acetylated. It is more potent than *Digitalis purpurea* and is used as a source for the manufacture of digoxin, lanatosides C and other cardiac glycosides.

The aglycones viz. digoxigenin and diginatigenin are specific to *Digitalis lanata*, while others are present in *Digitalis purpurea* also.

The inter-relationship of cardiac glycosides and their aglycones of *D. purpurea* and *D. lanata* are given in Table 4.2.

Table 4.2: Inter relationship of glycosides of *D. purpurea* and *D. lanata*

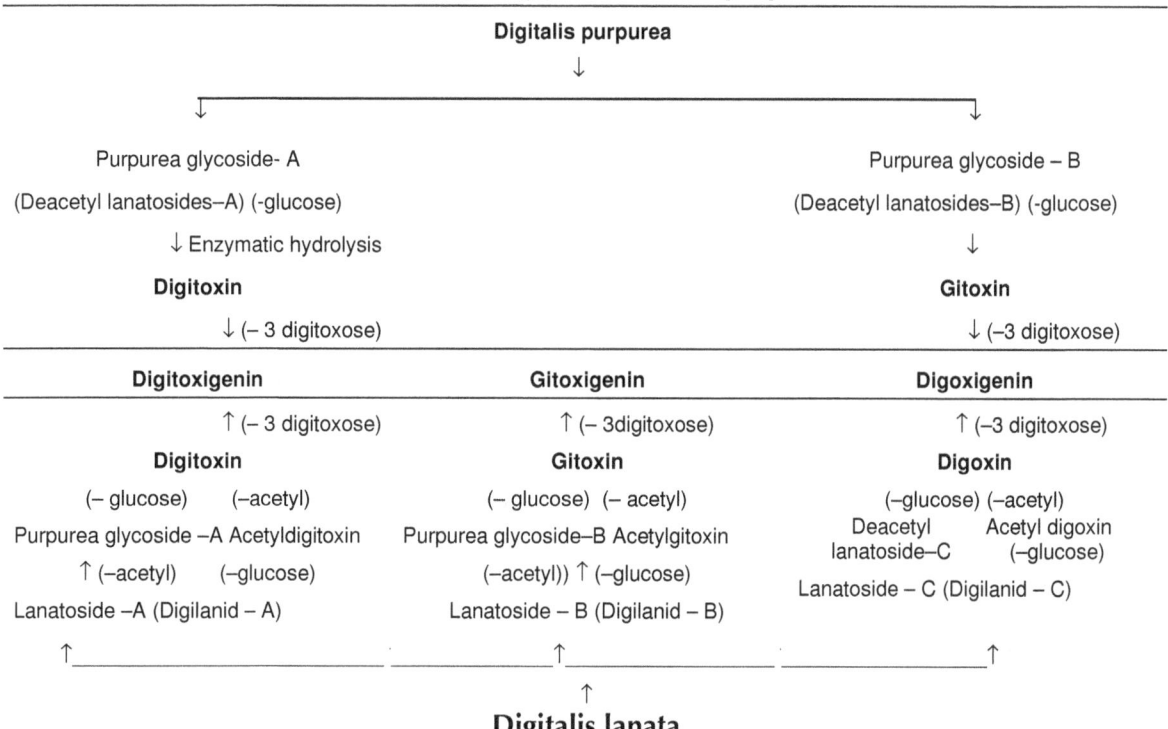

Uses

(1) *Digitalis lanata* is used as a commercial source for digoxin, lanatosides C, lanatosides A and a mixture of lanatosides. Lanatosides C and digoxin have the same actions as that of digitalis. Lanatoside C is poorly absorbed from gastrointestinal tract and it is less cumulative. Digoxin, by oral route, shows effect in about 1 hour and maximum effect is reached within 6 hours. Digoxin is used for rapid digitalisation in the treatment of auricular fibrillation and congestive cardiac failure. It is preferred because of less cumulative effects.

(2) *Digitalis lutea* (Straw Foxglove): These are the dried leaves of *Digitalis lutea* (Scrophulariaceae) grown in U.S.A. and Europe. Leaves are sessile, oblanceolate with serrate or dentate margin. The size of the leaves is 28 × 6 cm, but most of the leaves reach only 50 per cent of their size. The drug is as potent as *Digitalis purpurea*. It is used for the same purpose but, is supposed to have less irritation. The chemical constituents of the drug are not thoroughly known, but it is free of calcium oxalate. It is used as a common substitute for the official drug.

(3) *Digitalis thapsi* (Spanish Foxglove): It is found in Spain and Italy. The leaves are small (5 to 10 × 1.5 to 5 cm) in size. The leaves are yellowish-green in colour and lanceolate with crenate margin and decurrent lamina. Histologically, leaves can be identified by the absence of non-glandular trichomes and also due to the presence of very strongly striated cuticle. It contains calcium oxalate crystals. The drug is 1.25 to 3 times more potent than *Digitalis purpurea*.

The other species of Digitalis containing cardiac glycosides are *D. subalpina, D. dubia, D. grandiflora, D. ferruginea,* and *D. mertonensis.*

EUROPEAN SQUILL

Synonyms

Scilla, Squill bulb, White squill.

Biological Source

Squill consists of the sliced and dried scaly leaves from the bulbs of *Urginea maritima* (Linn.) Baker, belonging to family Liliaceae.

Geographical Source

It is indigenous to the countries near the Mediterranean region like France, Italy, Malta, Spain, Greece, Algeria, and Morocco.

Collection and Preparation

White squill gives the bulbs which are about 12 - 15 cm in diameter and 18 - 20 cm in height. They grow in half submerged condition in sandy soil in the coastal region. They are collected in spring or in August when the plant sheds all aerial leaves and flowering stage is completed. After collection, the external thin scaly leaves and central portion are removed and the remaining fleshy bulb is cut into transverse slices and then dried by sun rays or artificially.

Macroscopic Characters

It contains concavo–convex slices which are thick middle in the 3 - 6 cm in length and 4 - 8 mm in width. It has a slight odour. The drug appears as brittle, translucent and yellowish-white scales. It is hygroscopic in nature and becomes tough and flexible.

Microscopic Characters

The transverse section shows epidermis, mesophyll and vascular bundles. Epidermis consists of polygonal, axially elongated rectangular cells and the occurrence of stomata is almost rare. Mesophyll is characterised by mucilage present in large polygonal parenchymatous cells. The mesophyll also shows raphides of calcium oxalate. Mesophyll is interrupted by small vascular bundles.

Chemical Constituents

Squill contains the cardiac glycosides of bufadienolide type. It contains a number of glycosides, but most important is scillaren A, about two third of total glycosides in quantity. It also contains scillaren B.

The hydrolysis of scillaren A shows that it is a biglycoside (containing 2 sugars viz. glucose and rhamnose). The aglycone is called as scillaridin A (scillarenin A).

The drug also contains other cardiac glycosides in small amounts like glucoscillaren A, which is a triglycoside and Proscillaridin A.

Glucoscillaren A : Scillarenin A + rhamnose

+

glucose and

Proscillaridin A: Scillarenin A + rhamnose

+ glucose

Along with cardiac glycosides, the drug also contains xanthoscillide, flavonoids, mucilage, calcium oxalate, sinistrin (a carbohydrate similar to inulin), and a volatile substance which causes irritation.

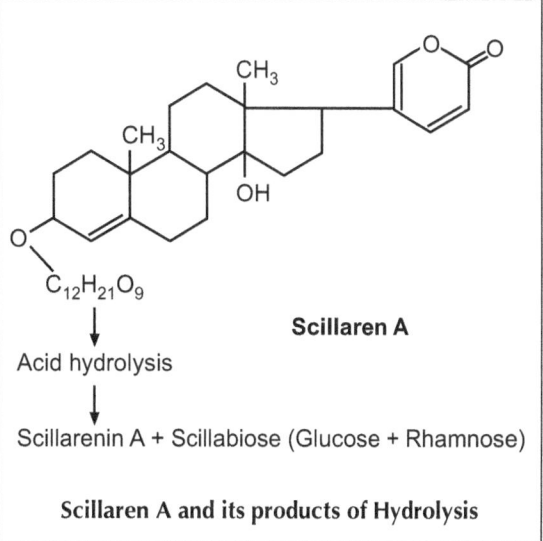

Scillaren A

Acid hydrolysis

Scillarenin A + Scillabiose (Glucose + Rhamnose)

Scillaren A and its products of Hydrolysis

Uses

It is a cardiotonic without cumulative effect. It is also used in chronic bronchitis as an expectorant in small doses, while in higher doses causes vomiting.

6 INDIAN SQUILL

Synonyms

Jangli pyaz, Sea onion, Scilla, Urginea.

Biological Source

Urginea consists of dried slices of the bulbs of *Urginea indica Kunth*, family *Liliaceae*.

Geographical Source

As the name indicates, it is found in India. It is grown along sea coasts including Konkan and Saurashtra and also in the dry hills of the lower Himalayas at an altitude of 1500 m.

Cultivation and Collection

It is not cultivated, scientifically. However, it is observed that the herb needs sandy soil and mean annual temperature of 15°C. Bulbs can be raised from seeds and the plant acquires full size within 5 years. Generally, the distance between two rows of plants is about 75 cm. Other agricultural practices followed are similar to that of the common bulbs like garlic and onion. The bulbs are collected after flowering in autumn. They are cleaned and cut into quarters which are further sliced. It looses about 80 per cent of its weight when the sun-dried. The bulbs are finally packed in bags or barrels.

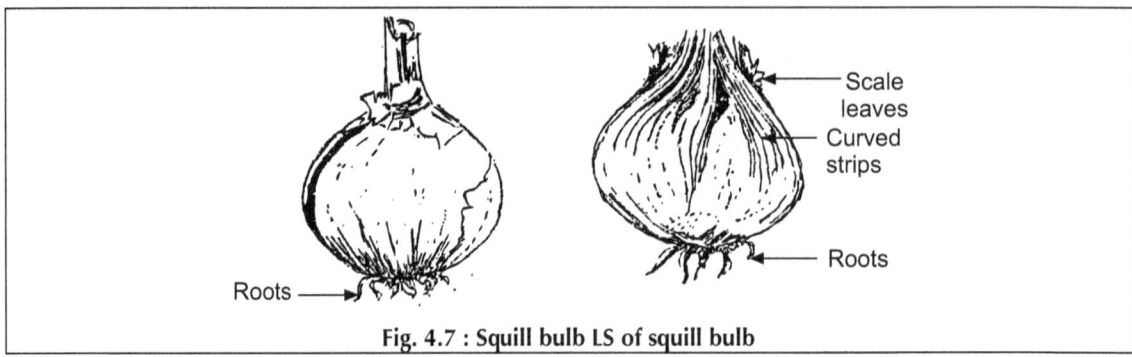

Fig. 4.7 : Squill bulb LS of squill bulb

Macroscopic Characters

Colour - The slices of squill bulbs are slightly yellowish to white.

Odour - Slight and characteristic.

Taste - Bitter, mucilaginous and acrid.

Size - 30 to 60 mm in length and 3 to 8 mm broad.

Shape - The slices of the Indian squill are united in groups of 4 to 8, which are curved.

Extra Features

The entire bulb of the Indian squill is about 15 cm in diameter. The slices of the squill are translucent and become tough and flexible after absorbing the moisture.

Microscopic Characters

The transverse section shows presence of polygonal axially elongated epidermis, parenchymatous mucilaginous mesophyll with raphides of calcium oxalate crystals and is interrupted by small vascular bundles.

Chemical Constituents

Indian squill contains about 0.3 per cent of cardiac glycosides. It yields to alcohol about 20 to 40 per cent of extractive. The other contents of the drug are mucilage (about 40 per cent) and calcium oxalate.

Scillaren A and scillaren B are the major cardiac glycosides of the drug. Scillaren A on hydrolysis (by an enzyme) scillarenase yields proscillaridin A and on acid hydrolysis scillaridin A, whereas scillaren B yields proscillaridin B and scillaridin B respectively. The drug also contains glucoscillaren A and an enzyme scillarenase.

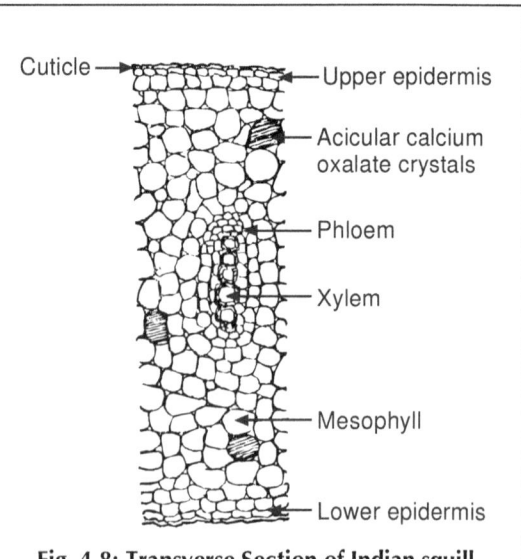

Fig. 4.8: Transverse Section of Indian squill

Chemical Test

Mesophyll stains red with alkaline colarin solution and reddish purple with 0.1 M Iodine solution.

Uses

It is a cardiotonic, stimulant and also an expectorant. It is diuretic in small doses. In large doses, it is emetic and cathartic. It resembles digitalis in its cardiotonic activities, but is less cumulative and acts rapidly. It is not a perfect substitute for digitalis, as it is associated with irritant effect and is poorly absorbed. It is used as a powerful expectorant in chronic bronchitis and asthma. It is also found to possess anti-cancer activity against human epidermoid carcinoma of the nasopharynx in tissue culture.

Adulterants

Commercial samples of Indian squill in the market, many a time, contain *Scilla hyacintoiana*.

7 STROPHANTHUS

Synonyms

Semino Strophanthi, Arrow poison.

Biological Source

These are the dried ripe seeds of *Strophanthus kombe* Oliver or of *S. hispidus* De Candolle, belonging to family Apocynaceae.

Geographical Source

Strophanthus is a climber indigenous to regions near the Shire river, Nyanza and Tanganyika lakes of Eastern tropical Africa. The tribals were using the extract of seeds as arrow poison.

Macroscopic Characters

The seeds are obtained from fruits with 2 follicles. The awns of the seeds are separated. The seeds are 10 - 20 mm in length, 3 - 5 mm in width and 2 mm in thickness. The seeds have bitter taste and unpleasant odour. The shape is lanceolate and awn is thread like extension of testa. The silky touch of the seeds is due to trichomes. The endosperm and embryo are quite oily in nature unpleasant odour.

**Fig. 4.9 :
Strophanthus Seed**

Chemical Constituents

The drug contains a mixture of glycosides called K-strophanthin. It contains K-strophanthoside (strophoside), β cymarin and cymarol. Except cymarol, all the 3 glycosides yield strophanthidin on hydrolysis. K-strophanthoside is considered as main primary glycoside which on hydrolysis gives aglycone K-strophanthidin along with 3 sugars cymarose, α and β glucose.

The drug also contains mucilage, resin, trigonelline, choline, and upto 30 per cent of fixed oil.

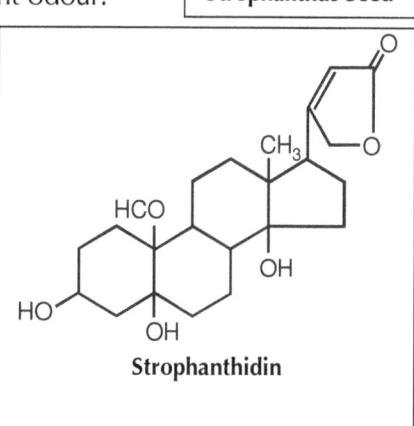

Strophanthidin

Chemical Test

The glycosides show emerald green colour on addition of 80 per cent sulphuric acid.

Uses

It is a cardiotonic. The drug is mainly considered as a source of K-strophanthin. These glycosides have less cumulative effect otherwise similar in actions as that of digitalis. It is given parenterally, because of poor absorption by oral route.

Allied drugs -

1. *S. gratus* – seeds contains 4 – 8 % G-strophanthin (ouabain) it is a rhamnose glycoside.

2. *S. sarnebtisys* – The seeds contain sarmentogenin as aglycone.

C. ANTHRACENE GLYCOSIDES

These constitute a major class of glycosides. They are mainly found in the dicot plant and families like Euphorbiaceae, Ericaceae, Lythraceae, Polygonaceae, Rhamnaceae, Rubiaceae, Leguminosae, Verbenaceae, etc. The family Liliaceae from monocots also shows the presence of C-glycosides. Some of the fungi and lichens also contain anthraquinone glycosides. But, it is observed that lower plants like Bryophytes, Pteridophytes and Gymnosperms are devoid of such glycosides. It is postulated that the aglycone part of these glycosides is formed by head-to-tail condensation of acetate units. This group of glycosides comprises of different aglycone moieties like anthraquinone, anthrone, anthranol, dianthranol, oxanthrone and dianthrone.

In different drugs like aloe, senna, rhubarb, cascara, aglycones are present in their derivate forms. The parent molecule for all these aglycones i.e. anthraquinone is present in different forms along with methyl, hydroxymethyl, carboxyl, dihydroxy phenol, trihydroxy phenol or free carboxylic acid groups. In a reduced form, anthraquinone is present as anthranol or anthrone which are isomeric with each other. Anthrone is a pale yellow substance insoluble in alkali while anthranol is brownish-yellow and soluble in alkali. Anthranol shows strong fluorescence in alkali, but anthrone is non-fluorescent by nature.

Some plants contain oxanthrone which is the intermediate substance from anthraquinone to anthranol. In some plants, the anthrone molecule orients in bimeric form called dianthrone which is therapeutically more important.

Anthraquinone   Anthrone   Oxanthrone

Dianthranol   Chrysophanic acid

The reduced anthraquinone are biologically more active. In a fresh drug, these aglycones are present in reduced form, but are hydrolysed and oxidized during their storage. They are present along with different sugars like glucose, rhamnose, arabinose and primeverose.

Borntrager's Test

Anthraquinone derivatives are generally detected by Borntrager's test. In this test, the drug is powdered and further extracted with ether or any water immiscible organic solvent. The filtered ethereal extract is made alkaline either with caustic soda or ammonia, by which the aqueous layer shows, after shaking, pink, red or violet colour. Borntrager's test is negative in case of anthranol (reduced forms). Anthrones are detected with their fluorescence tests.

ALOE

Synonym

Aloe, Kumari

Biological Source

Aloe is the dried juice of the leaves of *Aloe barbadensis* Miller (Curacao aloes), *Aloe perryi* Baker (Socotrine aloes), hybrids of *Aloe ferox* Miller and *Aloe africana* Miller or *Aloe spicata* Baker (Cape aloes), belonging to family Liliaceae. Indian aloe is obtained from wild growing plants of Aloe vera.

The official (IP, BP, EP, USP) varieties of aloes are Cape aloe and Curacao aloe.

Geographical Distribution

Most of the species of aloe are indigenous to Africa, but now introduced into West Indies and Europe. In Africa, it grows in Cape colony (South Africa) and on the islands of Socotra and Zanzibar. It is cultivated throughout India, but especially in North West Himalayas.

Preparation

Various methods are used to prepare aloes commercially in Africa, as well as, in West Indies. Following is the general method of preparation.

The fleshy and sessile leaves of aloe are cut near the bases and are arranged round in wooden trough or kerosene tin or vessels of goat skin as to form the V shaped cavity by placing the cut-end downwards. The leaves are allowed to drain fully. After 6 hrs all collected juice is transferred to a drum in which it is boiled and concentrated. Method of its concentration and cooling results in physical variations in aloes.

Organoleptic Characters

Colour : Depends upon the variety from which it is obtained. It is dark brown, brownish black or black in colour.

Odour : Characteristic.

Taste : Intensely bitter and nauseating.

Size : It is found in the form of masses of various sizes.

Microscopy

Transverse section of an aloe leaf shows following zones.

(1) Cuticularised epidermis with numerous stomata on both surfaces.

(2) Parenchyma containing chlorophyll, starch and raphides of calcium oxalate.

(3) Mucilage containing parenchyma cells.

(4) Vascular bundle will well marked pericyclic fibers and endodermis which i.e. at junction of two previous zones.

Extra Features

Three varieties of aloes can be distinguished from each other by their morphological characters.

Table 4.3 : Morphological Characters of Aloe Varieties

Cape aloes	Curacao aloes	Socotrine aloes
Dark brown or greenish brown or glossy mass; masses are transparent, when mounted in glycerin, the crystal particles are observed. Fracture is glossy.	Dark chocolate-brown, usually opaque fracture is waxy.	Reddish-black to brownish black; opaque smooth and conchoidal.

Solubility

It is entirely soluble in 60 % alcohol, and is partly soluble in water.

Standards

1. Water soluble substances   :   Not less than 25 %.

2. Alcohol insoluble substances   :   Not more than 10 %.

3. Loss on drying   : Not more than 10 %.

4. Ash   : Not more than 5 %.

Fig. 4.10 : Aloe Plantation

Chemical Constituents

All varieties of aloes contain a yellow coloured crystalline substance known as barbaloin (C-glycoside), resin and aloe-emodin. Aloin contains not less than 70% anhydrous barbaloin. Isobarbalion is present in Curacao and Cape aloes. Cape aloes are characterised by the presence of an amorphous compound, β-barbalion (80%), aloinosides A and B and capaloresinotannol with p-coumaric acid. β-barbaloin is absent in Barbados variety. Barbaloin is a C-glycoside which is not hydrolysed by heating with dilute acids or alkalis. It can be hydrolysed by oxidative hydrolysis with ferric chloride. This yields glucose, aloe-emodin anthrone and little aloe-emodin. (Modified Bornthrager's test).

In *Aloe* species, the content of anthra quinone is subject to seasonal variation.

The resin of aloe principally contain aloesin it is a c-glycosyl chromone. Aloesin is also responsible for purgative action of aloes.

Glucose

Aloesin (Aloe resin B)

Aloe-emodin   **Barbaloin**

Chemical constituents of Aloe

Identification

Prepare 1 % solution of aloes by boiling with water, add 0.5 % of kieselguhr to it and filter. With the filtrate, perform the following tests.

1. Heat 5 ml of the above test solution with 0.2 g of borax; add this solution to the test-tube containing water. A green fluorescence is produced (due to anthranols which are formed from anthrones i.e. aloe-emodin by isomeric change) **(Schoenteten's reaction)**.

2. To 2 ml of test solution, add equal quantity of freshly prepared bromine water. A pale yellow precipitate of tetrabromalion is observed.

Special Tests -

1. **Nitric acid test:** To 5 ml of test solution, add 2 ml of nitric acid. Different varieties of aloes produce different colours mentioned as under -

   (a) Cape aloes　　　　　　　：　Yellowish-brown to green.

   (b) Curacao aloes　　　　　　：　Reddish-orange.

   (c) Socotrine aloes　　　　　：　Pale brownish-yellow.

   (d) Zanzibar aloes　　　　　：　Yellowish-brown.

2. **Klunge's isobarbaloin test :** To aqueous solution (2 ml), add a drop of saturated copper sulphate solution, followed by sodium chloride (0.5 g) and alcohol 90 % (2 ml). (Cupraloin test)

   (i)　Curacao aloes　　　　　　：　Wine red colour.

   (ii)　Cape aloes　　　　　　　：　A faint colouration is developed.

   (iii) Zanzibar and socotrine aloes　：　Do not respond to the test.

3. **Nitrous acid test:** Crystals of sodium nitrite along with small quantity of acetic acid are added to aq. solution of aloes. The observations are as follows -

   (i)　Curcao aloe　　　　　　　：　Sharp pink colour

   (ii)　Cape aloe　　　　　　　　：　Faint pink colour

   (iii) Socotrine and zangibar aloe　：　No colour change.

   This test is for isobarboloin.

4. **Modified Borntrager's test :** To 0.1 g of the drug, and 5% solution of ferric chloride (2ml), and dilute hydrochloric acid (2 ml), heat on boiling waterbath for 5 minutes, cool and shake gently with benzene. Separate benzene layer and add equal volume of dilute ammonia. A pinkish-red colour is produced with all varieties of aloes.

Uses

Due to aloin (anthraquinone-derivative), it is used as irritant purgative. It is slow and uncertain in action. Now-a-days, aloin is preferred instead of crude drug. It acts on colon;

to counter effect the gripping action of aloe it is given with carminatives. It is an ingredient of compound Benzoin tincture.

Aloe-gel, a mucilaginous colourless, viscous juice of aloe, now-a-days, is used in cosmetics as a protective i.e. it prevents wrinkles (due to aging) on face and also in the treatment of radiation burns. It clears skin blemishes and grows new and healthy tissues. It stimulates the growth of hair. Externally, it is applied for painful inflammations.

Table 4.4 : Differentiation between Aloe gel and Aloes

	Aloe gel	Aloes
Part used	Mucilaginous tissue located in leaf-parenchyma of *Aloe* species. Family Liliaceae.	Dried leaf juice of *Aloe barbadensis, A. ferox* and hybrids, *A. africana, A. spicata,* Family Liliaceae.
Consti tuents	Mono and polysaccharides, tannins, sterols, cycloxygenase, saponins, vitamins and minerals. Polysaccharides contain xylose, arabinose and galactose. Lipids contain cholesterol, gamolenic acid and arachidonic acid.	Anthraquinones: 30 per cent mainly C glucosides known as aloin. Mixture contains barbaloin, isobarbaloin, emodin and aloe-emodin. Resins: Aloesin, aloesone.
Use	Used externally in the form of ointments, creams to assist healing of wounds, burns, eczema, and also in psoriasis.	In the treatment of constipation.

SENNA LEAVES

Synonyms

Tinnevelly Senna, Indian Senna

Biological Source

It consists of dried leaflets of *Cassia angustifolia*. Vahl belonging to family Leguminosae. It contains not less than 2.0 % of hydroxyanthracene derivatives calculated as sennoside B.

Geographical Distribution

Indian Senna is cultivated and collected in India. Its cultivation is mainly done in Tinnevelly, Madurai and Ramnathpuram districts of Tamil Nadu. Cultivation is attempted in Cudappa district of Andhra Pradesh, and to some extent it is collected from Kutch in Gujarat State. It has been successfully tried in Maharashtra.

Cultivation and Collection

Tinnevelly senna is obtained from *cassia angustifolia* grown in Tinnevelly district of Tamil Nadu, Andhra Pradesh, Gujarat and Maharashtra. The cultivation is done by sowing the seeds. The cultivation is done twice in a year March/April and November/December. It may be grown either in dry or well irrigated soil. It is a legume plant that usually adds nitrogen to soil. The crop is allowed to grow for 3-5 months. It is harvested by cutting and then dried.

Alexandrian seena is collected mainly in September from both wild and cultivated plant. Collected leaves and pods are separated by sifting. Therefore leaves are graded accordingly into following grades -

1) Whole leaves

2) Whole leaves and half leaves mixed

3) Siftings.

Preparation for the Market

The harvested leaves are spread on the floor under the shed without overlapping. The leaves are shuffled to attain uniform drying. Leaves loose about 50 to 60 % of their weight on drying. The yellowish green leaves, thus produced, fetch high value in the market. Complete yellow-coloured leaves are supposed to be of poor quality. The leaves are tossed to separate fruits and branches from leaves. The fruits are also dried in a similar way. The leaves are packed in the bales prepared by using hydraulic press and sent to the market or exported.

Organoleptic Characters

Colour :   Yellowish-green.

Odour :   Slight.

Taste   :   Mucilagenous, bitter and characteristic.

Size   :   7 to 8 mm in width and 25 to 60 mm in length.

Shape :   Leave are lanceolate, entire, apex is acute with spine at the top. Bases of the leaflets are asymmetrical with transverse lines, more prominent on the lower surface, while the trichomes are present on both the surfaces.

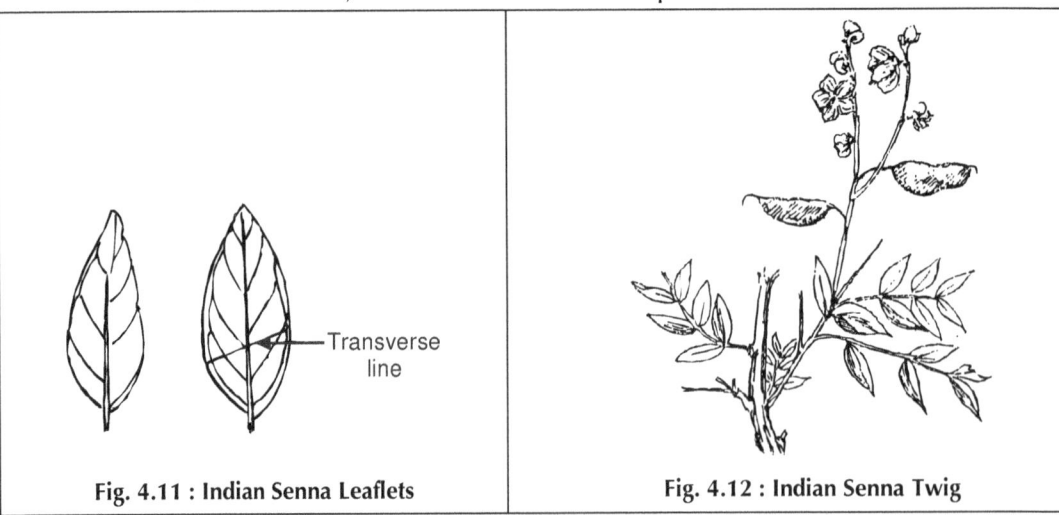

Fig. 4.11 : Indian Senna Leaflets   Fig. 4.12 : Indian Senna Twig

The another common variety which is official in British Pharmacopoeia bears the synonym *Alexandrian senna* and botanically consists of the dried leaves of *Cassia acutifolia Delile*. **Alexandrian senna leaves** are pale greyish-green in colour, 7 to 12 mm in width and 20 to 40 mm in length. Leaflets are ovate-lanceolate with entire margin, papery in texture, thin and without transverse marking. Alexandrian senna is indigenous to tropical Africa and is cultivated in Sudan. It is exported through port of Alexandria.

Microscopic Characters

Senna represents typical histological characters of isobilateral leaves which include the following - The epidermis shows presence of unicellular, conical, thick-walled warty trichomes. The trichomes are slightly curved at their bases and are present on both the surfaces. The rubiaceous or paracytic stomata are present on epidermal surfaces. Palisade tissue is present on both the sides, consisting of rectangular cells, enclosing cluster-crystals of calcium oxalate. The spongy mesophyll and conducting tissues are represented by leaves as shown in the figure. A patch of sclerenchyma towards upper epidermis and above the xylem (also known as pericyclic fibres) is present. The presence of cluster sheath and sclerenchyma are characteristic of the senna leaves. Vein islet numbers and stomatal indices can be used to distinguish the two species.

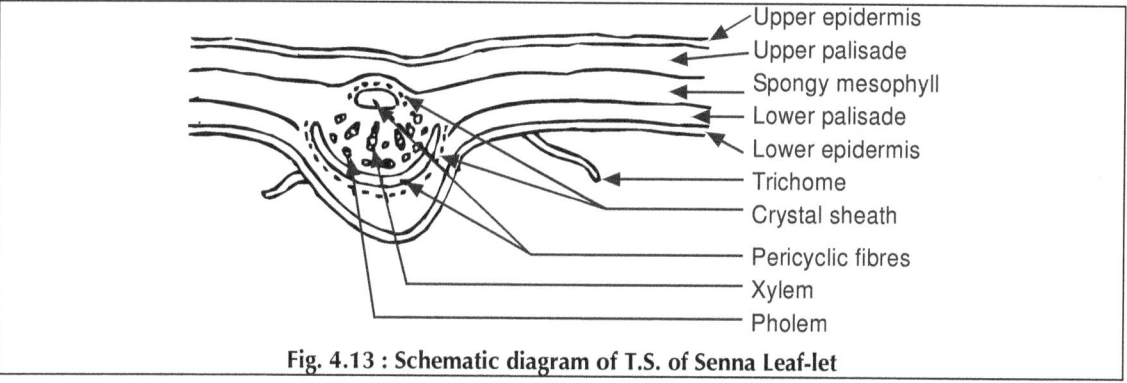

Fig. 4.13 : Schematic diagram of T.S. of Senna Leaf-let

The following are quantitative microscopic constants of Indian and Alexandrian senna leaves.

Table 4.5 : Comparison of Alexandrian senna and Tinnevelly senna

Alexandrian senna	Tinnevelly senna
Macroscopy Length : Upto 40 mm Colour : Greyish-green Base : More asymmetric	Length : Exceed 50 mm Colour : Yellowish-green Base : Less asymmetric
Microscopy Covering Trichomes More numerous Vein islet No. : 25-29-5	Less numerous Vein islet No. : 19.5 – 22.5

Stomatal index : 10-15	Stomatal index : 14 - 20
Usually 12.5	Usually 17.5
Palisade ratio	
Upper epidermis 9.5	Upper epidermis 7.5
Lower epidermis 7.0	Lower epidermis 5.1
Chemical Constituents	
Naphthlene elecivative	Tinnevellin glycoside
6 Hydroxy musizin glycoside	

Chemical Constituents

Senna contains mainly two anthraquinone glycosides called as sennoside A and sennoside B (not less than 2.5 per cent) which account for its purgative property. Tutin in 1913 isolated rhein and aloe-emodin. Stoll and his colleagues in 1941 reported isolation of crystalline sennosides A and B.

Sennosides A and B are stereoisomers of each other. They are dimeric glycosides with rhein dianthrone as aglycone. i.e. 10,10' bis (9, 10 - dihydro - 1 - 8 - dihydroxy - 9 - oxoanthracane - 3 carboxylic acid). In sennoside B the aglycone is in meso form, and in sennoside A, it is dextro-rotatory. They also differ by the way of linkage of glucose to the aglycone fraction. The purgative activity of sennosides A and B accounts upto 40 - 60 per cent activity of crude drug. It is also reported that, sugar part of these glycosides has transporting function for the aglycone upto large intestine and also protective action so that oxidation of aglycone to other very less active anthraquinone is prevented.

	R	10 – 10'	Glycoside
	COOH	*trans*	sennoside A
	COOH	*meso*	sennoside B

Standards

Foreign organic rnatter	:	Not more than 1.0 %
Stalks	:	Not more than 2.0 %
Sulphated ash	:	Not more than 12 %
Acid insoluble ash	:	Not more than 2.0 %
Heavy metals		
Lead	:	Not more than 10 ppm.
Cadmium	:	Not more than 0.3 ppm.

Chemical Test

Senna leaves can be tested for their chemical constituents. The test is known as *Borntrager test*, which is as follows.

Boil the powdered leaves with dilute sulphuric acid. Filter immediately, separate the filtrate and cool. Mix the filtrate with double volume of any one of the water insoluble organic solvents like benzene, chloroform or carbon tetrachloride. Shake it well and separate the organic solvent layer. To the layer of organic solvent, add equal quantity of dilute ammonia. The ammoniacal layer becomes pink and finally red indicating the presence of anthraquinone derivatives.

Uses

Senna leaves are used as a laxative. Senna is an irritant purgative due to presence of anthraquinone derivatives. Senna is free of astringent effect due to the absence of tannin. Purgative effect of senna is not followed by the constipation. The only disadvantage of senna is that it causes gripping, but it is overcome by admixing powdered senna with carminatives.

Substitutes and Adulterants

Indian senna is abundantly available and there are very few chances of adulteration. Comparatively, the cost of drug is also cheap. The following are common adulterants and substitutes for Alexandrian senna.

1. **Dog senna (Italian senna) :** It consists of dried leaves of *Cassia obovata* (Leguminosae). The leaves are broadly ovate and abruptly tapering towards the apex. Histologically, the lower epidermis of the leaves represents papillose cells.

2. **Palthe senna :** These are the dried leaves of *Cassia auriculata* (Leguminosae). The leaves are small oblong to obovate in shape. Histologically, leaves contain thick walled unicellular trichomes. The upper palisade consists of two layers. Chemically, it contains leucoanthocynidin giving red colour with sulphuric acid.

3. **Arabian senna :** These are the dried leaves of wild growing plants of *Cassia angustifolia*. It is found in Southern Arabia. The leaves are brownish green in colour, elongated, narrow and lanceolate in shape. The vein-islet number of leaves is 19 to 23.

Apart from the above substitutes, senna leaves are also adulterated with the leaves of *Ailanthus glandulosa*. They can be distinguished from the genuine drug by the following characteristics. The leaves are large, ovate and 70 to 100 mm in size. The leaves are covered with strongly striated cuticle with no stomata on the upper epidermis. The cluster crystals of calcium oxalate are present near the veins.

SENNA FRUIT

Synonyms

Senna pods; Sennae fructus

Biological Source

Senna fruits consist of dried fruits of *Cassia acutifolia* Delile, known in commerce as Alexandrian senna pods and dried pods of *Cassia angustifolia* Vahl, known as Tinnevelly or Indian senna pods (Family : Leguminosae). Fruits contain not less than 1.5 % of hydroxy anthracene derivatives calculated as sennoside B.

Pods are also obtained from *Cassia fistula*, family Leguminasae. This plant is indigenous to India but widely obtained from West Indies and Indonesia.

Geographical Distribution

Senna pods are collected in Sudan and Southern India from cultivated plants.

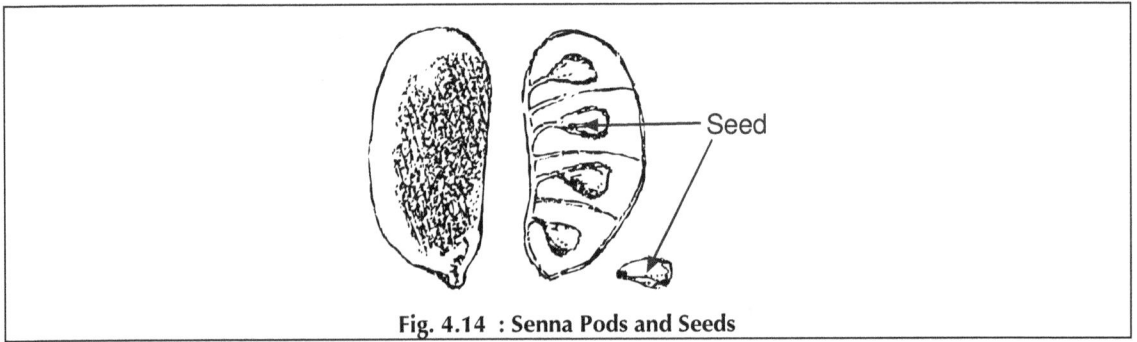

Fig. 4.14 : Senna Pods and Seeds

Organoleptic Characters

Colour   :   Pale green to greenish-brown.

Odour   :   None.

Taste   :   Slight.

Size   :   20 - 30 mm long and 20 - 25 mm in width.

Shape   :   Cylindrical indehiscent.

Extra Features

Seeds which are about six in number and obovate in shape are with bluntly pointed projection at hilum end.

Chemical Constituents

Senna fruit contains about 2.5 to 4.5 % of sennosides A and B. The pods are superior to leaves, as they contain more percentage of glycosides.

Uses

Senna pods are used as purgative due to anthraquinone derivatives. The pods do not contain mucilage and are easy to handle for the commercial extraction of anthraquinone glycosides. Sennosides are extracted as their calcium salts.

RHUBARB

Synonyms

Rheum; Rhizome-Rhei; Rhubarb-Rhizome, Revand-chini.

Biological Source

Rhubarb consists of rhizome of *Rheum palmatum* Linn. and other species of *Rheum*, excepting *R. rhaponticum*, belonging to family Polygonaceae.

Indian Rhubarb consists of the dried rhizomes of *Rheum emodi*. Wall or *Rheum webbianum* Royle. It is collected from six to eight year old plants, just before the flowering season and sold with cortex or in partially decorticated form. The drug should contain not less than 2.2 % of hydroxy anthraquinone derivatioves calculated as rhein.

Geographical Distribution

Rhubarb is cultivated and collected in China, Tibet, India, Germany and other European countries.

Indian rhubarb is a stout herb, about 1.5 to 3 m in height distributed in Kashmir and Sikkim at an altitude of 3600 to 5000 m. It is reported to be cultivated in Assam, but it is collected mainly from wild plants found in Nepal, Sikkim, Kulu and Kulaman. The drug is extracted in autumn or spring when about 6 – 10 years old plant dug and dried. The decorticated rhizomes are roughly cylindrical ('rounds') or if cut longitudinally ('flats') pieces.

Organoleptic Characters

Colour	:	Brown or yellow.
Odour	:	Fragrant.
Taste	:	Bitter and astringent.
Size	:	Pieces of rhubarb are 2 to 20 cm in length and 1.5 to 2 cm in diameter.
Shape	:	Rhizomes are sub-cylindrical, barrel-shaped, conical or in planoconvex pieces.

(a)   (b)

Fig. 4.15 : (a) Indian Rhubarb (*Rheum emodi*) *Twig* (b) *Rheum platinatum*

Extra Features

The rhubarb rhizomes are compact and firm with irregularly longitudinal wrinkles, furrows or ridges, while some pieces show transverse wrinkles or annulations. Fracture is granular, uneven and shows the presence of dark cambium lines.

Chemical Constituents

Rhubarb contains anthraquinone glycosides and astringent principles. The anthraquinone glycosides range from 2 to 4.6 per cent and are categorised into four groups.

(1) Anthraquinones with a carboxyl group like rhein and glucorhein.

(2) Anthraquinones without a carboxyl group like aloe-emodin, emodin, chrysophanol, physcion and also their glycosidal forms.

(3) Anthrones and dianthrone of aloe-emodin, emodin, chrysophanol and physcion.

(4) Heterodianthrones like palmidin A, palmidin B, and palmidin C. They are formed from two different anthrone molecules.

Palmidin A $\longrightarrow$ aloe - emodin anthrone + emodin anthrone

Palmidin B $\longrightarrow$ aloe - emodin-anthrone + chrysophanol anthrone

Palmidin C $\longrightarrow$ emodin-anthrone + chrysophanol anthrone

Rhein   **Chrysophanol**   **Aloe-emodin**

The astringent part mainly consists of gallic acid as glucogallin, along with tannin, catechin and epicatechin. The drug also contains rheinolic acid, pectin, starch, fat and calcium oxalate. The amount of calcium oxalate ranges over 3 to 40 per cent and hence the total ash also varies.

Commercial Grades

1. High grade or Chinghai or shensi-type; it occurs in round or flat about 15 cm long. It breaks with marbled fracture odour; aromatic, taste bitter and slightly astringent.

2. Medium grade or canton type: Some pieces are trimmed, granular fracture.

3. Third grade, very small pieces than higher grade.

Other Rhubarb Species

1. Indian Rhubarb (Himalayan Rhubarb, Revandchini)

It consists of dried rhizomes and roots of *R. webbianum* Royle, *R. emodi* Wallich or other related *Rheum* species found in India and Nepal. It occurs as unpeeled or partly peeled pieces. They resemble the Chinese variety, but are light in weight. Indian Rhubarb contains anthraquinone glycosides. It shows a strong deep violet fluorescence in ultra violet light. Indian Rhubarb contains hydrolysable tannins. It does not contain rhaponticin.

Rhapontic Rhubarb

It is obtained from rhizomes of *R. rhaponticum*. It is found in southern Siberia and the surrounding regions of Volga river. It is pinkish in colour and shrunken in nature. Rhapontic rhubarb lacks the presence of rhein, emodin or aloe-emodin, but it contains rhaponticin, which is a crystalline glycoside and is a derivative of diphenyl ethylene.

Rhaponticin

This glycoside has an estrogenic activity. It shows a blue fluorescence in ultra violet light.

2. English Rhubarb

Both *R. officinale* and *R. rhaponticum* were cultivated as drug but now it is obtained from *R. rhaponticum*.

3. Japanese Rhubarb

Hybrid of *R. Coreanum* and *R. palmatum*.

Chemical Tests

1. By addition of ammonia, it acquires pink colour.

2. With 5 % potassium hydroxide, blood red colouration is produced.

3. Under ultra violet radiation rheum-emodi gives brown colouration.

4. Borntrager's test for anthraquinone is positive with rhubarb.

Uses

Rhubarb is a mild purgative. It contains tannins and hence, is associated with the astringent effect after purgation. It is also stomachic in smaller doses.

Adulterants

Rhapontic rhubarb, obtained from *Rheum rhaponticum* is a common substitute for rhubarb. It is known as Chinese rhapontica in the market, as it comes from China. It has a distinctive odour and occurs as untrimmed pieces. Chinese rhubarb when examined under ultraviolet radiation flouresces bright blue (not observed in case of genuine drug). Raphntic rhubarb contains aglycoside "rhaponticin".

Chemical test for Rhapontic Rubarb

Alcoholic extract of drug shows blue fluoroscence when place on a filter paper and observed under UVs but official drug does not show such fluorescence.

CASCARA

Synonyms

Cascara bark, cascara sagrada, sacred bark, chittem bark, cortex *Rhamni purshianae.*

Biological Source

Cascara sagrada is the dried bark of *Rhamnus purshiana* de Candolle, belonging to family Rhamnaceae. It is collected at least one year before use.

Geographical Source

It is obtained both from wild and cultivated shrubs and small trees in North Carolina, Washington, Oregen regions of United States. It is also cultivated in Western Canada and Kenya.

Collection and Storage

The bark is collected from mid April to end of August. Longitudinal incisions are made in trunk and bark is removed, and dried in shade.

Such bark is known as "natural" cascara. While commercially it is available in small pieces known as "processed" or "compact" or "evenized" cascara.

Macroscopical Characters

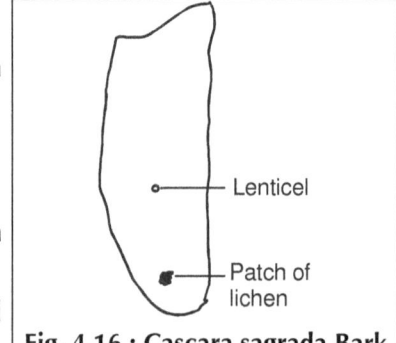

Fig. 4.16 : Cascara sagrada Bark

Colour : It is purplish-brown externally and reddish brown internally.

Odour : Characteristic nauseous.

Taste : Persistently bitter.

Size : About 1 to 4 mm in thickness with length about 20 cm.

Shape ; Usually, in the broken pieces which are small and flat. It occurs in quills or channels.

Extra Features

Outer surface of the bark is very smooth and shows the presence of scattered lenticels, lichens and cork. Externally, liverworts and sometimes, insects are also present on the bark. Bark shows internally, longitudinal striations and dull purplish brown surface.

Microscopic Characters

The transverse section shows cork, cortex, sclereid, primary and secondary phloem. Cork has several layers of cells which contain yellowish-brown substance showing purple colour with alkali. Cortex is composed of collenchyma, externally and cellulosic parenchyma on inner side. The latter contains a large number of rosette crystals of calcium oxalate. The cortex region also contains small and large groups of sclereid. The sclerids are irregular or avoid in shape. The major portion of bark is occupied by secondary phloem, in which phloem fibres are lignified and arranged in tangential bands, alternating with sieve tubes. Many cells of phloem parenchyma contain prisms of calcium oxalate and thus, form a crystal sheath to each group of phloem fibres.

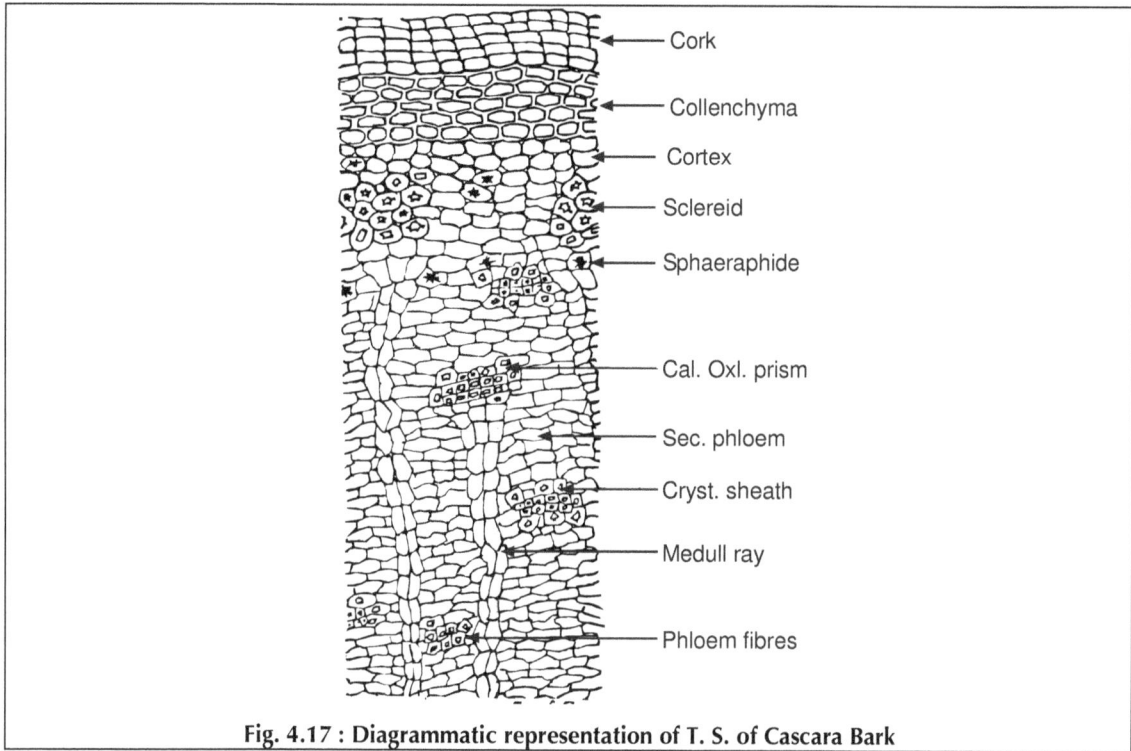

Fig. 4.17 : Diagrammatic representation of T. S. of Cascara Bark

Medullary rays are 1 – 5 cell wide and are radially elongaed.

Chemical Constituents

The freshly collected cascara bark contains anthranol derivatives which cause gripping and emetic effects. The drug becomes acceptable by storing for at least one year, during which anthranol portion is oxidised to anthraquinones.

Cascara contains both O-glycosides and C-glycosides. It contains four primary glycosides which are called as cascarosides A, B, C and D.

Cascaroside	Configuration	R
A	10 β	OH
B	10 α	OH
C	10 β	H
D	10 α	H

The bark also contains barbaloin and chrysaloin, various dianthrones of emodin, aloe-emodin, chrysophanol; heterodianthrones like palmidins A, B and C; free aloe-emodin, emodin chrysophanol and O–glycosides derived from them.

A lactone present in the drug makes it bitter in taste.

Glucose — O O OH

CH_2OH

H Glucose

Cascaroside A/B

Glucose — O O OH

CH_3

H Glucose

Cascaroside C/D

Chemical Test

As it contains C-glycosides, it gives modified Borntrager's test.

Uses

In the series of anthracene glycoside containing drugs, cascara is a mild drug. In small doses, it is used as a bitter stomachic and tonic and in larger doses as purgative.

Substitutes and allied drugs

Barks of *R. californica*, *R. fallax* and frangula bark are substitutes for cascara. The former bark has a more uniform coat of lichens and wider medullary rays than the original species.

Rhumnus cathartica : It has reddish or greenish brown cork and it does not posses sclerides. It contain frangula-emodin rhumnicoside.

D. MISCELLANEOUS GLYCOSIDAL DRUGS
KALMEGH

Synonyms

Andrographis, Kirayat, Bhui-nimb.

Biological Source

This consists of dried leaves and tender shoots of the plant known as *Andrographis paniculata* Nees (Acanthaceae). It yields not less than 1.0 per cent of andrographolide calculated on dry basis.

Geographical Source

Kalmegh is an annual herb found in Shri Lanka and throughout India, specifically in Maharashtra, Karnataka, Uttar Pradesh, Tamil Nadu, Andhra Pradesh and Madhya Pradesh. It is cultivated to some extent in Assam and West Bengal. It flowers in the months of September to December and is collected from November to December. Yield per hectare is 2.5 tones.

Cultivation and Collection

It grows well in tropical and subtropical regions. However, it is seen as a shade loving plant; as it grows abundantly in moist climate with well distributed rainfall.

It grows upto 1500 metres.

Temperature range between 25° - 40°C is suitable.

It can be grown in various types of soils, though sandy loamy soil with rich organic matter is suitable for its growth. It is also found growing on sandy clay soil. But soils with water logging condition are not suitable for its growth.

Cultivation details

It can be propagated either by seeds or vegetatively by using cuttings. But, seed propagation is economical and easy for commercial purpose.

For raising nursery, period before onset of monsoon i.e. May - June is suitable and for transplantation in the main field, period after onset of monsoon i.e. the months of July - August is favourable.

Total duration of crop is 100 - 120 days.

For nursery raising, either planting in polythene bags filled with soil, sand and organic manure in proportion of 1 : 1 : 1, or in beds of $3 \times 1.5 \times 0.15$ metre size is carried out. The beds are mixed well with cattle manure at the rate of 25 kg/m². About 5 cm apart lines are marked on the bed and the seeds are sown. The beds are watered daily. After sowing, the seeds germinate within 8-10 days and are ready for transplanting after one month of sowing.

The land is prepared by ploughing twice or thrice and levelled. Then, soil is mixed well with farmyard manure at rate of 25 to 30 t/hectare at the time of last ploughing. Irrigation channels are prepared in the prepared soil.

At the onset of monsoon, the seedlings are transplanted at a spacing of 15×15 cm. If seeds are sown directly, then distance of 30×15 cm is kept for healthy yield. On an average, 450 gm/hect. of seeds are required for sowing.

It is mainly grown as rainfed crop. In areas with well distributed rainfall, no special technique for irrigation is required. But in case of dry weather, it is to be irrigated regularly in initial stages with an interval of 3 - 4 days, later on after one week and once the crop stands in field, depending upon the requirement of crop.

To increase the yield and healthy crop production, kalmegh is fertilised even after application of 25 to 30 tonne/hectare of FYM during cultivation. Fertiliser dose of NPK is reported to be beneficial for good yield. 75 kg of nitrogen, 75 kg phosphorus and 50 kg of potash for one hectare are required. Out of this, 50% N and the entire dose of phosphorus and potash are applied as basal dose and the rest 50 % nitrogen is used as a top dressing after 30 days of transplanting / sowing.

During its initial stage of growth, the land should be kept weed free to promote growth of the crop. For this, first weeding is done after one month of planting. After this, one or two more weedings are required.

Plant - protection and pesticides

No disease or pests of serious nature been reported to attack kalmegh, as it is a hardy shrub.

Collection

Total 2 - 3 harvestings can be done in a period of one year. The crop is ready for the first harvest after 4 - 5 months of sowing/planting. The appropriate period of collection is when it starts flowering. For harvesting, the plants are cut at its base leaving 15 to 20 cm stem for regeneration of the crop. After first harvesting, the crop is again supplied with top dressing of nitrogen and irrigated. The procedure is repeated after every harvest. The crop is then ready after 60 - 65 days of first harvest. In this way 2 - 3 harvesting can be made within 100-120 days.

The plant or the harvested material is dried in shade for 3 - 4 days and stored.

Macroscopic Characters

Colour   - Leaves are dark green, while flowers are rose coloured.

Odour   - Odourless

Taste   - Intensely bitter

Size   - Leaves 7 × 2.5 cm, flowers 1.8 cm in length.

Shape   - Leaves are lanceolate and petiolate and with entire margin and acuminate apex.

Fig. 4.17 : Kalmegh Flowering Twig

The venation of leaf is unicostate reticulate and mid-rib is ventrally grooved. The stem bears numerous branches and many of them bear flowers. The calyx is about 3 mm long, linear, lanceolate, glandular and pubescent; corrolla, 1 cm in length, rose coloured and hairy. Flowers are arranged in axillary and terminal racemes, which are 7.5 - 10 cm in length. The plant flowers in the months from September to December.

Chemical Constituents

Kalmegh contains bitter principles andrographolide, a bicyclic diterpenoid lactone and kalmeghin (0.85 - 2.5 per cent).

Standards

Ash	- Not more than 20.0 per cent
Acid-insoluble ash	- Not more than 5.1 per cent
Foreign organic matter	- Not more than 2.0 per cent
Alcohol-soluble extractive	- Not less than 24 per cent
Water-soluble extractive	- Not less than 20 per cent

Andrographolide

Uses

Kalmegh is used as a bitter tonic, an alterative and anthelmintic. Green leaves are used as stomachic, anthelmintic and in the treatment of dysentery and dyspepsia. It possesses antityphoid and antibiotic activity. It has been proved to be hepatoprotective drug, mainly due to andrographolide.

Substitutes

Kalmegh is substituted with *Andrographis echioides*, found in tropical India and in dry districts of Maharashtra, Rajasthan and Tamil Nadu.

VISNAGA

Synonyms

Khella, Pick tooth fruit.

Biological Source

These are dried ripe fruits of *Ammi visnaga* Linn., belonging to family Umbelliferae.

Geographical Source

The drug is a native of Nile delta in Egypt. It has been cultivated in Egypt and Chile in South America.

Cultivation and Collection

The plant which is an annual herb growing about 1 to 1.5 metres in height, is propagated by means of seeds in loamy soil of nursery beds in August. After attaining a height of about 6 - 7 cm, transplantation is done into open fields. After 7 - 8 months, the plant bears flowers and harvesting is done at the stage of ripening of first fertilised flowers. The plants are cut and preserved in heaps, during which all the fruits are ripened.

Macroscopic Characters

Though, it is an umbelliferous fruit, very few cremocarps are entire. Otherwise they occur as separate mericarps. The latter are plano-convex in shape and ovoid-lanceolate in appearance. The fruit is greenish-brown in colour. It is about 2 - 2.5 mm in length, 0.7 to 1.2 mm in width and 0.8 to 1 mm in thickness. Mericarp shows 5 primary ridges and 4 secondary ridges.

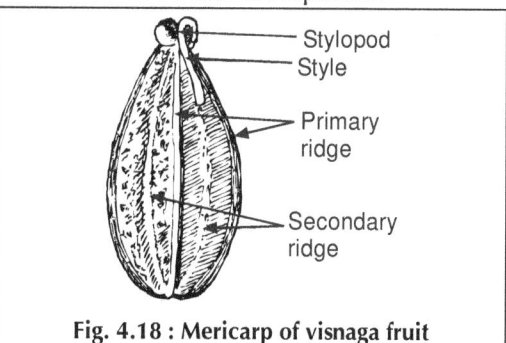

Fig. 4.18 : Mericarp of visnaga fruit

Microscopic Characters

The transverse section of mericarp shows characteristic parts of umbelliferous fruits. It has 5 vascular bundles and 4 oil glands. The section appears as a pentagon. A large lacuna is present in primary ridge on the outer side of vascular bundle. This is a distinguishing feature of this drug.

Chemical Constituents

The drug contains volatile oil about 1 per cent khellin, 0.1 per cent visnagin and 0.3 per cent. khelloside. They are furanocoumarin derivatives. Khellin occurs as odourless bitter tasting crystals and it is 2-methyl -5, 8 dimethoxy furanochrome. It is soluble in mineral acids and organic solvents except ether.

Glucoside	R_1	R_2	R_3
Visnagin	OCH_3	H	H
Khellin	OCH_3	OCH_3	H
Khelloside	OCH_3	H	O-glucoside

The oil present in drug contains samidine, dihydrosamidine, and visnadine.

Uses

Khellin is a smooth muscle relaxant and used as coronary vasodilator in angina pectoris, renal and uterine colic, bronchial asthma and whooping cough.

Samidine, dihydrosamidine and visuadine are strong vasodilators.

GENTIAN

Synonyms

Gentian root, Gentiana, Radix Gentianae.

Biological Source

Gentian is the dried partially fermented rhizome and root of yellow gentian i.e. *Gentiana lutea*, family Gentianaceae.

Geographical Source

Gentian is a perennial herbaceous tree native to hilly areas in Southern and Central Europe like Jura, Vosges mountains, and Yugoslavia.

Collection and Preparation

The large fleshy roots and erect rhizomes from about 2 - 5 year old plants are dug up. Collection is done in autumn, followed by cutting longitudinal into slices. At this stage, the pieces of roots and rhizomes are white in colour, without any odour. During slow drying or by keeping them in heaps and fermenting by slow heating, they become dark or yellow coloured and develop characteristic odour.

Macroscopic Characters

The rhizome is yellowish-brown and has transverse annulations and shows conical buds at the top. The root is narrower but continuous with rhizome. It is longitudinally wrinkled and has circular scars of rootlets. The drug has a peculiar odour. The drug first gives a sweet taste, followed by an intensely bitter taste. The fracture is short and smooth in dried drug, but tough and flexible in moist drug.

Microscopic Characters

The transverse section of rhizome shows bark, cambium, wood and pith. The root shows these parts but no pith, in place of which a triarch primary xylem is present. The cork cells are thin walled. Cortex has parenchyma with oil globules and calcium oxalate. Phloem is present in small groups and phloem fibres are absent. The xylem contains spiral and annular vessels and also shows presence of interxylary phloem. The drug does not contain sclereids.

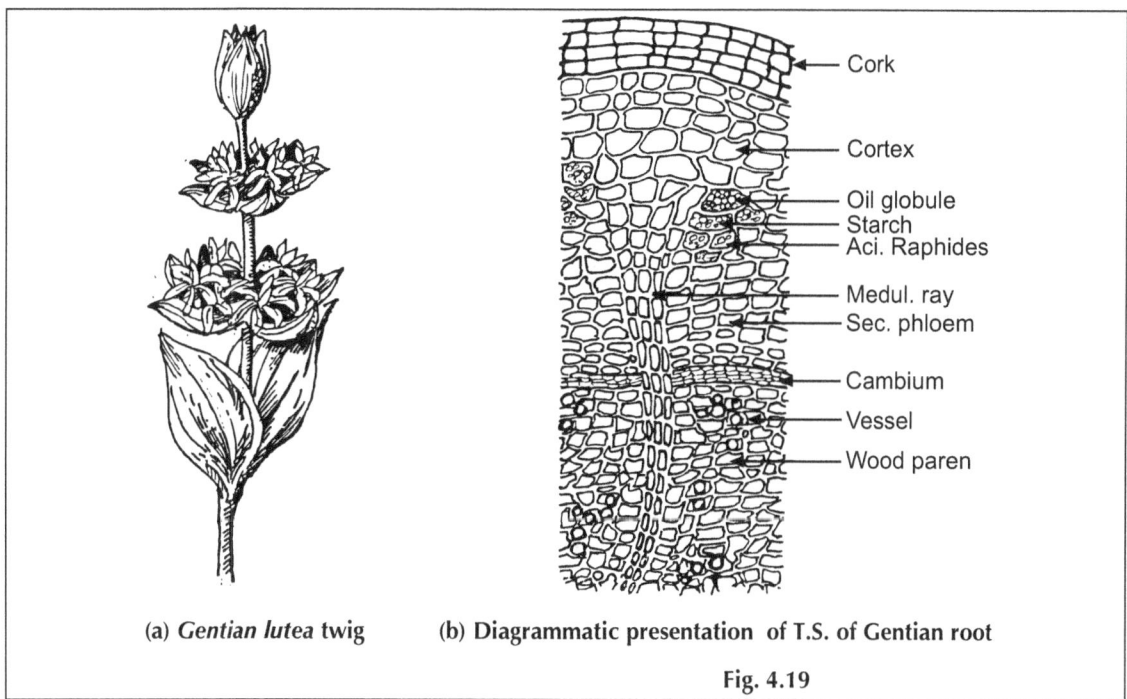

(a) *Gentian lutea* twig   (b) Diagrammatic presentation of T.S. of Gentian root

Fig. 4.19

Chemical Constituents

The drug contains bitter glycosides mainly gentiopicrin, which is also called gentiopicroside.

It is a water soluble, crystalline compound with a bitter value of 12,000. During fermentation and drying, it breaks down to gentiogenin and glucose.

The drug also contains amarogentin, amaroswerin, gentioside and a mixture of gentiopicrin and gentisin called gentinin.

Gentiopicroside   **Gentianin (Gentisin)**

In the natural products, amarogentin is considered as the bittermost substance and imparts a bitter taste in even 5.8 lakh times dilution. Although, most of the above mentioned constituents are bitter, the taste of the drug is mainly due to amarogentin. These glycosides contain monoterpene irridoids. The drug contains a flavonoid alkaloid called gentianine or gentisin. Gentisin gives yellow colour to drug.

The other constituents present in drug are gentisic acid, gentianose (a trisaccharide consisting two glucose and one fructose units), gentiobiose (disaccharide) and sucrose. The drug should yield not less than 33 per cent water soluble extractive value, due to sugars. It is decreased due to excessive fermentation.

Chemical Test: Under UV radiation gentian extract shows light-blue fluorescence.

Uses: It is used as a bitter tonic to stimulate the gastric secretion and hence improving the appetite.

Other Preparations

(1) **Concentrated compound gentian infusion:** It contains gentian, bitter orange peel, lemon peel and alcohol 25 %.

(2) **Compound gentian tincture:** It contains gentian, bitter orange peel, cardamom seed and alcohol 46 %.

ARTEMISIA

Synonyms

Annual wormweed, Sweet wormweed, Mugwort.

Biological Source

It consists of the aerial parts of *Artemisia annua* L. and other species of *Artemisia* belonging to family Asteraceae (Compositae). It should contain not less than 0.8 per cent artemisicinen.

Artemisia is a large, diverse genus of plants with between 200 and 400 species. The aerial parts have been used in traditional Chinese medicine for the treatment of: malaria; fever caused by tuberculosis; jaundice; "fever caused by summer heat"

Geographical Source

A. annua is widely distributed in the temperate, cool temperate and subtropical zones (mainly in Asia) of the world. It originated from China and grows mainly in the middle, eastern and southern parts of Europe and in the northern, middle and eastern parts of Asia.

It also grows in the Mediterranean region and countries in North Africa, North America, United States and in Canada.

Morphological characteristics of live *A. annua*

It is annual plant with aromatic, green, glabrous hairs. Stem is erect, ribbed, brownish or violet-brown, naturally grows to 30–100 cm high. Leaves 3–5 cm long and 2–4 cm wide, ovate, thrice pinnatley cut, their lobules oblong-lanceolate, short-acuminate, entire or with 1–2 teeth, 1–2 mm long and 0.5 mm wide, lower leaves are petiolate.

Fig. 4.20 : Artemisin species

Chemical Constituents

The chemical composition of *A. annua* consists of volatile and non-volatile constituents. The essential oil content is about 0.2–0.25%. The main compounds, which account for about 70% of the essential oils, are camphene, b-camphene, isoartemisia ketone, 1-camphor, b-caryophyllene and b-pinene. The main non-volatile ingredients include sesquiterpenoids, flavonoids and coumarins. It also contain proteins such as b-galactosidase, b-glucosidase, steroids like b-sitosterol and stigmasterol.

The main chemical constituents of *A. annua* are sesquiterpenoids, including artemisinin, artemisinin I, artemisinin II, artemisinin III, artemisinin IV, artemisinin V, artemisic acid, artemisilactone, artemisinol and epoxyarteannuinic acid.

Artemisinin

Uses

A. annua has a long history of medicinal use in China and also has various uses in other countries. The artemisinin compounds are effective against *Plasmodium falciparum* and *P. vivax,* including multidrug-resistant strains. They rapidly kill the asexual blood stages of the parasites, which are responsible for the disease manifestations (blood schizonticidal activity); they have some effect on the gametocytes (the stage which is infective to mosquitoes ingesting a bloodmeal from an infected person). In China it is also used for fever caused by summer-heat and jaundice. *A. annua* has analgesic–antipyretic effects, shows antibacterial, anti-inflammatory activities. The essential oil of *A. annua* also has insect repellent property.

CITRUS FRUIT

Synonyms

Nimbu, M¡ha Nimbu

Biological Source

It consists of fresh fruit of *Citrus limon* (Linn.) Burm. f. Syn. *C. medica* var. *limonum* Family, Rutaceae.

Geographical Source

The origin of the lemon is unknown, though lemons are thought to have first grown in Assam, Burma or China. Lemon is a cultivated as hybrid deriving from wild species such as the citron and mandarin.

Macroscopy - Organoleptic Characters

A lemon tree can grow up to 10 meters (33 feet), but they are usually smaller. The branches are thorny, and form an open crown. The leaves are green, shiny and elliptical-acuminate. Flowers are white on the outside with a violet streaked interior and have a strong fragrance.

Fruit is a berry (hesperidium) yellow when ripe, ovoid or globose, 5 to 10 cm long; external surface even or rugged showing openings of oil glands; usually with 9 mammillate extremity and thin rind; transversely cut surface shows thin rind and an inwardly grown endocarp forming 10 to 12 segments, each containing 2 or 3 seeds with pulp formed by succulent hairs; juice acidic.

Fig. 4.21 : Citrus fruit

Chemical Constituents

Fruits of Citrus limonum contain essential oil about 2,5 %: main components are: D-limonene (amount: 90 %) which gives their characteristic lemon smell and taste, citral (amount 3 – 5 %), nonanal, decanal, dodecanal, linalyl acetate, geranyl acetate, citronelyl acetate, anthranil acid methyl ester - flavonoids: naringine, neohesperidine, rutin, hesperidine, eriocritin.

Lemons contain significant amounts of citric acid; this is why they have a low pH and a sour taste. They also contain Vitamin C (Ascorbic acid) which is essential to human health.

Uses

Citrus flavonoids improve the permeability of vascular vessels, they show antiphlogistic effects and diuretic properties. Citrus flavonoids inhibit bacterial mutagenesis. Because of its high Vitamin C content it is used as a tonic for the digestive system, immune system, and skin.

Dried lemon peels are used as stimulant, carmenative and aromatic. They are also used as flavoring agent of choice.

Citrus Peels

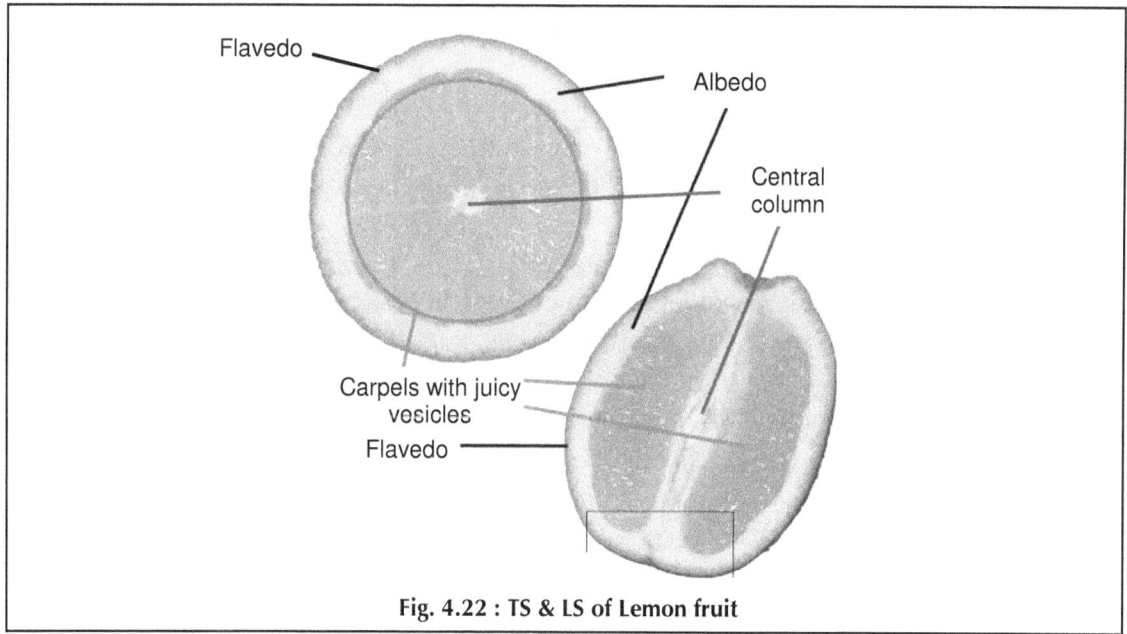

Fig. 4.22 : TS & LS of Lemon fruit

The peel is a by-product of lemon juice processing, with a high potential use. Two different tissues are found which is colloquially called lemon peel, i.e. flavedo and albedo. Flavedo is the peel's outer layer, whose colour varies from green to yellow. It is a rich source of essential oil and hence used by flavour and fragrance industry.

Albedo is the major component of lemon peel, and is a spongy and cellulosic layer laid under flavedo. Albedo has high dietary fiber content, flavonoids and vitamin C.

B. TANNINS

The term 'tannin' was first coined by Seguin in 1796. He denotes this term to the substances present in plant extract which are able to combine with protein of animal hide and convert them into lather. Therefore, tannins are detected qualitatively by tanning test (the glodbeater's skin test) and quantitatively by its adsorption on standard hide power. There are certain simple phenolic substances, that often present with tannins and may be partly retained by hide power. Such low molecular weight substances are calld as pseudo-tannins e.g. chlorogenic acid in coffee and nux-vomica, ipecacuanhic acid in ipecanuntia, and catachins in cocoa.

Both true as well as pseudo-tannins are astringent that precipitate proteins like gelatin. They are used in medicines as mild antiseptic, in the treatment of diarrhoea, in minor haemorrhages.

Tannins are poly phenolic compouds and have molecular weights of 1000 to 5000. The characteristics properties of tannins derive from phenolic compounds which are associated with o-dihydroxy and o-trihydroxy groups within a phenyl ring.

Tannins are non-crystaline rubstances that exhibit acidic reaction in water and forms colloidal solution. They are soluble in alcohol, glycerin, dilute alkalies but practically insoluble in organic solvents except acetone.

Some characteristic chemical reactions of tannins -

1) Tannins show colour reaction with iron salts. e.g. with ferric chloride gives bluish-black or brownish-green colour; with potassium ferricyanide and ammonia it gives deep red colour.

2) Gold beater's skin test : Gold beater's skin is a membrance prepared from OX intestine and it behaves similarly to an untanned hide.

   Soak a small piece of goldbeater's skin in 2% hydrochloric acid, rinse with distilled water and place in tannin solution for 5 min. Wash with distilled water and transfer to 1% ferrous sulphate solution. A brown to black colour on the skin indicate presence of tannins.

3) Gelatin test: Solution of tannins precipitate 1% gelatin solution. Gallic acid and other pseudo tannins also precipitate gelatin.

4) Tannins precipitate alkaloids in extract.

5) Phenazone test: To an aqueous extract of drug, add 0.5 g. of sodium phosphate, warm, cool and then filter it. To the filtrate add 2% phenazone solution. Bulky precipitate of tannins is obtained.

6) Tannins are precipitated by heavy metals like lead.

7) Tannins decolorise the coloured solution of potassium permanganate and bromine water.

8) Tannins are precipitated by strong potassium dichromate solution and chromic acid solution.

9) Test for catechin : Catechins from phloroglucinol when heated with acids and are detected by matchstick test.

Dip a matchstick in plant extract and dry it, then moisten with concentrated hydrochloric acid and warm. The phloroglucinol produced, turns the wood red or pink.

10) Test for chlorogenic acid : An extract containing chlorogenic acid when treated with ammonia, gradually develops green colour.

Classification of Tannins

Tannins are categorized as hydrolysable tannins and proanthocyanidins or condensed tannins.

A) Hydrolysable tannins -

These may be hydrolysed by acid hydrolysis or enzymatic hydrolysis (by tannase enzyme) They are formed from phenolic acids like gallic acid and hexahydroxy diphenic acid. They form esters within glucose molecule. Hydrolysable tannins are also known as pyrogallol tannins, as dry distillation of gallic acid and similar components get converted into pyrogallol. There are two principal types of hydrolysable tannins. One is gallitannins and another is ellagitannins. Gallitannins are composed of gallic acid while ellagitannins are composed of hexahydroxy-diphenic acid units. They respond to ferric chloride test producing blue colour.

Gallitannins: Rhubarb, clove, nutgall, hamamelis, bearberry leaves and chestnust.

Ellagitannins: Oak, myrobalans, pomegranate rind and bark, eucalyptus leaves.

B) Condensed tannins or proanthocyanidins

They are resistant to hydrolysis and are not readily hydrolysed to simplar molecules. They do not contain sugar moiety. They have polymeric flavan 3-one structure and are related to flavanoid pigments. Catechins and flavan 3,4-diols (leucoanthocyanidins) are the intermediate in tannin biosynthesis. They occur in monomeric, dimeric and trimeric forms.

Condensed tannins on treatment with acids get converted into red insoluble compounds known as phlobaphens.

The phlobaphens and their decomposed products give typical red colour to many drugs such as red cinchona bark. The condensed tannins on dry distillation yield catcchol, hence they are also known as catecchol-tannins. With ferric chloride they produce green colour.

They are distributed in different parts of plants. i.e.

Leaves	: Green tea, hamamelis.
Barks	: Cinchona, cinnamon, hamamelis, wild cherry.
Roots and Rhizome	: Male fern
Seeds	: Cocoa, cola, areca, guarana

Fruits   : Grapes (red wine), hawthorn.

Flowers   : Hawthorn.

Extract/Dry juices   : Pale catechu, black catechu.

They are extracted by solvent extraction using different solvents like hot water, methanol, acetone or ethyl acetate. The solvent and method of extraction depends upon the source of tannins.

C) Pseudotannins

They are low molecular weight componds and do not respond to goldbeater's skin test.

e.g. Chlorogenic acid in coffee and in nux-vomica, ipecacuanic acid from ipecacunha, catechins from catechu, cocoa.

D) Complex tannins

They are newly discovered group of tannins and are biosynthesized from both hydrolysable tannins and condensed tannins. They are found in Combretaceae, Myrtaceae, Polygonaceae, and Theaceae. They are not as such separate group of tannins.

PALE CATECHU

Synonyms

Gambier, Gambir-Catechu

Biological Source

It is a dried aqueous extract of the leaves and young shoots of *Uncaria gambier* Roxburgh, belonging to family Rubiaceae.

Geographical Source

The plant is indigenous to South East Asian regions like Arachipelago in Malaysia; presently, it is also cultivated in Singapore and Indonesia.

Cultivation and Collection

The cultivation is carried out in fields up to 170 m height and propagation is done by sowing seeds in damp soil. Nursery beds are raised and after 9 months, the seedlings are transplanted in open fields.

Fig. 4.22 : Uncaria gambier (herb)

The first harvesting is done when the plant attains an height of 2 m. The plant yields the drug up to 20 years. The leaves and young shoots collected are boiled in pot called *Cauldron*, made up of wood and with iron bottom for 3 hours and decoction obtained is concentrated till it becomes a pasty mass with yellowish-green colour. This mass is moulded in cubes and sun dried.

Different forms of catechu are used in Eastern market. It has 20 – 50% of rice husk, so it contains starch.

Description

Pale catechu occurs as reddish-brown coloured cubical mass quite friable in nature. When broken, it shows cinnamon brown colour and porous nature. The drug has no odour, but highly astringent taste which first is bitter and then sweet. When placed in water, it shows minute acicular crystals, of catechin. They dissolve on warming.

Chemical Constituents

The drug contains condensed tannins in the form of catechins 7.33 %, catechutannic acid 22.50 % and catechu red. The drug also contains quercetin and gambier fluorescin.

Standards

Loss on drying   : Not more than 15%.

Water soluble matter : Not more than 33%.

Chemical Tests

(1) It gives test for catechin by dipping a match stick in hydrochloric acid and warming it near flame similar to black catechu.

(2) Test for gambier-fluorescin: The drug is extracted with alcohol and sodium hydroxide is added to the extract, followed by addition of a few drops of light petroleum. The mixture is shaken and kept for sometime. Green fluorescence is observed in light petroleum layer (distinction from black catechu).

(3) Small quantity of drug is warmed with chloroform and filtered in a porcelain dish and evaporated to dryness. Due to presence of chlorophyll, it shows greenish yellow colour.

(4) With a mixture of vanillin and hydrochloric acid, it shows pink or red colour.

Uses

It is used as an astringent in treatment of diarrhoea and also as a local astringent in the form of lozenges.

Pale catechu is mainly used in dyeing and tanning industries, and also for protecting the fishing nets.

BLACK CATECHU

Synonyms

Kattha, Cutch, Khadir-catechu, Catechu

Biological Source

It consists of dried aqueous extract prepared from the heartwood of *Acacia catechu* wild and *Acacia chundra* wild family Leguminosae.

Plants used for preparation of catechu are grown in India and Myanmar.

History

Possibly, the use of black catechu could be traced back in history to the time of chewing betel leaf, wherein it has been used as adjuvant. In the bygone days, women used

Kattha to colour thier feet. Since 15th century, this natural material has been exported to Europe.

The old information about Catechu is by a Portuguese writer Garcia de Orta in 1574. Dr. Wrath first used the scientific process to extract catechu, and showed that catechu consists of two parts: kattha and cutch.

Manufacture of Black Catechu

In the traditional method, the separated heartwood is boiled in earthen vessels, fired by sap wood, till all the soluble portion is extracted from it. It is cooled naturally till it is converted to semi-solid mass. On cooling less soluble fraction separates out. The latter is removed as kattha and semi solid mass as cutch. It is transferred to rectangular pits, at the bottom of which sand and clay are placed. It is kept for several days, till the cutch part is absorbed by clay and solid mass, called kattha, is taken out and moulded into blocks.

In modern methods, the red heart wood obtained by felling the tree (Fig. 10.9) and separating the bark and sapwood, is cut into chips mechanically and put into extractors. The steam is passed through the drug for maximum extraction. The extract is concentrated under vacuum and is cooled by refrigeration. It is then centrifuged to isolate the cake of kattha. The cake is moulded in desired sizes and dried in proper condition. By this way, a good quality marketable kattha, ready for market is obtained. The mother liquor, left behind during centrifugation is concentrated, which on cooling gives cutch.

Description

Colour - Light brown to black

Odour - None

Taste - Very astringent

Size - About 2.5 - 5 cm

Shape - Cube or irregular fragments of broken cubes or brick shaped pieces.

Extra Feature

The cubes as well as brick shaped pieces of catechu show the presence of vegetable debris and break with a short fracture. The broken pieces are angular with pale cinnamon-brown colour. It is friable and porous.

Fig. 4.23 : Twig of catechu herb

Chemical Constituents

Black catechu contains about 10 per cent of acacatechin. It is distereoisomer of 5, 7, 3', 4' tetrahydroxy flavan-3-ols. Acacatechin is also known as acacia catechin. Acacatechin undergoes oxidation to catechutannic acid in presence of water and the latter constitutes about 30 per cent of the drug. The other contents of black catechu are catechu red, quercetin, gum and quercitrin. Black catechu does not contain chlorophyll and also the fluorescent- substance present in pale catechu.

Catechin   Catechol

Chemical Tests

(1) Because of the presence of catechin, black catechu gives pink or red colour with vanillin and hydrochloric acid.

(2) Catechin when treated with hydrochloric acid produces phloroglucinol, which burns along with lignin to give purple or magenta colour. For this purpose, tannin extract is taken on match stick dipped in hydrochloric acid and heated near the flame.

(3) Lime water when added to aqueous extract of black catechu gives brown colour, which turns to red precipitate on standing for some time.

(4) Green colour is produced when ferric ammonium sulphate is added to dilute solution of black catechu. By the addition of sodium hydroxide, the green colour turns to purple.

Standards

Ash value	- not more than 6 per cent w/w
Acid insoluble ash	- not more than 3 per cent w/w
Water insoluble residue	- not more than 25 per cent w/w
Alcohol insoluble residue	- not more than 90 per cent w/w

Uses

Kattha is used as an astringent externally for boils, skin eruptions and ulcers. It is also used in cough and diarrhoea. Kattha has cooling and digestive properties.

Cutch is not much used medicinally, but for other purposes like dyeing and colouring, water softening, reducing the viscosity of drill mud, removal of mercaptans from gasoline, protective agent for fishing nets and in the manufacture of ion-exchange resins.

AMLA

Synonyms

Emblica, Indian goose berry, Amalki

Biological Source

This consists of dried, as well as fresh fruits of the plant *Emblica officinalis* Gaerth *Phyllanthus emblica* Linn. belonging to family *Euphorbiaceae*. It contains not less than 1.0 per cent w/w of gallic acid calculated on dry basis.

Geographical Source

It is a small or medium size tree found in all deciduous forests of India. It is also found in Sri Lanka and Myanmar. The leaves are feathery with small oblong pinnately arranged leaflets. The tree is characteristic greenish-grey with smooth bark.

Cultivation and Collection

Intolerant to frost or drought, it is grown by seed germination; besides, Amla can also be propagated by budding or cutting. It is normally found up to an altitude of 1500 m. Commercially, it is collected from wild plants.

Now a days the newly released varieties are selected for better yield. These are known as Banarasi, Kanchan, Anand-2, Balwant, NA6, NA7 and BS-1. Seeds or seedlings are placed at a distance of 4.5 × 4.5 metres in red loamy or coarse gravelly soil. Proper arrangement for irrigation is required, Drip irrigation is most suitable. Fertilisers in the dose-range of 750 - 900 gms of urea, 1 kg superphosphate and 1-1.5 kg of potash per annum depending upon the quality of soil are sufficient. The above dose is divided into two equal parts, one part is applied in September / October and the second in April - May every year. Pruning is done regularly and only 4 - 6 branches about 0.75 - 1.0 metre above the ground are retained. Plant bears male and female flowers separately. Male flowers are reported in the axil of the leaf, in bunches while the solitary female flowers are the axil of the branches. The extent of fertilization is 25 - 30 per cent of flowers. Cultivated plants bear comparatively large fruits. The tree flowers in hot season and the fruits ripen during the winter.

Fig. 4.24 : Amla twig with fruits

Alternative crops to the extent of 7 - 8 years age of Amla trees can be undertaken. Black gram, tomato, gaur, sunflower, ground nut etc. are the common alternative crops of choice. Each plant can bear 175 - 300 kg of fruits and each of healthy fruit weighs approximately 25 - 35 gm.

Plant hormones like Gibberlic acid or planofix in the range of 30 - 50 ppm are most useful to increase the yield per hectare.

Pesticides

Diathase-78, DDT is useful to get rid of rust, blue mold or other fungal infections.

Macroscopic Characters

Colour   -   The green colour changes to light yellow or brick red at maturity.

Odour   -   Odourless.

Taste   -   The taste of Amla is sore and astringent.

Size   - The average size of an Amla is between 1.5 and 2.5 cm in diameter.

Shape   - The fruits are depressed, globular.

Extra Features

Fruits are fleshy obscurely 4 lobed with 6-trygonus seeds. They are very hard and smooth in appearance.

Chemical Constituents

Amla fruit is a rich natural source of vitamin C (ascorbic acid) and contains 600 - 750 mg per 100 g of the fresh pulp. Furthermore, fruits also contain about 0.5 per cent fat, phyllemblin and 5 per cent tannin. Amla fruits are also rich in mineral matters like phosphorus, iron and calcium. It contains appreciable amount of pectin. The fresh fruits contain about 75 per cent moisture. The fruits are dehydrated and stored. It is found that vitamin content of dried fruits is not lost considerably. It may be due to the presence of tannins, which retards oxidation of vitamin C.

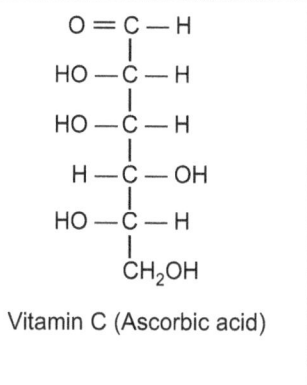

Vitamin C (Ascorbic acid)

Chemical Tests

1. Alcoholic or aqueous extract of the drug gives blue colour with ferric chloride solution.

2. Adding gelatin and sodium chloride in aqueous extract produces milky white colour.

3. In the aqueous extract of Amla add lead acetate to remove percipitate by filtration. To the filtrate add solution of 2 : 6 dichlorophenol – indophenols; the colour disappears.

Uses

Amla fruits are largely used in Indian medicines. It is used as an acrid, diuretic, refrigerant and laxative. Dried fruits are given in diarrhoea and dysentery. They are also administered in jaundice, dyspepsia and anaemia along with iron compound. Fruits are also used in preparation of inks, hair oils and shampoo. It is reported that fixed oil from fruits possesses the property of promoting hair growth. Seeds of the fruits are given in treatment of asthma and bronchitis. The leaves are used as fodder. Alcoholic extract of the fruit is anti-viral. It is a popular ingredient of 'Triphala' and 'Chyawanprash". Amla, being a rich source of vitamin C, is considered important to slow the ageing process. It improves skin health. Ageing is a cumulative result of damage to various cells and tissues, mainly by oxygen free radicals. Vitamin C is a scavenger of free radicals which breaks them down. It has an antioxidant synergism with vitamin E (which prevents peroxidation of lipids). Amla is a major ingredient of ancient Ayurvedic preparation Chyawanprash, believed to delay ageing process thereby adding to longevity.

BAHERA

Synonyms

Bellaric myrobalan, Baheda and Bibhitak.

Biological Source

It consists of dried ripe fruits of the plant *Terminalia belerica* Linn. belonging to family Combretaceae, and should contain not less than 0.3 per cent of ellagic acid and 0.75 per cent of gallic acid in dried form.

Geographical Source

The tree is found in all the decidous forests of India, up to an altitude of 1000 m. It is found in abundance in Madhya Pradesh, Uttar Pradesh, Punjab; Maharashtra and in Sri Lanka and Malaya as also.

Cultivation and Collection

Cultivation of Baheda, though not done on commercial scale, can be carried out by sowing the seeds. The seeds can retain the viability for a year and their rate of germination is about 80 per cent. The plant can also be raised by transplantation. It takes about 15 - 30 days for germination of seed. The maximum height of the plant is about 40 m and the girth is 2 - 3 m. The stem of the plant is straight and the leaves are broadly elliptic and clustered towards the end of the branches. Flowers are simple, solitary and in auxiliary spikes.

Macroscopic Characters

Colour   - Fruits are dark brown to black

Odour   - None

Taste   - Astringent

Size   - 1.3 - 2 cm in length.

Shape   - Fruits are globular and obscurely 5 angled

The fruits are pulpy with hard and stony seeds.

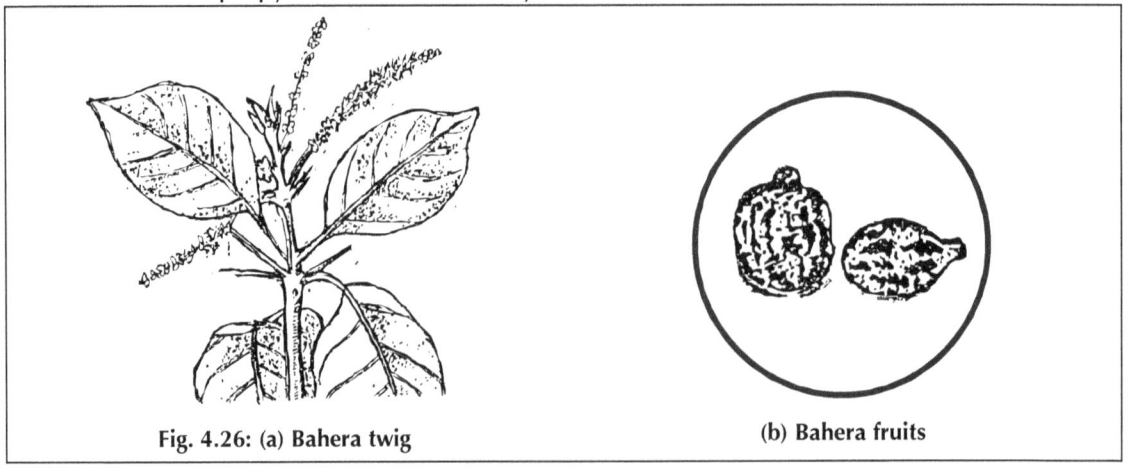

Fig. 4.26: (a) Bahera twig   (b) Bahera fruits

Chemical Constituents

The fruits contain about 20 - 30 per cent of tannins and 40 - 45 per cent water-soluble extractives. It also contains colouring matter besides gallic acid, ellagic acid, phyllemblin, and ethyl gallate and galloyl glucose. The seeds contain non-edible oil. The plant produces a gum. It also contains most of the sugars as reported in myrobalan.

Standards

Total ash	:	≯ 4.5%
LOD	:	≯ 10.0%
Acid insoluble ash	:	≯ 0.2 %
Alcohol soluble extractives	:	≮ 17.0 %
Water soluble extractives	:	≮ 26.0 %
Loss on drying	:	≯ 10.0 %

Uses

Bahera is used as an astringent and in the treatment of dyspepsia and diarrhoea. It is a constituent of triphala. The purgative property of half ripe fruit is due to the presence of fixed oil. The oil on hydrolysis yields an irritant recipe. Gum is used as a demulcent and purgative. Oil is used for the manufacture of soap.

MYROBALAN

Synonyms

Chebulic myrobalans, Harde, Haritaki

Biological Source

It consists of dried, ripe, and fully matured fruits of *Terminalia chebula* Retzr belonging to family Combretaceae. It contains not less than 5.0 per cent of chebulagic acid and not less than 12.5 per cent of chebulinic acid.

Geographical Source

Myrobalan tree is found in the sub-Himalayan tracks from Ravi to West Bengal, Assam and in all deciduous forests of India, specifically in Madhya Pradesh, Maharashtra, Bihar and Assam.

Cultivation and Collection

It grows at an altitude of 1800 m. It is not cultivated and fruits are collected from wild grown forest plants. It is a tree, 15 - 25 m in height, and 1.5 - 2.5 m in diameter. The tree is rounded, crowned with spreading branches and oxate leaves. It has yellowish-white flowers in the terminal spike.

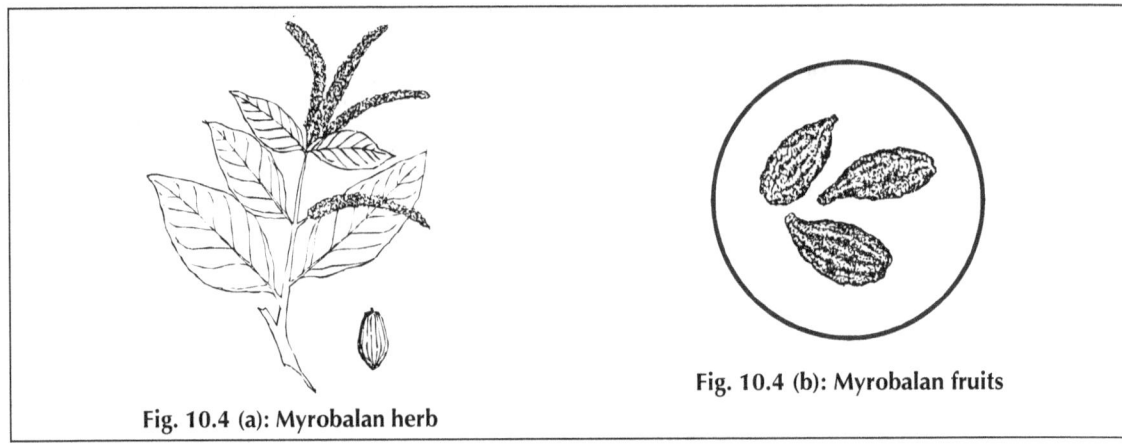

Fig. 10.4 (b): Myrobalan fruits

Fig. 10.4 (a): Myrobalan herb

Macroscopic Characters

Colour   : Fruits are yellowish-brown

Odour   : Odourless

Taste   : Astringent, slightly bitter and sweetish at the end

Size   : 20 to 25 mm long and 15 to 25 mm wide

Shape   : Ovate and wrinkled longitudinally

Extra Features

The fruits are hard and stony with single seed which is light yellow in colour and 15 to 320 mm in length. The pulp of the fruit is non-adherent to the seed.

Chemical Constituents

Myrobalan fruits are an important source of tannin. Depending upon the geographical source, they vary in tannin content and the fruits collected from Chennai are very rich in tannin. The approximate analysis of the fruits is as follows:

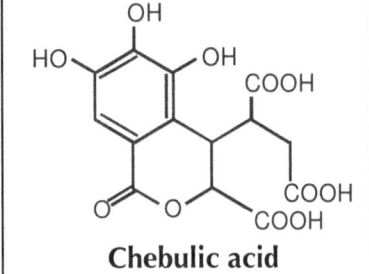

Chebulic acid

Moisture - 10 per cent;

Tannin - 25 - 32 per cent;

Water - insoluble matter - 40 - 50 per cent

The tannins of myrobalans are of pyrogallol type (hydrolysable tannins), which yield chebulic acid and d-galloyl glucose on hydrolysis. Chebulagic, chebulinic, ellagic and gallic acids are the other contents of myrobalans. Myrobalan also contains glucose and sorbitol (about 3.5 per cent). During the maturation of the tree, the amount of tannin decreases, whereas the acidity of the fruits increases.

Standards

Total ash   : ≯5.5 %

Acid insoluble ash   : ≯0.5 %

Loss on Drying   :   ≮9.0 %

Alcohol soluble extractives :   ≮40.0 %

Water soluble extractives   :   ≮56.0 %

Uses

Myrobalan is used mainly as an astringent, laxative, stomachic and tonic. The laxative property of Myrobalan is due to anthracene derivative present in the pericarp. It is also an anthelmintic. Fruit pulp is used to cure bleeding. It is an ingredient of ayurvedic preparation 'Triphala', used for treatment of variety of ailments.

Commercially, it is used in dyeing and tanning industry and also in the treatment of water used for locomotives. Myrobalan is also used in the treatment of piles and external ulcers.

 ❖❖❖

www.ingramcontent.com/pod-product-compliance
Lightning Source LLC
Chambersburg PA
CBHW080731020726
47503CB00010B/2867